Awoken

SERRA ELINSEN

For Him,
who has blessed me so completely.

CONTENTS

That is not dead which can eternal lie,
yet with strange aeons even death may die.

But love will never die…

Crashing

THE PRETERNATURAL LANDSCAPE WAS DESCENDED UPON by fog. Everything around me was hidden in misty grey. Even my own senses seemed distant, as if someone else were feeling for me. I stood on stone, ankle-deep in shallow water. The smell of the sea wafted in from far away.

How did I get here? And where *was* here? I couldn't remember anything—not my family, my friends, my home, my dark past or my murky future. Not a thing but my name.

"Andromeda," I named myself quietly. The word was louder than I thought it would be, breaking through the deep silence. The mist cleared slightly, as if listening, and stony ruins seemed to stretch on around me for miles. A new sound joined my echoing voice—the sound of waves crashing over rocks.

Crash.

Now in the foggy distance, I could see tall, crumbling

towers. A pale sun hid behind the cloudy sky. And beyond the cliff's edge just in front of me—I gasped for a moment—was a drop into the raging ocean. Five hundred feet? A thousand? I'd never been good at distances, but I knew the fall would kill me.

I took a few steps back, each one violating that sacred silence with another soft splash. Below, the waves:

Crash.

A cold wind slammed into me from across the sea, knocking me further away from the cliff's edge onto the ground. My head spun for a few delirious moments, and my hands grasped at the smooth, slippery stone to push myself up.

"*Gwher fhtagn y'osp silm Pso'dau ia…*"

I looked around for a moment. Nothing but the ruins around me. Then where was that murmuring coming from?

"*…y'osp tsem fhtagn Nor'Jarm Cthulhu Gr'der'si di ia…*"

I gasped. It was impossible! My heart pounded relentlessly in my chest.

The stone itself was whispering!

"*Fhtagn Nor'Farm Cthulhu Gr'der'si di ia! Ph'nglui ya mglw'nafh Cthulhu R'lyeh wgah'nagl fhtagn!*"

And then I heard something echoing in the distance. A reply. It was a mighty roar from the depths, like the proudest of whalesongs given form! "*Gr'dar Iscio jaq'te yr'ra!*"

It was so beautiful. Even though I didn't understand what the words meant, they sang to me. It was a song of freedom and release, of overwhelming joy and individuality. When it ended, the silence came back and I felt emptier than I ever had before.

"*Phrgl'nuima krafhys per'cluim nahnk'pui!*" The song

came back suddenly, longer and more triumphant! It was the sweetest sound I'd ever heard. The voice of an angel.

"*SGN'WAHL! SHA'SHOGG! THROD! CTHULHU'AI!*"

The ground shook again. I was so lost in that most beautiful of songs that once again I fell to the stone. I peered up from the ground… and marveled.

The ocean itself opened up below me, and rising from it— a vision in glistening emerald—was a gargantuan creature most people might call monstrous. Even through the mist, I could make out what looked to be huge, grasping squid-tentacles upon its face and enormous wings unfurling from its back. Its muscled body was like a man's, but strange and green-hued in the distance. Yet for all of the peculiar features, its eyes were the most strange and wonderful of all.

They were black but not black. All colors and no colors. Shining and lightless, warm and cold, loving and hating, good and evil, joyful and sorrowful. It was like looking into two glistening orbs of eternity, except on a cyclopean creature of wonder.

Crash, crash, crash!

The creature waded through the ocean with slow thighs, its eternity orbs focused on tiny, little me. Over the rolling sea, it towered above even my magnificent cliff. I watched with bated breath as it grew closer, closer, now close enough to crouch down before me and stare, sizing me up.

There was suddenly a burst of light and wind that knocked me to the ground. My eyes flooded with flashes of color as I tried to look before me.

Oh. Oh my.

On the stone, standing above me, was a boy. Or he looked like a boy, but how could he be? How could someone so perfect be a mere human? He had long, unkempt black hair, so black that it glistened almost blue in the misty light. It whipped about in the wind like a dark flag. He looked down at me with intense green eyes... eyes that seemed strangely familiar. Behind him, the monster was gone. Where was it now?

"Human," he muttered at me. His voice seemed to echo from everywhere at once... and yet it came from nowhere but him. "Why art thou upon this isle? Art thou a servant of Azathoth?"

"I..." I began, but my voice was caught in my throat. He was so intimidating... and yet...

My eyes made a trail down his lean, muscled chest, following droplets of water down his strong body. *He's like a Greek god...*

"Answer me, mortal!" he roared. I winced.

"No, no!" I squeaked nervously. "I don't even know who Aza-moth is!"

"Dost thou not know Azathoth, mortal?" said the boy derisively. "I find that hard to believe. *Indubitably* hard to believe." He turned around to stare out over the ocean, his hair tossing droplets of water.

I stared intently at him. "Who are you?" I asked carefully, startled by my own bravery.

"Who art I?" He stared into the distance. "That is not a revelation for a weak mortal such as thou."

"But—"

He turned around. His passionate eyes burned with viridian rage.

"BEGONE, DREAMING HUMAN! LEAVE ME TO MY THOUGHTS!"

The stone beneath me crumbled into slabs and the ocean vanished. The towers fell in upon themselves, and the sun dissolved beneath the grey mist.

And I was falling too; down, down, down, down…

~*~*~*~

Down, down, down…

…straight into my bed with a thump.

I lay still for a minute, panting, drenched in sweat. The dream had felt so *real!* The crashing of the waves, the smell of the saltwater, the monstrous creature and… *him.*

The boy. The otherworldly boy, with his bewitching emerald eyes, his shiny black hair, his perfect body. The way he looked out across the ocean, as if all the world were his. The way he looked at me, as if *I* were his…

"Sigh," I exhaled aloud. I knew why I'd had the dream, of course. It was because of my stupid, awful name. Andromeda. Ugh.

A sacrifice. A myth. A constellation. And the bane of my existence. I loathed it—and shortening it to Andi didn't help much. Sometimes I wondered how I ever made friends with a name like Andromeda. *The chained princess.* Only a hero could rescue her from the terrible monster of the deep.

So that's what I thought then. My dream had been about that handsome hero vanquishing the leviathan, saving me from certain death.

But I was wrong. So very, very wrong. The dream wasn't just a dream… It was a vision.

Because names don't just matter.

Names give you… destiny.

Chapter One
Colorless

I FELL BACK ONTO MY PILLOW, AND HEAVED ANOTHER sigh. I stared up at the ancient white wooden beams above me—my parents had been so excited to renovate this old ship maker's house when we moved in two years ago. They left the ceiling beams exposed because they said it gave the house character.

Personality. Depth.

"This *house* has more meaning than my life," I groaned aloud. I rubbed my eyes and groaned again when I rolled over and saw the time. The digital 6:53 a.m. taunted me. Not enough time to go back to sleep, too much time for getting ready for school.

I wrinkled my nose. *Ugh.* Insult to injury, it was Monday, too. Just another week, another day in 'quaint' little Portsmouth, surrounded by water and miserably far from anything interesting beyond the tourist pit stops on the way to Newport's mansions. My home.

"Now you're just depressing *me*," I moaned, chastising myself. Steeling my will, I rolled out of bed and to my feet. I grabbed my fluffy white towel off the door hook, and shuffled out of my room. The hallway mirror caught me mid-yawn, my brown shoulder-length hair a rat's nest, my dull grey eyes bleary.

Yikes! So not a morning person. I stumbled into the bathroom.

My bathroom at the end of the hall was small; the free-standing, clubfoot tub dominated what little space there was, a leftover from a late 19th century renovation. Even though my second anniversary living here had passed three months ago, it was still a surprise to look above the toilet and not see a water tank mounted on the wall. Instead, the brand new model sat crammed in the corner between the wall and the tub, completely out of place. But then again, anything younger than the 1920s just looked weird in this house.

I turned on the shower and brushed my teeth while I waited for the water to get hot. Of course, that would only be if I was lucky. Mom and Dad joked about how our house was like a grumpy old man who just needed a lot of love, but as far as I was concerned, it was a total pain. Nothing made me miss San Diego more than a temperamental New England water heater on a cold autumn morning.

When the pipes started knocking, I knew the water was finally ready. I tossed my pajamas into the hamper and stepped into the shower, carefully trying not to slip. I'd slipped so many times coming in and out of the tub, I could swear it was out to get me. I swear, someday I would knock myself unconscious with the faucet running, and drown. In a bathtub. How awful would that be?

The water was as hot as it could get, but it was just warm enough. The windows and mirror were fogging up from the steam already, but to step an inch out of the spray was to get hit by a wall of cold air. *Brrrrh,* I thought. It wasn't even October yet, but I could tell another New England winter was right around the corner. *Great.*

I reached for the shampoo and worked it into my hair, trying to tease the knots out. For hair that was so straight and dull, it was thick. Mom kept telling me I should try sleeping with it braided, but it just kept slipping out of the braid, or I would just plain forget. The last of the shampoo rinsed out, I slathered on the conditioner, letting it sit while I grabbed my loofah. My conditioner smelled like coconuts and my body wash like orange blossoms. I closed my eyes and tried to pretend I was back in California.

For a minute I could almost see the palm trees and beaches, smell the sun on the sand and feel the warm wind in my face. But as soon as it was there, it was gone, and I was back in Rhode Island.

I rinsed the conditioner out, and steeling myself, turned off the water. I started shivering as soon as I opened the curtain, and toweled myself dry as quickly as I was able.

I brushed my wet hair, scrutinizing my face in the mirror as I did. I suppose I was lucky to not really need special facial washes, toners or moisturizers like other girls my age, but at least other girls didn't have pale, wan faces like mine. There wasn't the slightest flush to my cheek, no freckles, no dimples, nothing. Just wide grey eyes, brown hair and pale pink lips. Snow White was I only in skin, and not in any of the other important descriptors. My best friend Bree always said makeup would really make my features pop, but I couldn't stand the stuff, and besides—what was the point of putting all those chemicals on your face if underneath you were still just uninteresting? Eventually the makeup had to come off, and then what?

No, it was just better not to bother.

My hair was still wet, so I tied it back in a messy bun. It would dry by the time I got to my first period class. Feeling more awake, I opened the door and turned toward my bedroom, and nearly ran into my dad.

"Oh, good morning sweetie!" My dad—Dr. Howard Slate to his students and colleagues—always the morning person. He was dressed and it looked like he was just about to run off to work. His Monday classes at Miskatonic University didn't start until 11:00 a.m., but he liked to offer open office hours for students in the mornings. If they thought their grades mattered, he always argued, they would drag themselves out of bed for them.

Dad's doctorate was in marine biology and he was primarily an oceanographer. Pretty much if it came from the depths, he found it fascinating. That was fine when we lived in San Diego, but a better paying position at MU dragged our entire family north—'Hook, line and sinker!' Mom had joked, and my dad had howled with laughter.

I loved my parents, but they could be *so* embarrassing sometimes.

"Morning Dad," I mumbled as I ran for my room, not wanting to stand in the hallway in my towel.

"Say, honey, I tested your car battery this morning and it's still not working."

I paused in my doorway. "Still?" I whined.

"Yeah, sorry, honey, looks like you're going to have to replace it."

"That's just great, Dad, how much do *those* cost?" I asked as I watched my Monday slide from bad to worse.

"We'll look it up honey, and it shouldn't take you too long to save up for a new one. Besides, I'm sure Bridget would be willing to pick you up today for school, give her a call," he suggested.

"I suppose. Or maybe even Vik could—"

"I'm sure Bridget could!" he interrupted. With a grimace, he continued, "Sorry, honey, I like the kid and all, but I just don't like that moped of his. Bridget's car is much safer."

"Dad, this is Portsmouth," I retorted. "What are we going to hit, the curb?"

"Please, honey?" he begged.

I sighed. "Fine, Dad, I'll call Bree first. But I'm sixteen you know!"

"I know, sweetie, and I just want to make sure you make it to seventeen," he admitted with a sheepish grin. "Have a good day at school?"

"Sure, whatever. Have a good day, Dad."

He headed down the stairs, and I closed my door. It was already 7:35 a.m. Class started at 8:25 a.m., but I still had to call Bree.

Crap.

I pulled some undies, a bra and socks out of my bureau. The bra and socks were white but the underwear was pink with the word 'FLIRT' over the rear. They were so embarrassing, but Mom had found them on sale. It was a little mortifying that my mom still bought clothes for me. I was always her little dress up doll, and I guess old habits die hard. Besides, it wasn't like Mom didn't have an eye for fashion—at least when it came to outerwear. For panties, however… well, it wasn't like anyone was actually going to *see* them. And just then I was glad to have them since I'd forgotten to do the laundry. Again. *Tonight,* I thought to myself. *I'll totally get it done tonight.*

I pulled them on, and dove for my Gap skinny jeans that were on the floor. I'd only worn them just this weekend, they were still good to go.

I grabbed my cellphone off the charger, and pulled Bree up in my contacts—I really needed to remember to ask Vik to add her to my quick dials for me. I'd had the phone since the first week of school, almost a month ago, but I kept forgetting, and my efforts to try to figure it out on my own had been laughable. Technology and I really just didn't get along.

It rang once, twice, three, *four* times and then Bree finally picked up.

"…S'up?" she mumbled.

"Oh god, are you still asleep?" I demanded.

"Five more minutes, s'okay—"

"Bree, look, I need you to pick me up. My car's still not working," I said as I searched my closet for a shirt to wear.

"But you could bike there in less than—" I could hear her sigh, and then grunt—she must have finally gotten out of bed. "Okay, okay, I can be there in twenty, don't worry."

"Thanks, Bree, you're a lifesaver," I said, and hanging up, tossed my phone onto my bed. I finally selected a shirt, a J. Crew light v-neck in teal. Boring, but simple. I had packed my bag the night before, so I grabbed my phone, threw on my black Converse sneakers, and I was ready for another wonderful, fabulous day. *Sigh.*

I headed down the rustic staircase. My mom—Professor Sonia Slate to her students and colleagues (except she was on a sabbatical for the year)—had one of those natural flairs for interior decorating.

When we'd moved in, she decided on a nautical theme for the old colonial place and she *ran* with it. The house was all wood and clean, cool colors, brass highlights, antique furniture, ocean-related artifacts and bookcases that spilled from room to room. Everyone was always saying how amazing it was that the house didn't feel too masculine or too feminine (which Dad always appreciated), and yet was still homey and inviting. Even though the end result looked effortless, I didn't really see the point of all the work Mom had done. A room is just a room after all, which was why I kept my own bedroom relatively plain. Just the furniture I needed, not really many decorations or curtains or anything. Stuff like that all just got in the way.

"Good morning, Andromeda," Mom sang as I entered the kitchen. She stood at the stove, waiting for her coffee water to boil, and caught the grimace that crossed my face at the mention of my name. After the dream, hearing it out loud pushed hard on the old sore spot.

"I don't know why you hate your name so much," she sighed. "It's a beautiful name. Classic."

I rolled my eyes as I leaned against the counter. She could never understand.

Mom just laughed. "Oh right, of course, I forgot—classic names are *lame*," she teased. Just then the teapot started whistling, and she turned to pour the water into the French press.

"I'm just not an Andromeda, Mom," I groused as I grabbed a coffee mug and a tea bag from the kitchen counter. It was my favorite tea, peppermint, and I used the last of the hot water to make myself a cup. I only added a little bit of honey and milk to it, and the way the aroma played with my nose was perfect.

"Not a soon-to-be sacrificed maiden rescued by a daring prince with a monstrous weapon?" Mom suggested. "I suppose that's fine then, but it's still a beautiful name and your father and I have no regrets giving it to you," she smiled.

A car horn interrupted the cozy silence of the kitchen— Bree had arrived!

"Later, Mom," I cried, running to grab my bag.

"Wait, you haven't eaten breakfast!" she protested.

"Not hungry!" I called over my shoulder.

"You will be in class. Hang on!" she ordered, and I paused, my hand on the brass doorknob. Through the window, I could see Bree sitting in her car, looking bored and texting. She honked again without looking up. *Geez, Bree,* I thought, *the neighbors are going to love that.*

"Here," Mom said as she jogged from the kitchen. She shoved a granola bar into my hand. "Something for the road, sweetie."

"Okay, bye Mom," I said as I opened the door and ran to Bree's car.

"Have a good day at school!" she yelled from behind me.

Not likely, I thought as I slid into the passenger seat.

After all, it was just another Monday in Portsmouth, Rhode Island.

Chapter Two
Clairvoyance

PORTSMOUTH HIGH WAS A COMPLETELY DIFFERENT shade of miserable than the rest of the town. With its off-white halls stretching around like a maze, antique stairs running up and down, old worn wooden finish, deep red curtains and a smell like dust and lead paint, it made me long for the days of living in the city and going to a school that didn't feel like a rejected haunted mansion. But those days—the neon lights, the laughter and the friends I'd left behind in San Diego—I had to accept that they were over and there was nothing to do but keep getting used to it. This was my life now, with all its bland, white blankness and bland, creaky old fishing boats and the bland, creepy old school I had to force myself to go to every single day.

Bree and I had somehow arrived early, and I sat down on the front stairs, postponing going inside for a few more precious minutes as I looked up at the iron-blue morning. A cold wind blew in like a message from the rising sun, tossing the gold and red leaves of autumn around like a crackling tornado.

"Bree," I said.

Bree, sitting at my side, gave me an inquisitive look as she cracked open a can of Pepsi.

Bridget Fifan was the very first friend I made in Portsmouth. We'd become inseparable over the past couple years, but I could still never quite figure out why someone like Bree would want to hang out with me. She was just so full of life in a careless way. She had the kind of fiery, curly red hair that should only exist in Disney movies. Her hazel eyes always seemed to shimmer with glee and mischief, and her face was dusted with freckles that everyone said made her adorable. She was as loud and quirky as her Goodwill clothes, and being the de facto leader of the school's 'thespians' (as she liked to call them) came naturally to her. On top of all that, she had the annoying habit of being crazy smart in just everything—nothing seemed too difficult for Bree, not even dealing with the taunts or catcalls that her edging-toward-marshmallow curves occasionally earned her. Instead she could just smile and laugh and flick her hair at whatever life threw her way. She was a perfect friend, the life of the party—

Being friends with Bridget Fifan could really make a girl feel inadequate. Not that that was her fault! Bree would never do anything to put a person down. I just couldn't help it. Bree was just so much... *more* than me.

I sighed deeply. "I had the weirdest dream last night."

She lifted a ginger eyebrow. "Was it the one with the guy in the panda mask again? Because that was kinda wicked hilarious."

"It wasn't funny, Bree," I snapped softly. "It was just… weird." *And nice*, I thought suddenly, surprising myself.

"It was *that* kind of dream, then?" Bree questioned, and took a sip of her pop. She set it down on the step and gave me a look. "Um, don't take this the wrong way, but I'd rather not hear about—"

"No, it wasn't like that!" I ejaculated exasperatedly. "There was this boy, and—"

"And no offense, Andi, but I think you should probably keep this to yourself," she said, her face reddening. "I'm glad you had a, er, 'weird dream,' but it's not like you're the only one. It's totally normal. So don't worry about it, huh?"

"No, you don't understand!" I exclaimed irritably. "Just let me explain, okay?"

Bree sighed in resignation and took another sip of her pop as I told her everything I remembered from the vivid dream. The eldritch stone ruins, the thick blanket of fog, the creature in the deep, the godlike boy who had saved me from it and the crashing of the waves that punctuated every moment.

"And then I was falling, everything crumbling away… and I was home," I said softly.

Bree nodded, taking one last swig. "That's actually pretty wicked," she said. "Sorry for assuming, Andi." She chuckled carelessly. "Pretty surreal stuff, though. Makes me wish I still had that dream interpretation book."

I sighed. Bree clearly didn't understand, or just didn't care. To her it was just one more weird quirk of Andi Slate, wasn't it? Just a silly little dream. Maybe she was right, too. What did it matter? I'd woken up once again to life in the town where excitement went to die, after all. There was no point in dwelling on dreams, no matter how entrancing they were.

The halls of Portsmouth High were bustling as everyone rushed to their lockers to grab books, papers, folders and such. I hurried to mine, and ran into an old friend waiting there. The only remainder of my San Diego life that was still with me.

He was standing beside my locker, frowning down at his watch. His face brightened when he saw me. "Oh, hi Andi! How are you? I've been waiting. I've got something to show you that you're going to love!"

"Hey, Vik," I replied, feeling too tired to be as excited as he was.

Bree wasn't, though. Maybe if she weren't so fond of sugary drinks so early in the morning, she'd learn to relax. "Heya, Vik! How are ya?"

Vik was short for Vivek Mayank, and it's what I'd called him ever since we were kids growing up in California. I'd known him for so long that he, being four months younger, was like a little brother to me (except Indian, of course). Our parents had been friends since his migrated from Bombay when we were in first grade, and when his mom and dad scored positions with Miskatonic's archeology department, they'd hooked my parents up with the biology department and our families moved across the country within a month of each other, just in time for me and Vik to start high school.

It seemed like he'd acclimated to life on the East Coast a lot better than I had—made friends, joined clubs, all that sort of stuff. Though I couldn't help but wonder why he'd never had a girlfriend. With his creamed-coffee skin, his cheesy bright smile, curly dark locks, deep amber eyes, lithe physique, the faint accent (almost British) that made him sound more sophisticated than I knew he was—you'd think he could have found someone. Sadly, poor Vik was a bit of a coward around other girls. If only he were as brave with them as he was with me, he'd probably have *someone* by now. My own lack of attachment, on the other hand, was no mystery. There just wasn't anyone that seemed to understand me here. Finding a friend in Bree had definitely been the exception, but don't even get me started on the Portsmouth boys.

"Very good, thank you," Vik answered Bree. "But listen, you won't believe what my parents got for Miskatonic!"

Probably some old broken pottery or slabs of concrete or something, I thought. Vik was always geeking out about ancient artifacts and figurines and all that. I could understand why. His parents were archeology professors, and growing up Hindu probably made him really big on mythology. I couldn't blame him too much for it.

"What'd they get?" inquired Bree nonchalantly as she ripped open a bag of chips.

"Well," replied Vik excitedly, "it's really famous. They say it's cursed, even! My parents have been wanting to get ahold of it for decades." He looked at me like he thought his next words would make my day. "It's this creepy old book called the..." He paused dramatically. "*Necronomicon!*"

A book? Now that, I hadn't expected. Vik knew how I loved books, especially old ones. When I usually thought of archeology and that stuff, I thought of pots and arrowheads and junk. But even if it were unreadable and ancient, a book was something I could get behind.

"What's it about?" asked Bree.

"If it's ancient," I said reasonably, "he probably doesn't know yet."

"Actually, I *do* know," Vik corrected. "They say it's an eldritch tome of forbidden magic!"

Bree laughed. "Spooky stuff!"

"I know, I know!" said Vik. "Who knows, though? It's so rare, maybe it *does* have some power."

"There's no such thing as magic, though," said Bree, munching on a chip. "They've done studies. Still sounds fun, though."

"I was thinking that later, after school..." Vik went on. Yet as he continued to talk, I found myself drifting off. The memory of the waves from my dream, crashing against the rocks. The memory of the majestic boy, gazing at me with royal, commanding eyes that shone with the emerald light of eternity. The sweet smell of saltwater in the moist air...

"You wanna do it, then?"

Bree's words shook me out of my reverie. "Huh?"

"We're thinking of going to the auditorium after school," Vik explained. "To actually read from the *Necronomicon*."

"Wait, you have it here?" I asked.

"Mother and Father won't miss it. They're not getting home until seven tonight."

"I bet Vik a good five bucks that nothing's going to happen," Bree smirked confidently. "And no matter *what* happens, I bet it's going to get interesting."

My life's been divided into one hour chunks, I thought. Class, class, class, forty minutes for lunch, class, class, class. Go home. Do homework. Eat dinner and try not to talk to my parents as they try not to understand me. Then try to amuse myself by reading or countless other empty activities before going to sleep. Then wake up, go to school, class, class, class…

It would do me good to mix things up a bit. Even if it meant staying at school longer than I had to.

"Why not?" I decided nonchalantly. "Right after school?"

"Yeah, I'll see—" Vik was cut off as the shrill ring of the bell crashed into our conversation.

He sighed laboriously and glanced down the hall. "I'm sorry, I've got to go. Spanish… ugh, we've got a quiz on the perfect tense. I'll see you guys in third period, okay?"

"See you there, Vik!" called Bree as he disappeared around the corner.

We had to hurry, too—English class for us, and I didn't want to miss a minute of it. I knew a lot of people my age hated reading, but I'd always loved getting lost in the romance of the old days.

~*~*~*~

I'd read *A Midsummer Night's Dream* a million and two times. Every time I read it was just as magical and strange as the first. But that day, in English class, I found myself drifting off. Faeries and magic, love and destiny… it was all so wonderful, yet all so distant from me. So unlike my own dull world. It was a sweet dream, like the one that kept fluttering around in my head with the gumption of a newborn butterfly.

Absentmindedly, I pulled out a clean sheet of paper and tried to imagine the boy from my dream on it. It was harder now, hours away from the land of sleep. The image came back to me, though, when Mrs. Phillips started rambling on about mythology in Shakespeare.

Mythology. The boy had looked like someone from mythology to me, so larger than life and so inhumanly handsome. He looked like an Adonis... Or even better, a Cupid—not that pudgy baby with angel wings most people think of, but the handsome young Greek god. I sighed heavily, remembering the story. Forbidden love. Cupid, romancing innocent, beautiful Psyche in the secret dark. The terrible things Psyche had to suffer before she earned the right to truly marry her Cupid. Most of all, though, I could envision Cupid standing in the dark... with those bright, gleaming green eyes.

And then I was gone for a moment in the darkness. Then I was Psyche, gazing into the emerald eyes of Cupid (and knowing that he had another name). The crashing of great waves came back as the Cupid consumed me with his simmering gaze, louder and faster this time...

"Miss Slate?"

Crap!

Mrs. Phillips, a frumpy old biddy with glasses that sank into her face, was giving me a look that Bree would have called 'wicked harsh.' I tried to grin back.

"Oh, hi. Sorry, what was the question?" I felt like I was about to melt with embarrassment. I glanced at my desk for my book... and found something else instead. A work of art. Somehow my hand had been drawing by itself, slowly tracing out the image of a very familiar, very impossible boy. He looked up at me from the paper with an expression that seemed too real for a mere drawing.

"The question," scolded Mrs. Phillips coldly, "was about the purpose of the scene in which Bottom turns into a donkey. Miss Slate, you are one of my best students, but that's no excuse for not paying attention... or drawing shirtless young men while we're supposed to be discussing a classic work of literature."

My face flushed red. I could feel the eyes of all the other students on me as Mrs. Phillips waddled up to my desk, snatched the drawing and tossed it into the trash can.

The rest of first period was spent in a haze of white-hot anger mingled with a fog of light-magenta embarrassment. I knew I should have been paying attention, but how could she make an example of me like that in front of the whole class? Then again, I *was* zoning out more than usual. Even though English was my best subject, was that really an excuse to just not pay attention?

My next class, French, was no better. Even sitting next to Bree didn't cheer me up, and Monsieur Cousteau dropped a mountain of homework on us right before the bell rang.

"Zis iz ze most important class you shall all take!" he proclaimed in his outrageous accent as we all zombie-shuffled into the hall once again. Right, my most important class. That would probably mean something if every single teacher didn't say the exact same thing about *their* classes.

"You're wicked distracted today," said Bree at snack break. (Her mouth was full of beef jerky, so it came out more like "Fuur wik destrak tuhd.") "What's up?" ("Fshup?")

"I told you about my dream," I snapped with a sigh. "That boy... he was otherworldly. Godlike, even. I just can't get it all out of my head..."

"It's bothering you, then?" Bree inquired concernedly, swallowing the last of her beef jerky.

Yes, I thought. And at the same time, I wasn't sure if I

knew. "Is it bothering me?" I muttered. "Or am I the one bothering it?"

Bree gave me an odd look. "Are you sure you're okay? Because that didn't... make any sense."

Maybe, I thought, *it doesn't have to make sense.*

The pounding of the bell cut our conversation short. It was time for Marine Biology, one of my least favorite subjects. I could blame my parents for that, but at least there was some consolation in sharing the hour with both Vik and Bree. Our teacher, old Mr. Cho, meant well, but he had an impenetrable accent and a terminal case of 'boring.'

Except Mr. Cho wasn't there today.

He usually stood at the front of the classroom, leaning on his cane and quietly waiting for all the students to arrive, occasionally greeting them with a formal bow or a hoarse "Ni hao." Today, though, someone else was sitting behind his desk.

The first thing that came into my mind when I saw her lounging at the front of the class was the look in her catlike hazel eyes. It was the half-lidded, tight-smirked look of a woman scorned. Her glossy auburn hair was coiled in an artful French twist. Under her half-slouched lab coat, her dress was glittery black, bare-shouldered and shone in the fluorescent light like it was covered in beetles. The moment I beheld her, I knew: whoever this woman was, she was utterly and completely heartless.

I sat down between Bree and Vik, unable to look away from the mysterious intruder in our classroom.

"Who is *she*?" Vik, gaped. "I've never seen her around before."

"I guess Mr. Cho's sick," said Bree, already taking

advantage of his absence to break class rules and sip on a juice box. "It happens."

"If she's our substitute teacher, I wouldn't mind if Mr. Cho took another few days off," said Vik with a smile. Bree rolled her eyes.

But even though they were joking, I could sense something was wrong. That look in the woman's eyes… Something about it chilled me to the bone. The last few students sat down, and she stood up instantly. She strode across the tiled floor, her stilettos clacking with every sashaying step, and slammed the door.

"Hello, my *dear* children." Her voice was low and husky, and her gaze crept across the room, lingering over every student predatorily. "I am your substitute teacher. Your principal's guidelines suggest that you should call me Ms. Epistola, but…" She laughed softly. "…I don't think there's a need to be so formal, do you? You may call me… Scarlett, if you wish."

"*Wow*," muttered Bree. "That's… not very professional."

"*Wow*," muttered Vik, and left it at that.

"I am to teach you about marine biology," Ms. Epistola continued in her sultry tones. "Though it is not my specialty, I will do my absolute best. Now, who can tell me about the main qualities of invertebrates?"

I raised my hand, as did Vik and five or six other students. It was easy stuff.

She glanced around the room for a strangely long time. Then her feline gaze fell on Vik, and I was certain that her eyes flashed with something like triumph. "You, boy—in the back!"

"Invertebrates are mostly found underwater," said Vik.

"They're heterotrophs, and their main quality is that they have no spine."

"*Very* impressive!" said Ms. Epistola. She grinned, her perfect white teeth shining. "Now let's talk about the difference between saltwater and freshwater animals…"

Ms. Epistola didn't seem to want to teach, not that most of the boys in class seemed to mind. She was apparently more interested in just asking questions, some of which didn't even qualify as marine biology. And more than anyone else, she called on Vik. Yes, he was always raising his hand, but so were a few other people. Why him?

"What is the primary characteristic of the mammal?" she asked Vik huskily.

"It's like Biology 1's greatest hits," whispered Bree.

"Except with an evil teacher," I whispered back.

Bree merely shrugged. "She's a bit weird, but she's an adjunct and a sub. She's probably just not used to teaching this subject."

Marine Biology dragged to a close, and Vik left with a huge goofy smile on his face.

"Thinking about our creepy substitute teacher?" asked Bree as we headed toward lunch.

Vik frowned. "She didn't seem creepy to me. She seemed nice." He shook his head, as if to clear his thoughts. "*Really* nice."

The rest of the day was almost as slow as Bio, or maybe my mind was racing so quickly that everything else just seemed sluggish. Finally, after an exhausting Algebra 2 class, Bree, Vik and I convened at his locker to collect his ancient book and wait for the hallways to empty. It was times like these, when the building was deserted and the day outside was deep grey, that the school truly felt like an abandoned asylum.

"Auditorium should be clear right now, right Bree?" Vik's voice echoed in the corridor. He sounded like he was speaking from somewhere simultaneously vast and far away, even though he was right there next to me.

Bree nodded. "No play practice today. In a few weeks I'm going to be wicked out of free time, but we're golden for now."

"Perfect," said Vik.

The words hung there in the air for a moment. So casual. So relaxed. To me, though, they had a strange heaviness to them that I couldn't place. The words sounded like they were just waiting to be contradicted. Golden. Perfect. But nothing was perfect, especially right then, in that empty place.

We were out of time. It was as if our entire lives, we'd been working toward that moment without knowing it. And so the three of us headed for the auditorium, *Necronomicon* in tow, our steps echoing on the tiles like the drumbeats of destiny.

Chapter Three

Convocation

THE AUDITORIUM WAS DARK, AND NO ONE WAS ABOUT.
It was the perfect place to read Vik's mysterious old book.
Well, it would have been if there had been more light. But
that problem could be easily solved, as I was never without
my portable clip book light. As we passed through the wings,
I noticed an abundance of strange, macabre props and
devices. Swords, bloody cloaks, tribal garments, skulls... a
grimy old bathtub.

"What is all this stuff?" I asked.

"It's for the Halloween play," Bree answered matter-of-
factly. "One of the seniors wrote it—Natalie. You remember
her, she was the lead in *Our Town* last year."

Ah, yes. She wasn't bad, as far as I recalled. In fact, she
had performed the role quite well. I just hadn't been so
pleased with the choice of production. It was a bit overdone.
I didn't think I'd ever heard of a high school that hadn't

done *Our Town* at least twelve times.

"Don't see it," Bree added, referring to the Halloween show. "It's horrible."

"The props are spooky, at least?" Vik observed uneasily.

They were incredibly creepy, actually. Not that I was scared or anything. But Vik, on the other hand was eyeing a skeleton like it was about to bite him.

I watched Bree creep up behind him. "Boo!" she yapped at his ear, prompting him to practically leap out of his corduroys.

"I hate you," he growled as we laughed.

"Would you prefer to do this somewhere else?" I teased.

"Actually," he responded, "why don't we just go out into the arts garden? It'll be easier to see out there, anyway."

Oh, the arts garden. Yet another reason why I couldn't stand my school. It was just too perfect. It had an actual, legitimate garden. With plants and a fountain and stuff. Outside, right behind the auditorium.

"If you insist," I answered, resigned.

As we filed out the back of the theatre, Bree plucked up an old, surreal-looking sword and used it to prop open the door so we could get back inside. We sat down on a swing bench beneath one of the small trees and Vik placed the book on the bench between us. In the afternoon light, the weighty tome at first seemed old, but harmless… until I took a closer look. The tanned leather of its binding was wrinkled with age but completely clean, as if no dirt or dust had ever dared to rest upon it. I wondered uneasily what animal the leather had come from. A raised design of dark stitching swirled around a flat piece of obsidian that was embedded in its center. I caught my faint reflection in its dull glassy sheen and leaned away from it instinctively. Looking into the black disc felt like looking into the deepest ocean—the sensation made me suddenly queasy.

"Wow, where did your folks find this thing?" I asked, trying to shake the nausea from my body.

"It's actually a family heirloom or something. It just came down to my mother when my great uncle died."

"Oh, Vik," Bree said. "I'm so sorry…"

"It's okay," he shrugged. "I didn't really know him. Mother was pretty broken up, though…"

I was too distracted by the book to listen to what they were going on about. My hand reached out to its cover, but I nearly recoiled when my fingertips grazed the leather—it felt… warm. As if it were… alive. I thought I saw something shimmer across the glossy disk, making an excited thrill course through me. I felt… beckoned…

"Well, go on, open it!" Bree's voice knocked me out of my reverie.

I reached for the cover with both hands this time—but was stopped as Vik put his hands over mine.

"You know, on second thought," he said, the unease evident on his face. "It's just a stupid old book. Let's just—"

"Yeah, so open it," Bree smirked.

"No, it's… Maybe I shouldn't have brought it here. I think I'll just take it back home," he said, though I realized he wasn't even looking at the book. He was eying my expression with confusion and concern.

I blinked and gave him an offended look. "What? *I'm* not afraid of it!" In that moment, I felt the very opposite of afraid.

"Yeah, Vik," Bree said. "If it's just a stupid book—"

"Legends say it's cursed," he mumbled, his excitement from this morning about that fact apparently dissipated. "Every story that surrounds this thing says it. I just... I just don't—"

"Vik, it's going to be fine," I slowly said, although to reassure him or myself, I wasn't sure. "Let's just look at it, and before you know it, you'll be paying Bree her five bucks."

"Yeah, so no backing out now," she added.

Vik sighed and released my hands, but he hardly looked relieved. "I almost hope you're right."

I nodded, and lifted the cover, opening to the first page. But before I could take in the words on the brittle vellum, Vik took the book from me.

"But I'll do the reading, thank you," he said.

I shrugged and folded my arms. "Go for it, archeologist boy wonder."

Vik's eyes remained on me for a moment, but then he shook his head with a faint smile and looked down. He turned to the center of the book with reverent fingers and found a place to begin. " 'In his house at R'lyeh,' " Vik read, his voice low, " 'Dead Cthulhu—' "

"Bless you," Bree interrupted.

Okay, maybe I didn't know what a Thalooloo was, but at least I could tell it wasn't a sneeze. Sometimes I felt sorry for Bree. Despite how smart she was, she was always so awkward and quirky. I loved her for it, but it must have been embarrassing for her when she was around other people. Maybe it was a good thing I was her only friend.

"What? No," Vik rolled his eyes. "Cthulhu is a mythical monster, a sort of giant octopus-dragon-thing that some ancient cult once worshipped."

An octopus-dragon-thing? I was immediately reminded of the sea monster from my dream. I glanced to Bree to see if she drew the connection as well, but she was focused on Vik. No... It had to have been a coincidence.

"Oh, sorry," came Bree's apology.

"Go on, then," I prodded, partially to distract Vik from poor Bree's misguidedness, and partially because I was even more intrigued by the mysterious book. "Keep reading."

Vik looked back to the page, and began again:

" 'In his house at R'lyeh, Dead Cthulhu lies dreaming. Yes, Great Cthulhu is dead, as much as he can be. But there is a hideous, unutterable gloom to this death. I was reminded of the inscription on the tomb in that terrible cyclopean city...

" '*That is not dead which can eternal lie, yet with strange aeons even death may die.*' "

Suddenly, a thunderclap shook the sky, and Vik jumped, dropping the book.

"Oh, great," I teased, "you didn't lose your place because you were scared of a little thunder, did you?" Honestly, I was a bit unnerved too. But I didn't dare show it.

Vik picked the book back up and pushed it onto my lap. "Alright, you read it then," he half-shouted as another roll of thunder pealed over us. "I still say it's cursed."

"Fine," I answered. I turned the book over and gave Vik a look. He could be such a baby sometimes.

I opened it up and came to a page that seemed near to where he was before.

"Okay, um... 'I felt a great force overpowering my mind, as if a thousand Eldritch horrors were pressing against my skull. I fell, and the world darkened. And then, the voices. Those dreadful voices began to speak in my head, and they have not since stopped. Even now, I can hear them.

" '*Sgn'wahl! Sha'shogg! Throd! Cthulhu'ai!*' "

The wind began to pick up, blowing my hair into Vik's face. I realized that the words I had just read were not printed in English, yet I had no difficulty pronouncing them, despite their deficiency of vowels.

I read on, growing fascinated by the author's hallucination.

" 'He calls to me! Dead Cthulhu shall rise again!

" '*Uln Cthulhu! Wgah'n ya!*' "

And then I realized—I was speaking the same language I'd heard in my dream. Impossible as it seemed, I was sure of it. Was this book somehow related to my dream? Maybe it was mystical, after all. It almost seemed as if the very words I spoke had a direct effect on the sky, which was getting darker, the wind growing more furious.

"Um, guys, maybe we should stop," Bree winced. "It looks like there's a wicked bad storm coming."

But I hardly heard her, and I ignored the powerful wind; I simply kept reading. I had to keep reading. I could not stop. I felt as if I were falling into a trance. The only thing that existed to me at that moment was the book, the *Necronomicon*.

" 'The Daemoniac cries never cease!' " I read. " 'He shall rise from the depths of the sea, and the Earth shall be no more!' "

I was vaguely aware of birds taking off all around us, as if trying to escape the magnificent, mad manuscript from which I read. The effect was empowering, and my voice grew louder as I recited more of the strange language which somehow in that moment seemed to make so much sense to me.

" *'Ch'ftaghu shugg Cthulhu! Thr'throd!*
Ch'ftaghu shugg Cthulhu! Thr'ngli!
Ch'ftaghu shugg Cthulhu! Thr'ghlfnaw!' "

As I spoke the last word, the loudest clash of thunder I'd ever heard rang out directly above us. The sound shook through me, reverberating straight into my core. The skies flashed with jagged streaks of lightning and a powerful gust of rain attacked me, forcing the book closed. Bree screamed, and Vik muttered something in Hindi that was lost beneath the riotous wind.

"Andi, we have to get back inside *now!*" Bree said worriedly as a branch was blown off of a tree behind us.

Where did such a storm even come from? The forecast hadn't mentioned anything of the kind. It couldn't have had anything to do with the book…

Could it?

The *Necronomicon* did seem to describe things eerily similar to what I saw in my dream. That Cthulhu thing sounded almost exactly like the huge green squid monster that the beautiful boy had saved me from. But how could reading it have had any bearing on the weather? Unless Vik was right, and the book was cursed? In that case, Bree owed him a good five bucks.

Bree's second prompt of "GUYS" brought me out of my thoughts. Vik took up the *Necronomicon*, and we hurried back inside the theatre.

Bree pulled the sword from the door and we ducked into the green room (which, despite its name, only had a vaguely greenish carpet). We sat in a circle, catching our breath, and

Vik put the book down in the middle of it. He crossed his arms and frowned in much more than annoyance. He was not happy.

"I don't know why I let you talk me into this," he chastised Bree.

She rolled her eyes dismissively, but her freckled cheeks were red and splotchy. "Whatever," she muttered. "It's just a storm."

"This was a stupid idea," Vik said with a frown. "I should have left this thing at home. All I wanted to do was show it to you, Andi. I know how you…" He hesitated as he looked up at me. "You shouldn't have read from it like that. Who knows what you just did…"

"What!? Me!?" I stared at him in disbelief. Swiping the thing from his parents and bringing it to school had been his idea in the first place! "I read your book and it started raining, Vik. That's all that happened. Why is this a big deal?"

He shook his head and lifted a hand to ruffle some raindrops out of his curly hair. "Because the book is powerful," he muttered. "And cursed."

"Right, Vik," I answered blankly, "you just keep telling yourself that."

"What if he's right, though?" Bree abruptly inquired. "What if, somehow, it actually is," she hesitated at the word, "cursed?"

I gaped at her. Now Bree was suddenly on his side? She was the one who'd bet against him! Why was it that whenever Vik and I disagreed, Bree always joined with him? She was supposed to be *my* best friend.

"Whose side are you on?" I demanded. "What happened to 'there's no such thing as magic?' "

34

"Nobody's side!" she replied. "There don't have to be sides here. I'm just pointing out that, *if* the book actually is cursed, we could be in big trouble. I mean, if this were a horror movie, we probably would've just summoned up the mighty demon Beelzebub or something."

While those sorts of movies weren't exactly the kind of thing I ever chose to watch, I'd heard enough about the clichés to know how they all worked. "Yeah," I retorted, "and the token ethnic guy would be the first victim, and the awkward best friend soon after. Okay, now I see why you're siding with him."

Vik's expression darkened. "This is serious, Andi."

"No, Vik. It's stupid," I snapped.

"Look," Bree answered, trying to defuse the situation, "let's just leave it. Vik, you can take your creepy book back home, and we'll just forget all this ever happened, okay?"

I suddenly realized that I wanted to protest. Something within me burned for more time with the *Necronomicon*. I wanted to see if it contained anything else that might relate to my dream. But if I asked Vik to let me see it again, then I'd practically be admitting that I thought it was a magic book. Which I didn't. Except...

Ugh, I didn't know what to think.

"Fine," I said as inoffensively as I could.

It didn't have any venom behind it, really. I didn't mean to sound angry or even annoyed. I actually meant it as a sort of resignation. But as Vik stood up with the book and left the room without another word to either of us, I couldn't tell whether or not he interpreted it as such.

"Are you alright, Andi?" Bree queried, clearly concerned.

I wondered for a moment why she was asking me that; it

was hardly the first time Vik and I had disagreed, and it wasn't exactly a huge argument. I knew we would make up tomorrow, or even tonight if we saw each other online later. We'd have our usual "No, it's my fault, really" back-and-forth for a minute, and then life would go on as normal.

"Andi?" Bree prompted. "You look like you're about to pass out."

I looked to the mirror on the green room wall, and realized that she was right. I was pale, shaking. Suddenly, I felt incredibly weak, as if all my energy had instantly been drained away. As if... as if the experience with the book had stolen a bit of my soul. Everything became a blur, and then darkness.

~*~*~*~

I was back on the cliff face of my dream. There were the waves crashing on the rocks below. And there was the creature, the giant green winged monster. It began to reach for me with a webbed hand, tipped with long jagged claws, but then I heard my own voice echoing everywhere, though I did not speak.

"*Ch'ftaghu shugg Cthulhu!*" my voice cried out from the distance.

Just like last time, the beast vanished in a chaotic flash of darkness and nothingness, a flash that was strangely blinding, yet wonderfully beautiful in spite of its chaos.

When I could again see, I once more beheld the boy. That beautiful, immaculate boy. I gazed into his eyes, even as he glared back at me. We shared each other's gaze for what seemed like eons before I blinked, and he was replaced by...

Vik?

"Andi?" Vik called. "Wake up, Andi!"

But I didn't want to wake up! I wanted to remain in the dream, with the boy.

But he was gone...

"What... what happened?" I asked groggily as I sat up in the school nurse's office.

"You fainted," Bree answered.

After that enlightening statement, the nurse riddled me with questions about whether or not I was eating sufficiently, if I'd suffered any blows to the head recently and so on and so forth.

When I was finally set free from the confinement of the bleached white room, Vik, ever the humble pal, offered an apology.

"I am really sorry, Andi," he admitted. "I shouldn't have blamed you."

"It's okay," I answered. "I forgive you."

The storm had apparently passed as quickly as it came, and as we left school, we talked for a few minutes about class and Mr. Dunleavy's latest barrage of horrible history puns and everything that wasn't the *Necronomicon*, before eventually parting ways in the parking lot.

Vik took off on his Vespa, but as I walked with Bree to her car, I had the oddest sensation that I was being watched. I looked behind me, but the place was deserted. All the other students had left campus long ago and only a few lonely faculty cars remained.

"What is it?" Bree asked, always quick to jump in with the third degree.

I shook my head dismissively, but as I went around to the

passenger side of her car, the feeling struck me again—an icy chill that made my flesh crawl. I twisted back to look over my shoulder, and this time, I saw someone standing on the school steps.

Across the expanse of the parking lot, his eyes met mine, and I instantly felt an overwhelming sense of *hatred* emanating from them. I tensed and pulled the car door open, scrambling inside. For a moment, I wasn't sure if I even knew the guy. But then I realized... It was *him*.

The boy from my dream.

Chapter Four
Consternation

MY ALARM WENT OFF AT 7:30 A.M. THE NEXT MORNING, just like it did every school day. The smell of fresh coffee wafted up from the kitchen. Outside my window, a bird chirped. It seemed that the world would keep on turning, indifferent to my personal crisis.

It was all in my head, I decided, staring up at my bedroom ceiling. I'd just seen a guy who happened to resemble the one from my dream. Nothing strange about that. After all, there must have been hundreds of tall, handsome guys with black hair and green eyes in the world.

I sat up in bed. I could see myself in the mirror over my dresser, and the sight made me wince even more than usual. There were dark circles under my eyes, the result of a night spent tossing and turning more than sleeping.

"Your mind is playing tricks on you," I told my reflection sternly. "Just forget about it and get on with your day."

As usual, I didn't waste much time picking out clothes after my shower. I opened my closet and, after only a moment's deliberation, pulled out a green cashmere sweater. Emerald green, like a certain pair of eyes… I shook my head. *Focus, Andi!* I put on the sweater, along with dark blue jeans and my favorite boots (brown suede with little brass buckles on the sides), brushed my hair and went down to the kitchen for breakfast.

By the time I got to school, I had finally managed to push all thoughts of the raven-haired boy from my mind. So it was a bit of a shock when I got to first period and found him sitting in the desk directly behind mine.

I stopped dead in my tracks, my heart pounding.

The boy looked straight at me. Suddenly, I understood what people meant when they described eyes as 'piercing.'

"Whoa," Bree whispered in my ear. "Who is that?"

So I wasn't hallucinating; the boy was really there. He looked exactly the same as he had in my dreams, except… dry, and wearing FUBU. Also his hair was shorter than I remembered and appeared expertly styled in a way that made it look effortlessly mussed. The florescent lights of the classroom brought out the almost-blue highlights in its black waves. But where had he come from? What was he doing in my class? *And who was he?*

I got no answers that day. Mrs. Phillips didn't even acknowledge the presence of the new student, nor did he introduce himself. The exact same thing happened when I got to French class. And Bio. And History. And PE.

Bree and I weren't the only ones to notice him. Over the next couple of days, I heard a dozen variations on the same conversation:

"Have you seen that new transfer student?"

"The tall guy? Really pale, with black hair?"

"Yeah. He is so wicked hot! Did you catch his name?"

"No. Any idea where he's from?"

"No, but I heard he's a European model."

"No way, his parents are diplomats, and totally loaded."

"They must be!"

Everyone was curious and rumors abounded, but for some reason, no one was able to glean any actual facts on him. At first, the other girls could talk for hours just about how attractive he was. This resulted in a lot of jealous grumbling from the guys. However, the gushing died down as everyone started to realize what I'd known from the start: there was something off about the boy.

The fact that his schedule matched mine so perfectly might have been a coincidence, but that didn't explain the way he stared at me. Just me. Constantly.

At first, I was oblivious because he always sat behind me. But Vik noticed right away, and he wasted no time in telling me.

"It's totally creepy," he said. "You need to be careful, Andi. Don't let that guy get too close."

"Vik, you're overreacting," said Bree. "It's not a crime to *look* at someone."

My brain agreed with Bree, but my gut was with Vik. There was definitely something unsettling about the boy. And maybe it was just my imagination, but from then on, I swear I could feel his piercing eyes always on me. I began to empathize with animals in the zoo.

~*~*~*~

"Riley Bay!"

Bree said the name as though it were the answer to a riddle she'd been puzzling over for days. As it turned out, it was.

I looked up from my cafeteria lunch (veggie pizza, a bright green apple and chocolate milk) in confusion.

"Huh?"

"Riley Bay," Bree repeated, plopping onto the bench across from me. "That's your not-so-secret admirer's name."

My heart skipped a beat, but I tried to play it cool. I rolled my eyes. "He's not my admirer, secret or otherwise. Have you seen the way he glares at me? He's clearly the exact opposite of an admirer."

"I wouldn't say he *glares* at you. He just *stares* at you. That could be good or bad." She smiled slyly. "Maybe he's just captivated by your beauty."

I rolled my eyes again. "I sincerely doubt that."

"No, seriously," she continued, "I think he might like you, Andi. He may be weird, but he's still a teenage boy. Maybe he's just shy."

I honestly hadn't considered that possibility, nor did I give it much thought now. It was hard to imagine any guy noticing me in that way, but a guy that gorgeous? No way.

"You must be at least a little curious about him," Bree prodded. "After all, it's not every day a girl gets her very own stalker."

"Just what I always wanted," I said sarcastically.

The truth was, Bree was more right than she knew. For two nights in a row, I'd lain awake, wondering about this mystery boy. But who could blame me? I wasn't used to getting attention from boys, except for Vik, and he didn't count. For that matter, I wasn't used to getting this kind of attention—silent, but intense—from anyone.

So he had a name: Riley Bay. That didn't seem right to me. I was expecting something a little more exotic, like Balthasar or Demetrius or Fabio. How could such an unusual person have such an ordinary name?

In my head, I went over the facts I knew about Riley Bay: he was new in town, so new that no one seemed to know anything about him. He was in every single one of my classes. He was extremely, ridiculously good-looking. He was a total jerk.

Okay, so those last two were technically opinions, not facts. But I didn't see how anyone could dispute them.

"Has he spoken to you yet?" Bree asked. Or at least, I think that's what she said. It was hard to tell, given that she was talking through a mouthful of corn dog.

I shook my head. "I haven't heard him talk to *anyone* yet."

"Weird," said Bree.

"What's weird?" Vik queried, sitting down next to me.

"Nothing," I said hastily, but at the same time, Bree blurted, "Andi's mystery man."

Instantly, Vik's face darkened. "He hasn't been bothering you, has he?" he asked me urgently.

I shot Bree a dirty look. Why did she have to go and mention Riley to Vik? Now I was going to have to put up with his overprotective pseudo-brother shtick for the rest of lunch.

"He hasn't done anything other than glare at me in every class," I reassured him.

Vik relaxed visibly. "Well, speak up if he does," he said sternly.

I rolled my eyes. "Sure. Whatever. Can we please change the subject?"

Of course, changing the subject didn't help me forget about Riley Bay, because the boy himself was sitting on the other side of the cafeteria. And, as always, I could feel his eyes fixed on me.

~*~*~*~

The next day, Bree passed me a note during third period:

'Craving lobster rolls like u wouldn't believe. Etta's 4 lunch?'

Henrietta's was a little cafe down by the harbor. Naturally, it specialized in seafood. It was the kind of picturesque locale that drew tourists like flies to honey, but on a weekday afternoon in September, it would be relatively empty. Bree was obsessed with the place, which she insisted was the only really good restaurant in the whole town.

I frowned, and not just at Bree's text speak. Only seniors were allowed to leave campus for lunch. Underclassmen sneaked out all the time, but knowing my luck, we'd be the first students in history to actually get caught and punished. I caught Bree's eye and shook my head.

Pleeeeeeese? she mouthed.

I sighed deeply. Well, I *was* getting pretty sick of cafeteria food. I passed the note on to Vik, who nodded enthusiastically.

When the bell rang, I bolted out the door. If we were going to drive to Henrietta's, eat and get back in time for fourth period, we couldn't spare a minute. I was halfway down the hall before I realized Vik and Bree weren't following me. I retraced my steps and found Bree hovering outside the Biology classroom.

"What's the holdup?" I asked.

"Vik is talking to Ms. Epistola," she said.

I blinked in surprise. "About what?"

Bree shrugged.

Vik emerged from the classroom a couple minutes later, looking thoughtful.

"What were you talking to the sub about?" I asked.

Vik didn't look me in the eye when he answered. "I just had a question about the exam next week," he mumbled, blushing.

I stared at him in amazement. Was it possible Vik was lying to me? How could he do that? *Why* would he do that? What could he have been discussing with our substitute teacher that he couldn't share with me?

Before I could interrogate him further, Bree started pulling us both down the hall.

"Come on!" she wailed. "I'm freaking starving!"

Vik looked relieved at the interruption. This raised my suspicions even more, but I decided to let the issue drop for the time being. I had enough on my mind without worrying about Vik.

Ten minutes later, I was parking Bree's car in front of Henrietta's while Bree and Vik bickered in the backseat.

"I'm not saying she's a bad teacher," Bree said indignantly. "I'm just saying she should dress more professionally."

"Ms. Epistola is a grown woman. She should dress

however she wants," Vik shot back.

"You just like being able to see her cleavage!"

"Guys!" I hissed. "Cool it! You're going to attract attention."

I peered cautiously through the glass door of the restaurant. There were only a handful of patrons inside, but they were clearly locals, not tourists. Which meant that any one of them might recognize us and realize that we were breaking school rules.

"Calm down, Andi!" said Bree. "Even if someone notices us, what are they going to do? Call the cops? No one cares that much about some dumb school rule except the vice principal, and he's not in there."

Without further ado, she and Vik strolled into the restaurant. All I could do was sigh and follow them. It turned out that Bree was right. No one even spared us a second glance.

"What can I get you kids to drink?" the bored-looking waitress asked.

"Just water for me," I said.

"Same," said Vik.

"I'll have a Pepsi," said Bree.

The waitress nodded and went back to the kitchen.

Just as I was starting to relax, everything went wrong.

I was sitting with my back to the door, so I didn't see him walk in. But I knew who it was immediately from the looks on my friends' faces: looks of surprise and, in Vik's case, rage.

"That does it," he growled. "I'm confronting this psycho."

He started to get up, but Bree grabbed his arm, pulling

him back down to his chair.

"Confront him about *what?*" she challenged. "He's only guilty of leaving campus for lunch—which we are also doing!"

"You know that's not it!" Vik snapped. "He's *stalking* Andi. This proves it. Why else would he choose this place, on this day?"

"Maybe because it's the only decent restaurant in town, and he's been here long enough to get sick of our crappy cafeteria food?"

From behind me, I heard the scrape of a chair being pulled across the wooden floor and knew that Riley had taken a seat nearby. I didn't have to look to know that he had positioned himself for optimal Andi creeping.

"What can I get you to drink, hon?" I heard the waitress ask him. After a long pause, she added nervously, "Um... some water, maybe?"

"That will suffice," said Riley. It was the first time I'd actually heard his voice. He had just the hint of an accent that I couldn't begin to place, and the pitch was deeper than I would have imagined. Somehow... more *resonant*, like it belonged to a much larger body.

"Hey, Riley!" Bree called. "Come join us!"

Vik and I both looked at her like she'd lost her mind, but it was too late to say anything; Riley was already standing before our table.

"Good afternoon." He directed this oddly formal greeting to me and only me.

"So you snuck off campus, too, huh?" said Bree. "Well, we won't tell if you won't."

Riley's eyes flicked to Bree for only a second before

returning to my face. "A reasonable agreement."

After an awkward pause, Bree asked, "So are you going to Jerrid's pool party on Saturday?"

"Pool party?" Riley repeated slowly, as though he'd never heard the term before.

Underneath the table, I gave Bree a warning kick, but she blathered on, "Yeah! It's the social event of the season—one last shindig before it gets too cold for swimming."

Riley turned back to me. "Will you be attending this... pool party?"

"We all will be!" Bree said cheerfully. "Practically the whole school is going."

"Very well," said Riley. "I will see you Saturday." Then, without another word, he turned around and walked out of the restaurant.

Vik, who had been silently fuming the whole time Riley was at our table, burst out angrily, "What the hell, Bree?"

"What?" said Bree. "Is it a crime to make an effort to be friendly to people you inexplicably don't like?"

I was just as angry as Vik, but not at Bree. Who did Riley Bay think he was, following me to Henrietta's just to stare at me creepily? And now he was going to ruin Jerrid's party for me, too?

I rose from the table and started walking toward the door.

"Andi? Where are you going?" Vik called after me, concerned.

"Wait here," I called back.

I caught up with Riley in the parking lot.

"What the heck is your problem?" I demanded angrily.

Slowly, he turned to face me.

"I beg your pardon?"

The words flowed from my mouth in a furious torrent: "You come here out of the blue, acting like you own the place. Suddenly, you're in all of my classes, and you're constantly staring at me, like I'm some kind of sideshow freak. Now you're following me around outside of school, too? Just to stare at me some more? I repeat, *what is your problem?*"

Riley's mouth fell open. It was the first time I'd seen him look anything but one hundred percent composed.

"You insolent wench!" he hissed. "*You* dare to question *me?*"

I was so shocked by the venom in his voice that the strangeness of his vocabulary almost didn't register.

"Insolent wench?" I repeated incredulously. "Who the heck—"

I was cut off mid-sentence by a tremendous crash of thunder. I turned just in time to see a bolt of lightning hit the water in the harbor less than a hundred yards away. It was really weird, considering there wasn't a cloud in the sky. Even weirder, when I turned back, Riley was gone. I don't mean that he was running away, or driving off. I mean that he had vanished without a trace. I was alone in the parking lot.

I didn't know how he'd pulled that trick, any more than I knew where he'd come from or why he hated me so much. Only one thing was certain: I now had an enemy, whether I wanted one or not.

Chapter Five

Contradictions

AFTER THURSDAY'S DEBACLE AT HENRIETTA'S, I SPENT Friday doubling down my efforts to avoid stumbling into Riley's line of sight, at least whenever possible. I resolutely refused to look over my shoulder in any of our classes; miraculously, I managed it. Though it wasn't easy.

I nearly had a slipup almost from the get-go in second period when Monsieur Cousteau called on Riley. Even though I was braced for it, his resonant voice three rows behind me sent chilly shivers down my spine as he conjugated the verbs perfectly, his accent flawless.

"*Très bien, Monsieur Bay! Vous êtes un crédit à cette classe.*" Even Monsieur Cousteau was awed by Riley's command of the tongue. "Perhaps some of your classmates might benefit eef you offered your services as tutor, *non?*"

I heard some of the girls in class giggling and repeating the word "services." In the desk next to mine, Bree fanned herself, perhaps only half in mockery, and I rolled my eyes. But even I had to bite the end of my Lisa Frank pencil to keep from following every other eye in the room when Riley responded.

"*Ce serait mon plaisir.*" The words rolled off his tongue like French honey. It would be his *pleasure*.

How had I managed to never hear his voice (outside of my dream, that is) before yesterday? Maybe the teachers had been going easy on him for his first days of classes at a new school, but now it seemed like every single one of them was part of a conspiracy to make me break my resolution. They all called on him at least once the rest of the day.

Hearing him behind me sent increasing strata of tingles over my flesh each time. I kept my legs tightly crossed under my desk, my teeth all but permanently clenched. The tension in the air was almost unbearable. I wondered if anyone else could feel it. Like at any moment he might suddenly say something nasty about me out of nowhere. I knew I was probably just psyching myself out, but I wouldn't put it past him. If yesterday had been any indication, despite his usual strong-silent-type routine, when he did open his mouth, he apparently didn't have much of a filter. Especially where I was concerned.

By the time school was out for the week, I was exhausted, and wanted nothing more than to just crash and forget all about the past five days. My parents attempted to goad me into watching a movie with them, Mom wheedling me with a batch of her homemade apple cider that she was perfecting for the annual Portsmouth Pumpkin Festival the weekend after next, but I just didn't have the energy to deal with them, and I managed to escape.

Typical Andi Slate, in bed by 9:30 p.m. on a Friday night. At least I was too tired to spend much time stressing over the dreaded pool party. But the weariness didn't keep me from dreaming about *him*.

Of course.

~*~*~*~

Saturday afternoon found me staring at the three bathing suits I owned as they lay splayed across my bed. I'd known about Jerrid's party since the first week of school, and had been planning to wear my white sundress with the navy-style buckles on the straps and the little embroidered anchor on the pleated skirt. It would have been the perfect goodbye-to-summer outfit paired with my rope-heeled wedges. I hadn't even considered bringing a bathing suit. I certainly wouldn't be swimming at the party.

When it came to water, I was all oil. We just didn't mix. Swimming was simply something I did *not* do. It was kind of ironic considering my parents' life vocation and where we lived, but the dark truth was that the ocean terrified me.

There's a word for people like me: Thalassophobic. And I was a textbook example. When I was a kid, I used to have nightmares about being swallowed up by stormy waves, devoured by serpentine sea monsters or drowning under my parents' research boat while they were too busy with their binoculars and notebooks to notice I'd even slipped off.

I suppose the dreams hadn't exactly ever stopped, had they?

I shivered as I pushed away the image of the statuesque boy that threatened to surface from the sea of my mind, and I focused instead on the swimsuits on my turquoise argyle comforter. Needless to say, none of them had ever touched water outside of a washing machine. Jerrid's extravagant swimming pool with its three-tiered stone waterfall and elevated hot tub was a far cry from the ocean of my nightmares, but I definitely wouldn't be going within five feet of it if I could help it.

For that matter, I wouldn't have even been going to the party at all if I could help it. I knew I wasn't going to fit in. Even though Jerrid and most of his meat-head friends were seniors, a year above me, I always just felt so... *old* around them. But avoiding the event was out of the question. When the grand poobah all-high, Madam Bridget Fifan decided to go to a party, she always found a way to make sure I suffered through it with her. But despite all that, I couldn't explain my sudden desire to wear a bathing suit.

Perhaps there's someone you want to impress?

I glowered daggers at the inner voice that dared to nag me. No. It was because I knew Bree would berate me if I didn't wear one, whether I swam or not. That was the only reason.

I strongly considered the boyshort tankini set I usually donned whenever I attempted to sunbathe, but then I found myself fingering the material of my royal purple bikini. I'd bought it while Under The Influence Of Bree when we'd been shopping at the Victoria's Secret outlet in Newport last summer. Bree was always pushing me to 'be more spontaneous.' But despite the fact that I'd owned it for over a year, I'd never been brave enough to actually wear it.

Perhaps you just never had a reason to before now?

I bit my lip hard and snatched up my aquamarine one-piece with the wrap top.

Part of me was still furious with Bree for spilling the beans to Riley. What had she been thinking? That maybe he was just lonely and only needed to feel welcome and then he'd suddenly open up to being social like a magical moonflower and somehow become anything other than an insufferably conceited jerk? It wasn't going to happen.

But maybe he wouldn't actually show up at the party after all. He clearly had no interest in getting to know anyone else at school. I couldn't see why he would even want to come. Just to stare at me some more with his hate-filled gaze? Didn't he get enough of that during school hours? You would think he'd at least want a break on the weekend.

But that was too much to hope for.

When Bree and I walked into Jerrid's sprawling backyard (fashionably late, as per Bree's plan), the party was in full swing, and Riley was impossible to miss on the far side of the patio, looking like an Abercrombie and Fitch billboard idol in deep green swim trunks and absolutely nothing else.

I heard Bree release a low whistle next to me. "I didn't think it was humanly possible for real people to look like that."

I rolled my eyes. "I'm still not convinced he's not some kind of cyborg."

Bree gave me a look but then shook her head. "Well, *they* sure don't seem to mind."

She was referring to the veritable harem of string bikini-clad girls that surrounded him, laughing like jackals at everything he said. I couldn't imagine what they could be talking about. He certainly didn't look like he was saying anything funny. He had the same cold, hard expression as always. But he *was* talking to them, and I wasn't sure what to make of the oddly bitter taste that realization left in my mouth. He was actually engaging in conversation, and not looking at me. For once. I should have been thrilled. But instead I only felt simple and invisible in my comparatively conservative bathing suit and sheer sarong. I almost gagged as one of the tanned blondes at Riley's side handed him a bottle of coconut oil and gestured to her back.

"Jerrid's got the grill going!" Bree chirped. "I'm going to say hi and get a hotdog. Want one?"

I shook my head and she bounded off.

I ignored Riley completely and wandered through the throng of partiers toward the arrangement of comfortable lounge chairs that took up most of the expansive raised wooden deck. They were a good enough distance from the pool where I didn't have to worry about falling victim to any wayward splashing.

"Hey Andi!" Vik called, intercepting me as I passed by one of the artfully-displayed snack tables. A fluffy purple towel was slung over his broad brown shoulders. "I was wondering when you'd get here. I just about to jump in, but—"

"Yowza," he was cut off by Travis, Jerrid's best friend from the football team. He had clearly just come from the pool. "Lookin' scrumptious, Andicakes."

I blinked, then shrugged. "Um, thanks?"

Vik's expression darkened and he stepped over to Travis. "Hey *dude*, don't talk to my friend that way."

Travis lifted his hands and flashed Vik a bleached smile. "Chill, man! No disrespect." He turned to me and ran his tanned fingers back through his wet blonde hair. "Heading poolwards?"

"Andi doesn't swim," Vik snapped.

I groaned internally. There he went again. The protective brother thing could really get beyond awkward sometimes. Outwardly, I just shook my head and managed an inept half-smile. "You boys have fun though."

I waved a goodbye, then skirted the snack table to finish my trajectory to the deck where I contentedly spent the next hour stretched out on one of the lounge chairs, engrossed in rereading my well-worn copy of my favorite classic book (*The Phantom of the Opera* by Gaston Leroux) and cajoling my helplessly pale skin to at least try to soak up some sun. It was a useless effort; I couldn't tan if my life depended on it. Even if I did get any color, it would be gone by tomorrow.

"So why don't you swim?"

I almost jumped in my cushioned chair. I'd been so caught up in the tragedy of the Phantom and Christine's forbidden love story that I hadn't even heard Travis approach.

He grabbed one of the deck chairs and flipped it around, straddling it backward right up against the side of my lounge. He folded his beefy arms on the chair's back and looked down at me. He'd dried off, but he was close enough that I could still smell the chlorine on him.

I shook my head and quickly tried to concoct an answer that was anything but the truth. However, my train of thought completely left the station as I suddenly couldn't help noticing that Riley was standing about twenty feet behind Travis, just at the edge of the deck, like a chiseled marble statue come to life. His pack of bleached-blonde hyenas was gone and he was staring at me again.

Except... no. This time he was staring at Travis. And if I thought his eyes were filled with hate when he looked at me before, they were brimming with unadulterated vitriol now. If I didn't have prior knowledge of how thick Travis's head was, I would have been baffled that he could manage not to feel that blazing green gaze burning straight through the back of his skull.

Travis glanced over his muscled shoulder to see what I was looking at, but he didn't notice Riley or didn't care. I don't know how he possibly accomplished either.

He looked back down at me. "Uhuh, I see. Yeah, that's pretty much what I thought."

I repressed a shudder and blinked to focus on him again. "Huh?"

"You don't have a reason."

It took me a moment to remember what he was talking about, but then the thought train came back into the station and hit me. I shook my head. "Oh, um, I just can't swim. I never learned."

He let out a jocular laugh. "It's only like four feet deep!"

"Not all of it." I glanced to the end of the abstractly shaped pool nearest to us. I knew it must be the deep end, because at that moment I happened to catch Bree doing a colossal cannonball off the diving board there. She almost landed on Vik who was treading water nearby. Everyone laughed and then they started a race to the far side of the pool.

"So what are you reading?" Travis inquired.

I lifted my book, just to show him the cover, but he took it right out of my hand and flipped idly through the pages. "Looks interesting." He was clearly not in the least bit interested.

I shrugged, playing it cool. "I like it." No way was I going to tell him that it struck chords in my heart that no other story ever had. A guy like Travis couldn't possibly ever understand.

"Oh yeah?" His blonde eyebrows rose on his tan forehead and he stood up, taking the book with him.

I pushed myself up when I realized he was heading for the pool. "Hey!"

Travis laughed. "Then you probably wouldn't like it if I accidentally dropped it in the water." He pretended to teeter on the edge. "It sure is slippery over here!"

"Travis!" I snapped, leaving the safety of my chair to go after him.

"Whattaya say, Andi? I think one of you is gonna go swimming. You or your book."

I felt my stomach drop. I'd owned that copy of *Phantom* since I was thirteen and read it more times than I could even remember. It was battered and dog-eared, sure, but it was a dear old friend to me.

I folded my arms tightly and glared at him. "You're acting like a child."

He grinned at me as he wagged the book over the water. "C'mon, just spill it. Why don't you wanna swim? Afraid your hair will get frizzy?"

"I just don't like it, okay?"

"How do you know unless you try it?"

"Just stop."

"C'mon, Andicakes, do it for your precious book!"

I threw down my arms with a groan of frustration and stepped up, reaching around him to try to snatch the book back. I realized an instant too late what a grave mistake I'd made. I felt his thick arm lock around my waist and I gasped, jerking back on instinct. I don't know if he actually slipped or if he did it intentionally, but either way, he was laughing as the ground disappeared beneath us.

The next thing I knew, we were slamming through the water, and then we were submerged. And I was instantly more terrified than I'd ever been in my life.

I thrashed at first and opened my mouth to scream, but when the chlorinated brine rushed down my throat, my body locked up. Only distantly could I tell how quickly I sank, like a stone. The seacrest hues that surrounded me began to blur, and I saw the shape of my book float by the corner of my eye for a second before fuzzy white overtook my vision.

My heart combusted in my chest and needles stabbed every inch of my skin. My body burned to move, but it couldn't—and then, I *knew*. This was it. Every one of my worst nightmares had finally come true.

It was no use... no use fighting... I *knew*. And I gave in. I could hear nothing but the crashing of my pulse in my ears, but it too faded and soon everything around me was soft and floaty. I found myself drifting into a long-forgotten memory. A summer afternoon when I was very young, on my parents' boat, bobbing on the gentle waves off the San Diego coast. The sun warm on my cheeks, the ocean breeze whispering through my hair...

Look Andi, whales! Do you see the whales? No sweetie, look further. Out there... beyond...

A distant splash of a body diving into the water above me broke through the soft stuff of the memory, but then it too was gone.

Don't lean over too far, Andi... If you fall in, we'll never be able to get you back...

Suddenly, I felt Travis wrenched away from me. I hadn't even realized he was still holding me until he was gone, and for an instant, the water's chill assaulted my back. But only for an instant. And then arms were around me. I must have been beyond delirious because it felt like more than two. Countless arms—an impossible number of them, surrounding my frame, enveloping me, completely entwining me—strong and protective, gathering me against a hard, firm body like the most precious of pearls from the darkest of depths, buoying me to the surface, where I burst forth into the glorious air with a tremendous gasp.

I gulped in mouthfuls of air, sweet and beautiful, and was faintly aware of Vik's voice shouting my name from afar. My vision began to clear as I felt the strong arms pull me up out of the pool as if I weighed no more than a child. I coughed and sputtered as the arms sat me down gently on the ledge. And then I realized that there were only two of them, and that they belonged to Riley Bay.

He released me and crouched at my side, his face inches from mine, his hair dripping down his forehead. His black brows knit deeply as he peered intently into my eyes. It was as if he were searching for something, demanding an answer to a question I could never begin to fathom.

I was too shocked to react. My mouth fell open and I stared back at him.

"Andi!" Vik's voice called, closer now. I heard splashing.

Riley's eyes flashed and he pulled away from me with a noise under his breath that sounded almost like a growl. I must have still been pretty disoriented because he was suddenly several feet away from the edge of the pool faster than I thought anyone could possibly move.

I heard more splashing and angry voices arguing. I looked back to the pool and drew my feet up from where they still dangled in the water, wrapping my arms tightly around my knees and immediately beginning to shiver as if the air temperature had suddenly dropped twenty degrees.

"What's the matter with you!? Are you crazy?!?" Vik was shouting at Travis, who looked like he'd only just surfaced, about fifteen feet from where we'd gone in.

Travis pushed his bangs out of his face while treading water and opened his mouth as if he'd answer Vik, but then... it just kept opening. And opening. I didn't know a mouth could open that far. His tongue lolled out, his lips curled back and his eyes bulged as if they'd come right out of their sockets, his face contorting in a gruesome display of excruciating agony. A moment later, a ragged, earsplitting howl escaped his throat and tore icicles up my spine. His hands shot up to clamp against his own ears and he sank straight to the bottom of the pool.

Even once he was submerged, I could swear I could still hear the screaming. A second later, a bloom of red erupted around his shadowy shape below the choppy surface.

Vik's eyes went wide and he dove after him. I scrambled back from the edge of the pool as pandemonium broke out around me and everyone else fought to escape the water. Some girls started shrieking and other people shouted for help. My back hit the wooden edge of the deck and I looked up. Riley was standing above me, as still as a statue, his hands clenched at the sides of his dripping swim trunks.

But no, as I looked closer, I realized he wasn't still at all. His entire frame was trembling. And his face was intensely focused into an expression of what could only be called sheer black loathing, his smoldering eyes fixed on the spot where Travis had disappeared.

I gasped and pushed myself to my feet. If he noticed me there, he didn't show it. I followed his gaze back to the pool and saw Vik and another boy bring Travis to the surface. He was still howling, and burgundy blood was streaming from his ears. They got him up onto the ledge, where he curled into a ball and began to claw at his own eyes. Three of his friends from the football team jumped to stop him, pinning him down, and Vik backed away in dismay as a crowd gathered from all sides. I saw Vik crouch at the edge of the pool and fish something out of the water. Then he seemed to look around amid the swarm of frightened people. He looked lost. I knew he was looking for me.

I turned my attention back to Riley. His gaze remained deadlocked on where Travis was, though there was no way he could possibly see him through the crowd. But if anything, the look in his eyes had become even darker. His lips were moving just slightly, as if he were whispering to himself, though I couldn't hear anything despite how close I was.

What was he doing? What was wrong with Travis?

I looked back to the crowd. Someone shouted to call 911. I put a hand over my mouth as I drew in a gasp. I shook my head in denial.

No... it wasn't possible.

I looked back to Riley. His jaw was clenched now, but his look was the same. I started to back away. "You..."

His head snapped in my direction and I bit back a gasp. But when his eyes met mine, the dark look was gone. It was only the usual glower of contempt that greeted me. He seemed to study my face for a moment, but only briefly, and then his lip curled into a disdainful sneer. He turned on his heel and stalked away, disappearing into the crowd.

Oh god. *What* was *that?*

"Andi, are you alright?" It was Vik, at my elbow.

I turned to him, suddenly trembling head to toe. His face was filled with concern, his warm ochre eyes pained as they took in my bemused expression.

"Here." He gently wrapped his fluffy purple towel around me. "You're alright, right?"

I tried to nod, but I suddenly felt on the verge of tears.

"Hey, it's okay." He put an arm around my shoulders, pressing the towel against my back. I tried to swallow what threatened to be a sob and dropped my forehead against the front of his wet shoulder.

He gently patted my back, his voice soothing. "You were only under for a few seconds. I saw the whole thing from the other end of the pool. I was on my way over, but then that... that guy dove in and dragged you out."

A few seconds? It had felt like so much longer. And it hadn't felt like dragging... It had felt like floating, like flying... I shivered as I remembered the feeling of Riley's arms around me... the look in his otherworldly eyes as his face had been so close to mine at the side of the pool.

But then... Travis... It was like Riley *did* something. Something to Travis.

Oh god, *what had he done?* And why?

I bit my lip hard and looked down. It was then that I noticed Vik held something in his other hand.

The waterlogged remains of my book.

Oh god.

What had *I* done?

Chapter Six
Confrontation

THOUGH I BARELY SLEPT AT ALL, I SPENT THE REST OF the weekend in bed. I saw no point in getting up. I knew I wouldn't be able to focus on anything but my own thoughts, and I could just as easily do that lying down.

My mom came barging in every couple of hours, asking questions and looking at me as though I were dying. I must have said, "I'm fine, Mom," a dozen times. Of course, I *wasn't* fine, but she didn't need to know that. There was nothing she could have done to help me, except leave me alone with my thoughts. Again and again, I went over the events of the past week, trying to make sense of it all, but it was like trying to solve a jigsaw puzzle without all the pieces.

Riley had made Travis lose his mind. I was sure of it.

But how? And, more importantly, why?

I thought about Thursday in the parking lot at Henrietta's, when he'd vanished into thin air. The way he talked, like he was from another era. The fact that he'd appeared in my dreams before I'd met him in real life. The conclusion was as obvious as it was terrifying.

Riley Bay wasn't human.

But if he wasn't human, then what was he? An alien, sent to Earth to learn about humanity in preparation for an invasion? Riley was certainly weird enough to be an alien, but I didn't see why the mother ship would send him to Portsmouth, Rhode Island, in the guise of a high schooler. Surely, he would learn more by infiltrating our government or something, right?

If he wasn't from outer space, then he had to be from Earth. But if any native of Earth could do the things he did, then the world was a much stranger place than I'd been led to believe.

In my head, I made a list of every mythical beast I could think of, but Riley Bay didn't resemble any of them. He went out during the day, so he couldn't be a vampire. He was in school during the full moon, so he wasn't a werewolf. He didn't have wings, so I could cross both faery and angel off the list. What did that leave? Leprechauns? I snorted at the very idea.

And what was his motive? What interest could such a creature have in me, the most ordinary girl in the world? Why did he despise me so? And why punish Travis for taunting me? If anything, he should have reveled in seeing me humiliated like that. The more I learned about Riley Bay, the less he made sense.

A big part of me wanted to pretend the whole thing had never happened, but that was impossible. Even if my mind had let me forget, my classmates wouldn't have. On Monday, everyone was talking about Travis's unexpected mental break.

"They're saying it was drugs," Vik informed us at lunch.

"He didn't seem high to me," said Bree. "I mean, until he started screaming about tentacles."

"I guess whatever he took needed time to kick in," said Vik, shrugging.

"What did he take?" Bree asked. "LSD? Bath salts? Mushrooms?"

"I've heard conflicting things," said Vik. "But whatever it was, he must have way overdone it. They're saying his brain is permanently fried."

No one said a word about Riley. Apparently, I was the only one who'd noticed the look on his face as Travis went insane. That made sense when I thought about it. No one else had any reason to be looking at Riley at that moment. Even if they happened to glance in his direction, they probably wouldn't recognize the significance of his expression. Only I had reason to be wary of him already.

By the time the 3:35 p.m. bell rang, I couldn't take it anymore. I had to confront him.

Cornering Riley wasn't hard since, as usual, he had chosen the desk directly behind mine. I waited just outside the classroom door, gesturing wordlessly for Vik and Bree to go on without me. Then, when Riley came out, I ambushed him.

"We need to talk," I said bluntly.

Surprise flicked across Riley's face, but a second later, he'd regained his composure.

"Yes?" he asked coolly.

I looked around. The hallway was swarming with students, but Mr. Price was still in his classroom, as most of the teachers would be. In the end, I pulled Riley into a nearby janitor's closet. It seemed faintly ridiculous, discussing such fantastic events surrounded by mops, brooms and various other humble objects, but it was better than the hallway. It was going to be awkward enough without an audience.

"I want to know how you did what you did to Travis, and why," I said.

He looked at me the way you'd look at a poodle that suddenly started reciting *Hamlet*.

"I… I know not what you mean," he said.

"Don't lie to me!" I snapped. "I saw the way you were looking at him."

Riley's lip curled. "That's your damning evidence?" he sneered. "That I *looked* at him?"

My cheeks flushed. Now that I'd said it aloud, it sounded ridiculous. But my gut was still telling me Riley was to blame.

"It had to be you," I protested weakly. "Who else could have done something like that?"

"I think you'll find the question is not *who*, but *what*. The boy foolishly ingested a most potent drug, or so believe the authorities."

I shook my head. "That doesn't add up. There were a hundred people at that party, and none of them saw Travis take drugs."

"Perhaps he did so while hiding in the lavatory."

"Or perhaps he didn't take anything at all," I said mockingly.

Riley only smiled patronizingly at me.

"I suggest you leave the detective work to the police, Miss Slate. You clearly have no aptitude for it."

He started to walk out of the room. Furious, I called after him, "That's not all I've seen you do!"

He froze, his hand on the doorknob.

The next instant, I found myself pushed up against the closet wall. Riley was gripping me by the shoulders, his face so close to mine that I could practically count the eyelashes framing his unearthly eyes.

"What do you mean?" he demanded, his hot breath warming my cheeks. I was seriously freaked out, but there was no turning back now.

"Last week, in the parking lot at Henrietta's," I said. "You just vanished. I only took my eyes off of you for a second. No normal person could have run away that fast."

For the first time, Riley Bay was at a loss for words. I would have smiled triumphantly if I wasn't so scared of what he might do next.

"And that's not even taking into account the weird way you talk, or the fact that your past is a complete mystery, or—" I stopped short. I didn't want to tell Riley that I'd seen him in my dreams. That seemed too... intimate. He might get the wrong idea.

"You... you noticed these things?"

"Of course. I'm not blind."

He shook his head. "But you're just a girl. One utterly insignificant girl. How could you...?"

Riley trailed off. He was looking at me in a completely different way then: with wonder and—was it possible?—a touch of fear.

"Perhaps the prophecy is true, after all," he murmured, more to himself than to me.

"What prophecy?" I asked, baffled.

Riley just stared at me some more. The gears in his head were clearly turning a mile a minute, but I couldn't guess what they were producing. Finally, he seemed to come to a decision.

"They'll never believe you," he said. "They'll think you've been ingesting drugs as well."

I opened my mouth, then closed it again. He was right. If I was really the only person who'd noticed all of the strange things about Riley Bay, then trying to tell people would be pointless. They'd find it much easier to believe that I'd gone insane than that I'd actually witnessed any of it.

Riley finally released his viselike grip on my shoulders.

"Go home, little girl," he said. "Enjoy your mundane little life while you still can."

And with that, he was gone.

Chapter Seven

Conspiracy

THE NEXT DAY, RILEY WASN'T IN ENGLISH CLASS.

He wasn't in French class either.

Tuesday passed.

During the few minutes we had for a mid-morning snack between French and Biology on Wednesday morning, still no sign of him. The logical part of my brain told me that I should be relieved.

So why didn't I feel relieved?

"Andi?" said Bree. "Are you okay?"

I'd almost forgotten Bree was there. It was hard not to, with thoughts of Riley racing through my mind. "I'm fine," I said mechanically. But I wasn't.

Bree, as always, took that at face value and started going on about something else, munching Cheetos while talking about the new episode of this or how Natalie said that, but I found myself drifting away. Was I fine? No, I wasn't. I *couldn't* be. This feeling in my heart, radiating outward across me, choking me up, holding up Riley's toned body and his cocky smile in my mind's eye... Surely I was sick.

But why? After he'd been so weird and smug and then downright threatening, *why* couldn't I just be relieved that he wasn't at school anymore to give me that smoldering look of disdain he had reserved special for me? *Why* couldn't I just stop thinking about him?

"Are you sure you're okay?" said Bree. "You don't look so good."

How could I explain it to Bree? She wouldn't understand. She *couldn't* understand. I didn't even know if I understood. And outside of things like schoolwork, spelling, history or general knowledge, there was very little Bree understood that I didn't.

"Hey," said Bree, gazing longingly at the granola bar I'd forgotten to even unwrap, "are you gonna eat that?"

We stepped into Biology. Vik was there, in an unusually aloof, dreamy state, but still no sign of Riley. And, to my ever-sinking heart, Mr. Cho wasn't there either.

Looked like we were going to get to enjoy Ms. Epistola as our substitute again. Goody.

As the bell rang signifying that we needed to be settled in class, her red lips curled into a sultry smile.

She was wearing an even more form-fitting shirt under her lab coat that made me wonder if it even fit the dress code, and her hair was no longer up in a bun, but flowing in luxurious, auburn locks down her back, looking like she'd just stepped off the set of a shampoo commercial.

I looked over to Vik at the table next to me and Bree; he seemed captivated by her. And who wouldn't be? We were mortals in the presence of a goddess.

How could anyone ever be interested in someone like me with women like her in the world?

She lifted a piece of chalk up to the board with her perfectly-manicured fire engine-red nails, and wrote:

'Ph'nglui mglw'nafh Cthulhu R'lyeh wgah'nagl fhtagn.'

Those words, that language!

"Are any of you familiar with the legends… of the Elder Gods?"

The class sat in awkward silence.

"It is fortunate, then, that Mr. Cho was discussing the deep sea this week, as that is a special interest of mine," said Ms. Epistola as she took gliding steps back and forth across the room in her stilettos. "It pertains not only to the mysteries of the deep, but also to those of archeology and anthropology. They are the Great Old Ones, giant creatures that are said to have large houses beneath the sea. It is said that mortals sometimes sense the presence of the Old Ones, meeting them only in their dreams, the one place where they can be truly comprehended."

I tore my thoughts from lamenting how pale and awful my skin was compared to hers at the mention of dreams. *Dreams.* What she was saying seemed like a bunch of inane babble, but the bit about dreams felt all too familiar. Meeting in my dreams incomprehensible creatures of the sea, the place I feared most and yet was inexorably drawn to. And that language she was using, so similar to what I had heard in my dream. I couldn't escape the feeling that maybe there *was* something to what she was saying.

And that it might have something to do with Riley.

"We've pieced this information together based on artifacts

from primeval cults." Ms. Epistola's eyes flashed. "And of course, ancient books. Old innocuous-seeming books with special significance to the Great Ones. Books so significant that their mortal owners, small-minded and well-meaning though they might be, may not even grasp their power."

Bree raised her hand. Ms. Epistola glared at her. "Miss Ficus?"

"Fifan," corrected Bree. "Aren't we supposed to be learning about marine biology? Wouldn't these old lessons belong in like, an anthropology or archaeology course or something?"

Ms. Epistola's eyes flashed with that unmistakable intensity of a woman scorned. "This is the lesson your teacher left me," she said, her voice wavering for a fraction of a second before regaining her calm, cool composure. She smoothed out her blouse, tossed her hair and smiled, her white teeth in sharp contrast against her dark red lips. It all only reminded me of how goofy I looked whenever I tried to wear cosmetics, like a doll a little girl tried to crayon her mother's makeup on.

The lesson continued from there, but I hardly paid attention. She was going on and on about archaeological stuff, some old tribal things that happened down in Louisiana or something and then some blather about ships disappearing and sailors losing their minds in the South Pacific. I only caught tidbits; I had to force myself not to stare at the clock, willing it to move. It was bad enough to feel so uncertain about Riley, but sitting through Ms. Epistola's lectures, watching every guy in the class drool over her?

Ugh.

Thirty-five torturous minutes later, I was finally saved by

the bell.

"I'll see you tomorrow, class," said Ms. Epistola. Somehow it felt more like a threat than a promise. "Provided Mr. Cho is still feeling unwell." She sashayed out of the room.

"I'll meet you guys in the cafeteria," said Vik, his bag already packed as he dashed out of his chair to follow Ms. Epistola. "I need to ask Scarlett some questions."

"About what?" I inquisitioned him, but he was gone in a flash. "Scarlett?"

My heart did a little flip, my blood starting to simmer. There was something I really didn't trust about Ms. Epistola, and I *really* didn't like Vik going after her like that.

"She's really into this whole Atlantean deep sea archaeology stuff!" said Bree, oblivious as always. "Even if it really has nothing to do with marine biology."

"Yeah," I said, shoving my notebooks into my bag as quick as I could. I was still really anxious about Vik, but thoughts of Riley soon butted their way back in, demanding my attention. He hadn't been at school for two days now. The slight thrill of relief I had felt at first yesterday was now replaced with dread; what if, in confronting him about Travis's madness, I had driven him away? What if he *never* came back?

There were so many questions left unanswered, so much I still desired to know of him. After what had happened at the pool party and then those things he'd said to me Monday? There was something very fishy about Riley Bay.

Wednesday passed.

Thursday morning, he still wasn't in English or French. And come third period, Ms. Epistola, true to her word, was our teacher again. She was still going on about the glory of her 'Elder Gods.' Bree kept shaking her head and saying that it didn't have anything to do with marine biology, but all I could think about was Riley. Well, Riley and Vik. Vik was transfixed by Ms. Epistola in a way that was starting to seem almost religious, like he was bowing piously before some kind of goddess at an altar.

Was she really *that* beautiful? Oh, who was I kidding, of course she was. Although if it were possible, it seemed that her skirt under the lab coat had gotten even shorter, and her red knit top was so *tight!* If it hadn't been for the white coat, there would have been nothing left to the imagination.

When the bell rang for lunch and Ms. Epistola gave her signature sensual wink and sashayed out the door, once again Vik scooted after her like a loyal puppy. Though before he made it into the hall, he stopped and looked back at me. "You're going to lunch now, right?"

What kind of question was that? "Of course."

"We need to talk." With that, he dashed out of the room after our curvaceous substitute.

Uh oh, that couldn't be good. I wondered what it could be about, then I remembered the look Vik gave me Saturday when Riley pulled me out of the water after Travis had attacked me. The look he had given *Riley*. Maybe Vik had some insight to Riley's mysterious disappearance?

"C'mon, um, I think Vik wants to talk to us about something in the cafeteria," I mumbled to Bree.

"About what?" Apparently she had not heard him.

"I dunno, something! He didn't say." I started to hurriedly stumble toward the door. I wondered if she could see right through me. I knew exactly what Bree would say: *"Typical Andi Slate. Just can't stand up for yourself and say what's on your mind.*" And she was right. I just was not the confrontational type, and it never did me any good when I tried. I was nothing like loud and boisterous Bree. The one time I tried to be like her, I'd made an enemy for life in Riley.

"What's the big hurry?" yelled Bree, still at our desk putting her things away. I hadn't even realized she wasn't following me. I was so buried in my own thoughts, so concerned with keeping my head down, I didn't look where I was going until it was too late, and I slammed right into a wall of rock-hard abs sheathed in a tight, black t-shirt.

Riley.

"Sorry!" I stammered, jumping back. His green eyes were cold, vast and mysterious as the ocean. "Y-you weren't in class the last few days."

"I was studying."

"Studying? *During* school?" I tried to stand up straight. "What were you studying, your *prophecy?*" I dared myself to cajole him.

His eyes burned. "You know not of what you speak, little one."

"Why not?" I squeaked. I had wanted it to come out stronger than it did. "Because I'm just an 'insignificant little girl?' "

His gaze was white-hot, it was all I could do not to cower under it. So overwhelmed was I that I scarcely heard Bree come up behind me.

"Hey, there you are, Riles!" she said. "Shame you weren't in class the last couple of days. You missed Substitute Hottie, PhD going on about all sorts of conspiracy crazy stuff."

"Crazy stuff?" he inquired.

"She's not *that* hot," I retorted.

"Walk with us to lunch?" asked Bree.

I did not get her! How could she be so unquestioningly blind and nice to people? Did she not *see* what he'd done to Travis?

Maybe Riley was right. No one *would* believe me.

"I have already feasted upon my required daily sustenance," said Riley, his burning eyes aglow.

Bree laughed. "You're cute," she said. "I can see why the Andster likes you."

I felt my face go sheet-white. Riley seemed nonplussed, moving on without a word. I marched toward the cafeteria like a robot, eyes wide, waiting for the blood to return to my face.

"Hey!" said Bree, playing catch up.

"Why would you say that?" I demanded once inside the bustling cafeteria.

"Oh, come on!" said Bree. "It's obvious what's going on. I know it, he knows it. It's time to sweep those seashells off the table and give in to the passion!"

"You know I'm afraid of the ocean, Bree!"

"It was a joke, lighten up!"

I scoffed, turning from her to go find Vik. He sat at our usual spot on the far side of the room. I suppose Bree was a bit humbled after the incident at Henrietta's a week ago; she didn't even begin to suggest that we leave campus to find something more palatable. As I sat down with my veggie burrito, carrots and banana, Bree went to go stand in line, probably to get her usual double helping of ultra-processed half-plastic school pizza. I didn't know how she could stand to stomach the stuff, but that topped with ranch dressing was one of her favorites.

"I can't believe her," I snapped. "I just can't believe her! Telling Riley to his face that I *like* him? While I'm standing *right there?*"

Vik's eyes shot up like I'd smacked him.

"I mean," I amended. "It's not true! I don't like him. So uncool for her to tell him that. With me *right there!*"

"How could you like him?" asked Vik, concerned.

"I don't! I just told you."

"I don't trust him," said Vik. "He's so broody and possessive... He talks weird, he just gives me a bad sense. I don't like you around him."

There Vik went *again*, playing up the protective brother routine. "I can take care of myself, you know."

"Can you?" he said. "Normally I would agree, but I can't take into account crazy people."

"He's not crazy!" I snapped, perhaps a little too quickly. "He's just... Yes, I agree, there is something very strange about him. But I don't think he's violent, or would hurt anyone." *Not me, anyway,* I thought, remembering Travis.

Vik huffed. "I don't like the way you defend him."

I scowled. "Well I don't like you following around Ms. Epistola like a lovesick kitten every day after class, speaking of weird people with possibly eeeeeviiill motives."

Vik blushed, and he frowned deeply. "I'm not a lovesick kitten. She's my tutor and I have things to discuss with her. *Academic* things."

I couldn't help myself; I gasped, sucking in air as I did. "She tutors you? When?"

"After school," he said, a little smug. I could tell he liked how upset it was making me. "She comes by to see my parents—"

"She was at your *house?*"

"Yes, she wanted to see some of our family's heirlooms, particularly the *Necronomicon*." He hesitated, but then shook his head. "But when I looked for it I couldn't find it. I'm afraid it may have been stolen."

"She visits you at your *house?*"

"She is my tutor, Andi!" he ejaculated. "Yes, and I just told you the *Necronomicon* might have been stolen!" He looked me levelly in the eye. "Do you know anything about it?"

"No, and why should I care?" I didn't mean it. I had ached to look through that book again, to unlock the mystery of my dreams. A part of me, a big part, thought that perhaps it all was a piece in the greater puzzle of Riley Bay. He had only appeared *after* I read from the book, after all...

I shook my head. That was absurd. It was just some old book. "Maybe Riley stole it. If you hate him so much, go ask him," I snapped.

"Maybe he did!"

"I was *joking!*"

"Well I wasn't! He showed up right after we read from it!"

"Well maybe your *tutor* stole it."

"What do you suspect her of?" demanded Vik. "Why are you so threatened by her? She's *just* my tutor!"

"Tutoring you in what? 'Marine biology?' Well she's teaching the wrong class if all she's interested in is that archaeology and weird religious stuff!"

"I find that stuff interesting," retorted Vik. "And for your information, she's an adjunct at Miskatonic and that's what she teaches in her night classes. She works with our parents. They all know her and she knows them. So yes, 'marine biology' but also that 'archeology stuff' that you're too much of a philistine to care about."

I scoffed, hurt. He shook his head. "Look," he said, "I'm upset, Father was really mad at me. He blamed me for losing the book and… Look, I'm going to go. We can talk later."

I moved to stop him, but stayed silent, watching him as he grabbed his tray, dumped his uneaten food into the trash and left the cafeteria. As he went, I saw Bree approach, an expression of concern on her face and small mountain of food on her tray.

"What's with him?" she asked, sitting across from me where Vik had been not thirty seconds prior.

I sighed. "A few things. Did you know he's being tutored by that…" I didn't feel like she deserved the dignity of being referred to by her surname like a real teacher. *Ms. Epistola.* She wasn't a real teacher *or* a real professor, just a cheap cheerleader Barbie substitute. "That Scarlett lady?"

"Yeah, apparently she knows his parents. He's totally into that stuff she talks about during class. You know, that stuff that totally has nothing to do with marine biology…"

"I don't trust her," I said, scowling at Bree angrily. "And I don't like that Vik's spending all this time with her." A picture of Riley flashed into my mind, and suddenly I remembered *why* I had been mad at Bree when I sat down. "And I can't believe you told Riley that I liked him!"

"What's the big deal?"

"Well it's not true, for one."

"Suuuure it isn't." Bree took a big bite of her ranch-soaked pizza. I sulked.

"Okay," she relented. "I'm sorry, I was just... I didn't think I was out of line, but I'm sorry, okay?"

I continued to sulk, crossing my arms and looking away.

Bree's face brightened. "Hey, there's going to be another party tomorrow after school."

"Not another pool party..."

"Well, we do live in a port town," reminded Bree, "this one's on the beach."

"That's even worse!"

Bree sighed, exasperated. "You don't have to go *in* the water." A sly smile crept onto her face. "It's a college party. So no high school idiots to do dumb, idiot things like drag people into pools."

College party. That somehow sounded *even* worse. If it wasn't bad enough to be surrounded by my peers, hollow-headed morons who didn't even know the name of the *original* author of my favorite book, which they then proceeded to ruin by dumping me in pools, college guys were their own kind of awful by being intimidating. Judging me for still being in high school, judging the way I looked and how I dressed, assuming I never knew what they were talking about (and they were *always* wrong).

"C'mon..." said Bree. "It's going to be wicked awesome, and It'll get your mind off Riley and Vik."

My eyes perked up. "You sure Riley won't be there?"

Bree shrugged. "Not unless he knows the same people I know, which I doubt. He doesn't seem to know anyone."

"And you can *promise* not to invite him?"

"Of course!" said Bree. "I promise."

Unexpectedly, my heart sank. I wasn't sure why. I didn't

want to think about him, or Vik, or 'Ms. Epistola,' or Vik's stupid book. In theory, meeting new people, even if they were intimidating, judgmental college kids, would be good for me, right?

So why did it make me feel so low to hear Riley wouldn't be there?

"Okay," I said, ignoring the deep sense of foreboding in my heart.

"I'll go."

Chapter Eight

Contaminated

I COULD HEAR THE OCEAN'S ROAR ON THE OTHER SIDE of the dunes before we even saw it, and it made me shudder. *Ugh.* The sheer vastness of it, the terrible creepy crawlies that lived in it, the unsavory feeling of salt clinging to my skin on the rare occasions I'd ever dared to step into it. And it seemed like every time I had, something awful happened. One time, as I ran out of the waves my first summer here (having been dragged in by Bree, of course) I stepped on a jellyfish. Not the stinging kind, but I still slipped and fell, and it was *disgusting!* Worse was the time a shark nipped at my heels. I avoided the water for two years after that. It didn't draw blood, and its dorsal fin didn't break the surface, but I just *knew* it was a shark that had gone for the gold and missed. I just *knew.*

The second I stepped onto the beach to join the party, I could tell I was in over my head. I couldn't begin to fathom how Bree carried herself with such confidence, striding onto the sand, her curvy hips bobbing back and forth. I sighed, swallowing my doubts. I wanted to do this. I wanted to be here.

Didn't I?

"Bridget Fifan!" One of the college boys, a tall, slender black guy, stood up from the bonfire he was stoking. He definitely had the aura and swagger of someone older. He approached Bree, giving her a high five. I stood back, apprehensive.

"What is up, my sista?"

"Keepin' it real, Jamal!" said Bree. "Allow me to introduce my friend, Andi. Andi? Jamal." She pointed to some of the other college kids. The guys were all shirtless, and the girls were all in string bikinis. Bree had talked me into finally wearing my bikini as well, the wide-banded grape-colored one, but it was downright modest compared to what the college girls were wearing and it was currently hidden under my big baggy t-shirt.

"And that's Tyler, Skylar, Saoirse, Kigawe, Miracle, Melanie, Steve, Ta-Nehisi and Ryan."

I waved awkwardly. A couple waved back, but most of them stayed focused on the bonfire they were dousing in lighter fluid.

"It's been forever, girl!" said Jamal to Bree. "Come sit, make yourself at home! *Mi casa es su casa*. And hey." He reached into a large blue cooler by the fire and pulled out a metallic bag that looked like a Capri Sun. "Can I interest you ladies in a… wine cooler?"

"F'sho!" said Bree, snatching it hungrily. Jamal tossed one to me before I had the opportunity to respond. *Oh crap*. Now

I *really* felt in over my head. Except for having snuck a sip of my parents' Bud Light Lime once or twice, I'd never even tried alcohol! And to have a whole wine cooler to myself? I didn't want to look uncool in front of Bree's college friends, but I felt so out of my league!

And something in me told me Riley wouldn't want me to drink it.

I scoffed. Riley, of all people? Why did I care what *Riley* thought about whether I had a couple of wine coolers? He was just some weird guy I barely knew. Really, we'd barely even spoken.

Then why does he consume your thoughts?

I ripped the tiny straw off of the baggie, peeled off its plastic casing and jammed it into the beverage, droplets of inebriating sweetness popping out. "Thank you, Jamal," I said. I wasn't about to let what Riley thought—no, what I *thought* Riley would think about this party—dictate what I would and wouldn't do. "For real."

One wine cooler became two. Bree was having a high old time, regaling the college kids with stories about her trip to Brazil with a women's literacy group, but I kept to myself, sipping on my straw, trying not to think of Riley.

"Hey, you alright?" asked Bree, taking a break from showing her friends the pictures of some of the kids she'd taught on her phone.

I took a deep breath and forced a smile. "Fine!" I said.

"You're not thinking about Riley again, are you?" she asked. "You seem so unhappy when you think about him."

There it was again, the Bridget Fifan third degree. Did she just have to know every single excruciating detail of my inner workings? "No... well... maybe."

"Get him out of your head!" she said, sitting down next to me and giving me a pat on the back. "I brought you out here to have fun, and you *specifically* said not to invite him."

"Yeah, but it was *you* who invited him to the pool party in the first place."

Bree sighed and smiled, typical smile of can't-get-me-down Bree. "Oh, I was just trying to be nice! I'd never seen him talk to anybody... or be friendly to anyone, for that matter." She shrugged. "C'mon, don't worry about it! Let's have fun!"

Her idea of fun seemed to be more wine coolers. I took another, and as the afternoon wore into evening, the bonfire grew higher and the raucousness of the college kids grew more debauched, I found myself starting to relax. Was it the effects of alcohol, or was my mind genuinely finally starting to drift from thoughts of Riley?

"Is there anything to eat?" I asked, standing up and brushing the sand off my behind. I shivered; the sun was setting, and it was starting to get a little chilly, but I couldn't find where I'd left my t-shirt after tossing it off half an hour ago in a surge of wine-cooler induced boldness. But now, I felt *strange*. Standing up made me realize just how woozy I was.

"I think everyone ate all the chips and stuff," said Bree.

"Word," said Jamal. "But you can jive on up to the taco hut on the boardwalk if you hungry, dig?"

"Okay," I said, trying to take a step and finding my legs seemed to be made of rubber.

"Whoa, are you okay? How many did you have?"

"Three," I said.

"Three beers?"

"No… wine coolers… pretty good!" I said. Jamal and Bree seemed confused.

"Wow, girl, you a real lightweight!" said Jamal.

"I'm a what?" I asked.

"I can come with you," said Bree. "I'm a little hungry myself. I could go for a burrito."

"No, it's okay," I said. "I'm good, just a quick taco and I'll be back." Eyeing another wine cooler, I snatched it as I headed off in the direction of the boardwalk, ignoring the part of me that felt guilty, the part of me that felt that Riley wouldn't like it. Maybe I was underage, but I knew how to take care of myself. And besides, I still couldn't get a beat on what his fascination was with me. A part of me felt he hated me, and yet another part felt that he wanted to protect me.

The biggest part of me felt that he saw me as an ant and wanted to crush me. But if that were the case, why did he keep showing up wherever I happened to be?

Whatever he wanted to do with me, why couldn't he just get it *over with?*

I clamored up the wooden stairs and onto the boardwalk—no 'taco hut' in sight. I took another swig from my drink and started stumbling down the boardwalk, hungry for tacos. As the sun sank lower, everything seemed to be either closed or in the process. I continued to amble on, sipping my wine cooler and trying to keep my increasingly drunken thoughts off of Riley.

I came upon an alley, a light at the end of it. Was that the elusive taco hut? It was almost entirely dark now, and I was starting to lose hope that I would ever find a taco, let alone my way back to the beach! I was so stumbly and—

"What up, girl, you lost?"

I turned around. There stood three men, blocking my way back to the boardwalk. One of them looked like Jamal, but darker. Another looked Hispanic, and the third had blonde hair and was smoking something that was definitely not a cigarette. All three wore polo shirts. Had they been down at the bonfire?

No... those guys were all shirtless.

Speaking of which, I looked down. *Oh god.* I'd forgotten I'd taken off my baggy t-shirt. Here I was in an alley by the boardwalk wearing nothing but my bikini. I moved to hide my shame.

"No, girl," said the Hispanic guy. "You look good. Real good. Good enough to eat."

"Um, I was just looking for the taco stand."

"It's closed, girl," said the blonde guy. He took a drag from his marijuana, and then tossed the half-smoked joint onto the ground.

"Yeah," said the black guy. "Everyone's headed home except for the guys partying on the beach... and you're a long way from them."

A sense of dread began to well up in the pit of my stomach. I gulped. "Well then..."

"Don't worry about a thing, girl," said the blonde guy. Even in my drunken state I couldn't mistake the intent in his eyes. In all of their eyes. Want. Hunger. Dominance.

Lust.

They came closer to me, slowing as they moved, like a pack of lions about to pounce upon their prey, their predatory looks unmistakable. "We'll take good care of you."

I ran, not waiting for them to come another inch. The second I split, I stumbled, but I tried to shake off the effects of the wine coolers. I could hear them come after me and I cried out. My flip flops were slowing me down, and I had no idea where I was, dashing from alley to alley, the tenement buildings climbing higher and higher.

Not another human in sight.

I could hear them behind me, laughing cruelly. I tried not to think of what they'd do if they caught me, but I was in panic mode. I had no idea where I was going. Such was my indiscretion that I didn't realize the dead end until it was upon me.

A tall fence, unscalable. I felt like it was laughing at me, laughing like the evil, leonine, lustful boys on my heels.

"Don't worry, girl," said one of them right behind me. "We're just here for a good time."

"Just leave me alone!" I shrieked, backing up against the fence. Why, god, *why* did I let Bree talk me into wearing this bikini?

Now they were upon me, surrounding me. I could feel their breath against my face, smell the beer on it. I winced, tried to turn from them, but they were everywhere.

"Shhh," said one, resting his finger on my lip. I jerked away. "Like we said, we're just having a little fun."

"Yeah," echoed the blonde one. I felt his eyes crawling up my body, touching me with his lecherous gaze. "A little bit of fun."

For a split second, time seemed to slow to a stop. It seemed as though all sound had been sucked out of the world, and we were in a vacuum.

And then, like a light coming on, all three of their faces contorted, melting from expressions of lust and amusement into abject *terror*.

One grabbed his hair and ripped it out in large, painful chunks. Another dragged his fingernails down his face. The third fell to the ground, ramming his forehead into the pavement.

"*No!*" he screamed. "*Nooooooo!!*"

I was at first too stunned to react, or to even think. Soon all three of them were on the ground, abusing themselves, shrieking incoherently. The effects of the alcohol were still on me, as well as the terror from my sprint from the horny wolf pack. My mind was in a haze until I looked up, and there he was.

Riley.

It might have been the alcohol, but I could swear his piercing green eyes were glowing, and I *knew*. He was doing this. He was doing this to these guys, just like he had done it to Travis at the pool party.

And he had saved me.

Overwhelmed, I began to collapse, and suddenly he was there next to me, catching me. Just like at Henrietta's, it was as though he moved space and time, stepped right through it, or stopped it so that he could effortlessly cross that distance in a split second to catch my fall. Insignificant, stupid, drunk me, collapsing because of a situation that I alone had gotten myself into. I had no one to blame for them coming after me but myself. I knew that. Riley had to have known it.

But he caught me anyway.

"Riley," I whispered.

"Tiny thing," he said. I could barely hear him over the screams of the three guys losing their minds. "Tiny, insolent, inebriated creature."

"I know," I said. He began to carry me away from them,

back toward the boardwalk. "I'm sorry, it was stupid for me to get myself into that situation…"

"It was," he said. I could see him now up close, and unless I was losing my mind too, I knew it wasn't the alcohol—his green eyes were *definitely* glowing.

"It is clear to me now that I cannot leave you alone," he said. "You will only hurt yourself!"

"Riley, I—" I felt wretched. Twice now I had needed him to rescue me from situations that I had brought upon myself through my own miserable stupidity. "I'm sorry!"

"I cannot allow you to hurt yourself," his voice broke as he said the words, as though the mere idea pained him. I looked into his glowing, verdant eyes, hoping in them I would see answers.

Instead, I only saw pain.

"I cannot allow it…"

And then everything faded to black.

Chapter Nine
Captivated

I HAD BEEN DREAMING.

Dreaming of Riley once again.

Dreaming of being in his impossibly strong arms as he carried me to a safe, dark place. The dream had already begun to fade, but I clung to it with all my inconsiderable might. I did not want to let that beauty go...

I didn't know how long I'd been out, but as I came back to consciousness, I turned my head—left and right, up and down. My breath caught in alarm. I could not see! All was darkness, even though I could swear my eyes were open. I raised my trembling fingers to my face and discovered that it was covered with a delicately soft, silken blindfold. It reminded me of an expensive necktie.

As my fingers ghosted over the strange fabric, I discovered a second unnerving circumstance: my wrists were bound. I explored the binding awkwardly with my nose and mouth; it felt like a rope woven from the same silky material. Despite the bewildering context, the texture of it wasn't altogether unpleasant.

I took a moment to digest my discoveries. Obviously, I was in the process of being (or had already completed the process of being) kidnapped. How long had I been unconscious? I felt like I'd been out for hours, though my head was still spinning somewhat from the four wine coolers I'd had, and the hideous chain of events that transpired afterward.

Oh god, I thought, *have I been kidnapped by those creeps from the alley?*

The beauty of the dream had made me forget, mercifully yet far too briefly, everything that preceded my fall into blissful oblivion. But how much of it had only been a dream? I couldn't remember exactly what had happened in the alley, the memory was already so hazy and filled with gaps... Why had I gone off by myself? Something about Bree? Had she been there? Someone named... Kigawe? That couldn't be a real name, could it?

One thing though was blazing crystal clear in the eye of my mind—the horrible memory of those frat brats, reeking of their body spray and tanning lotion. The thought of them, the hideous knowledge of their very existence, made me shudder. I must have made a sound, because at that moment, *he* spoke.

"You're awake."

It was Riley, his voice like a thousand cellos made of gold. The sound made me shiver in a very different and unfamiliar way.

"Riley? Is that you? What's..." I nearly finished the

sentence... *going on?* But I didn't want to sound like a hysterical girl, to look a fool before him. "What's... up?"

He made a strange sound, somewhere between a chuckle and choke. "What is *up*, young one, is this: you disgraced yourself last night." The words, though spoken softly, percussed me like a backhanded slap. He continued, "You imbibed the spirits of the grape in quantities far too great for your slight flesh. You wandered from the protection of your group, like an idiot wolf cub who misplaces her pack, and you allowed that..."

He made the strange sound again, and when next he spoke, his voice was harsh as diamond on steel. "You allowed that... *filth*, that vile *scum*, that *muck* that I would sooner scrape from the heel of my *boot*—"

There was a great sound, like a large piece of wood splintering, as though he had lashed out at something in violent anger with the need to wreak destruction however inconsequential. His motion set me to rocking, and I realized we were on a water vessel of some kind. The fading echoes of the sound implied a great, cavernous space around us.

Riley was silent for a long time. Perhaps it was only my imagination, but it seemed that his being and mine were in some kind of synchronicity, set off by the rocking of the boat. I could *feel* the tension in his body, so very close to mine. I could sense him trying to seize control of some great and overpowering emotion. I could *feel* the clenching of his muscles, the grinding of his teeth, the burning in his heart. And I experienced, just as I imagine he did, the slow slackening of his rage, the careful and deliberate cooling of the fire, the return of normal pace of breath.

Finally he spoke again, his voice having taken on its

previous deep and calm timbre. "You allowed yourself to be in the position... you *placed* yourself in the position of prey to hungry and salivating predators. And... worst of all, young one..."

Did his voice crack, or did I imagine it?

"I was not invited to the party."

I was devastated. I, by my selfish and thoughtless actions, had caused pain for this beautiful boy. This dear boy who had now saved me twice. In that moment *I* was the filth, *I* was the vile scum, *I* was the muck to be scraped from the boot of some Roman-statue-made-flesh. "Oh... oh, Riley, I'm so sorry that I hurt your feelings!"

"Don't... concern yourself with that right now." I felt him turn away from me. "Be quiet, now... this is the difficult part."

Difficult part? I couldn't pretend to understand what he meant, but I obeyed. I leaned back and tried to make myself comfortable in spite of my restricted movement and obscured vision. I was playing out an unfamiliar... but also, somehow *strangely* familiar... scenario. But with Riley as my pilot, I did not fear coming to any harm. I attempted to open up my senses to my surroundings, to take in as much as possible. I could hear the water lapping at the boat, the rhythmic sound of what I assumed was rowing and faint echoes of what might be some squamous cave-dwelling creature going about its business in the distance. The gentle rocking of the boat felt like a mother's loving embrace of a fragile newborn.

Then, impressing with great urgency upon my senses, came the most beautiful sound I had ever heard. A wavering, delicate, yet somehow mighty and thunderous melody. It was like birdsong one moment, whalesong the next. It was Riley.

Rileysong. The sound of it was simultaneously heartbreaking, energizing, forlorn, joyous. It was the song from my dream. I was bathed in it, my body pulsing with a thousand subtle emotions...

...When suddenly the air was alive with static electricity, and the bottom fell out of my stomach. I distinctly heard the sound *b'chhk'tch*, as though the universe were expelling something rotten and sinister from the depths of its gullet. Riley had ceased his singing and the boat had ceased its rocking.

"We have arrived," he said.

"Oh god," I gulped as my stomach continued to flip. "I might be sick. Please don't look if I get sick. Where have we arrived, Riley?"

"R'lyeh," was his unfathomable reply.

"What... Riley. That's what I said."

"No, it is not my name, it is the name of this place. My home. R'lyeh."

A thrill shot through me, helping somewhat with the roller-coaster feeling still coursing around my body. Riley had brought me back to his place?

"Your house is named after you?"

"...If that helps you. Now please, be quiet. I am... drained."

He didn't feel drained though, as his incredibly strong hands grasped my shoulders. My skin danced at the touch of his fingers, but there was something else as well. It was a sensation like being brushed lightly by a cat's tail made of smoke. He lifted me and placed me in what felt like an ancient stone chair hewn from the rage of a millennium of violent waves. I felt a rope, woven from inexplicably soft and silky material, being looped about my chest and arms, binding me to the chair. And again, that strange feeling, like wisps of steam evaporating from my skin.

"Is this really necessary?" I queried, my voice as even as I could make it and my face pointed in what I assumed was Riley's general direction. I wriggled my shoulders against the rope. "I hardly intend to run away."

He finished tying the last knot with a sharp and precise motion, binding me fast. "I restrict your freedom for your own protection," he said.

That seemed reasonable. I was in an unfamiliar place, after all, a place where Riley was apparently at ease. I relaxed. The chair was not terribly uncomfortable, and I felt in my heart of hearts that Riley knew best in this matter. He grasped the back of the chair and I was tilted back forty, perhaps forty-five degrees. He began to drag me. Once again, I was dumbfounded by his strength, the ease with which he moved over any uneven terrain. And we *were* moving over uneven terrain, that much was certain, the chair bumping, thumping, scraping and catching on various topographical features we crossed. I became aware that we seemed to be going uphill. Riley was utterly silent. Even his footfalls were apparently swallowed up by the vast space we inhabited. The only sound for many, many minutes was the dull metallic cacophony of the chair moving over the ground.

Then the noise stopped, and the front feet of the chair slammed down. I was unprepared, and I made a rather unflattering sound as the rope across my chest squeezed the wind from my lungs. For a long time, all was silent. But I could feel Riley there, watching me.

At last, he spoke. "Twice now, young one, have I

prevented you from coming to the harm which you seem to seek out, like the imbecile moth seeks the scorching flame. Why do you think that that is?"

"Well…" I was flustered. I was alone with the most unusual and indescribably unordinary boy I'd ever met. My feelings were all jumbled up, all *new*. For the first time in my entire life, a boy had gotten under my skin. And though I felt an incredible connection with him, a synchronicity, I did not know at all what *he* felt.

I did not know how to answer his question.

What hidden motivations were the engine of his actions? Yesterday I'd been convinced that he hated me. That he considered me but an insignificant ant. But now, as the remaining dregs of last night's drunkenness finally dispersed, I remembered with crystal clarity the words he had spoken as he took me from the alley.

I cannot leave you alone. You will only hurt yourself…

He could not leave me alone. Did that mean… that he couldn't bear to be away from me? And, whatever it was he'd done to those creeps in the alley, he'd saved me. That much was clear. Could it be that he… no. No, it could not be. Could it? No. But maybe…?

"Well," I started again, but I suppose I'd spent too long in contemplation, because his voice cut mine off sharply.

"I shall tell you. I shall shine a bright light upon you, and I shall share with you great truths which you shall understand by only half. And I shall lay myself bare before you. Because I have been left with no *choice!*"

With that, my blindfold was torn harshly away. He stood before me. His eyes pierced me. They were luminescently green, deep, fearsome and… unnatural.

Beautiful.

Indescribable.

"Look about you," he said.

I obeyed. We were in a great space, a vast cave of size beyond size, filled with darkness and inky shadow. It was also utterly, unspeakably *impossible*. We were atop a massive formation of pocked and puckered stone, like volcanic rock. I could easily trace the path we had taken from the boat, which I could now see was a jet-black gondola. But the gondola, the dock it was tied to and the black water in which it floated were somehow *above* me, even though I was looking *down* at them.

Around us, I could discern objects which might have been a table, a couch, a doorway, a bed, a bookshelf. But the angles were all wrong, the perspective skewed, everything stretched and compressed in hideous and abominable ways.

The darkness that filled the space seemed to pulse, to contract, to flow, to *breathe*. I began to feel ill again, but worse, like my insides were trying to claw their way out of me, my veins in a frenzy, twisting and tangling themselves.

I started to moan, to hyperventilate. I hated that I was allowing myself to be so weak in front of Riley, but I had lost all physical control. I strained against my bonds, pitched my gaze all about in an attempt to find something, anything to latch on to, anything I understood that could anchor me. Even Riley seemed twisted and distorted to me... he was fading, receding into the black seas of infinity, *leaving me. Oh god!*

"Andromeda." My name on his lips brought me back from the brink, and in the melodious timbre of his resonant voice, for the first time in my life, it sounded... beautiful.

"Station your gaze upon this." He placed something in my hands.

It was a statuette, heavy, about eight inches tall. It was hewn from some greenish-black stone with a texture that reminded me simultaneously of marble and bar-soap. It depicted a girl, sitting atop a cubic base covered in arcane runes. It was unmistakably me, skinny limbs and all. Andromeda Slate, carved in stone.

I looked up at Riley curiously, my sensory overload immediately forgotten. He knelt before me, so that our eyes were level, our knees not quite touching. Again, I experienced that sensation of too-solid smoke against my skin, but I could see nothing there. He held up a hand, inches from the tip of my nose.

"These hands created that figure. Almost two weeks ago." He moved his hand to tap his temple. "But this mind did not. I awoke from a dream to find *that*," he pointed at the statuette, "upon my bedside table, the tools of its creation still scattered about this place. I do not remember carving it. But upon gracing it with my eyes, I remembered *you*."

"Me? But we only just met..." But I knew what he was going to tell me, because I had had the same experience. My drawing in Mrs. Phillips's class the morning after my dream. My heart fluttered. We really were synchronized in some impossible way. Linked in a way that no one had ever been.

"I remembered you..." he said, "from my dream."

We talked for a long time after that, him cross-legged on the ground, me in my chair, the bonds forgotten. He told me of his dream, which I recognized as the mirror image of my own. We truly had met outside of time, outside of space, in a shared universe belonging only to us! I could tell that he had a hard time opening up, so I filled the empty space with stories of my life. Bree, Vik, my parents. I told him about how frustrating Mom and Dad could be when they got so involved in their jobs and each other and my private life. Riley just sort of half-smiled as he listened, somewhere between laughter and sadness, as though he well understood the difficulties that came part and parcel with family.

After what felt like mere minutes but was probably more like hours, I kind of ran out of things to tell him about myself. Not surprising, what with my existence being so terribly ordinary up until last week.

"Ordinary?" he said with that same sad half-grin. "You, young one, are anything but ordinary." His gaze swept over me and I felt a shiver of delight coil inside of me. So different from the way he'd always looked at me before.

He seemed to hesitate, as if it took great will for him to speak his next words, but when he did, they were firm. "I believe that I have waited as long as possible. The time has come to bathe you in the light of unutterable truth."

He stood with a single movement, the embodiment of lithe grace, his clothing rippling across his body as if trying to get even closer to his skin. My breath caught in my throat as he seemed to grow taller, his already muscular frame seeming to swell almost to the point of bursting the seams of his clothes. His face took on a searing hardness—an expression I was more familiar with. His eyes narrowed upon me, and I felt they saw through to my very core.

"Sgn'wahl!" he said with great force. "Sha'shogg! Throd! Cthulhu'ai!" Each of the alien words rang like a gunshot. I knew them all. "These are the words which called out to me, rousing me from slumber," he said. "Uln Cthulhu! Wgah'n

ya! Ch'ftaghu shugg Cthulhu! Thr'throd! Ch'ftaghu shugg
Cthulhu! Thr'ngli! Ch'ftaghu shugg Cthulhu! Thr'ghlfnaw!
These are the words that rang out to me, in your voice!"

His viridian eyes blazed like a rainbow in the dark. From
the back pocket of his jeans, he produced a long, thin,
vicious-looking knife that glistened like ebony. He took a step
toward me. For the first time since I woke, I felt something
resembling the thrill of fear. He placed the flat of the blade
against my upturned forehead.

"Words have power. Words *cut.*" With a blindingly fast
motion, the blade swooped down and neatly divided the rope
that bound me to the chair. "All reality, the planet within
which we stand and the universe within which it spins, *all* are
shaped by words. Some believe the very universe itself was
created with a word. Well, Andromeda," the sound of my
name upon his lips made me tingle, "open your mind's eye to
this hideous truth: the universe shall *end* with but a word."

He turned his back to me and began to walk into the
darkness. "Come," he said, without breaking stride.

I rushed after him, still clutching the statuette in my
bound hands, my legs somewhat wobbly after sitting for so
long. I caught up, and we walked side by side into the
foreboding black. After a while, I couldn't even see the
ground before me, but trusted in Riley's steady footfalls that
I should not stumble. Eventually we seemed to reach our
destination, because Riley's voice boomed:

"Stop."

I stopped.

"Look about you."

I looked about me.

"What do you see?" he asked.

"Um… I don't see anything."

"Precisely. *You* do not see anything. *You* perceive only the lack of *thing*. But I… I see the overpowering presence of *nothing*, beautiful in its infinite and absolute negation. We now stand in a pocket of primordial chaos, where everything is but a swirling pool of nothing. What you now see creeps rapidly to envelope your world, young one. Such was prophesied aeons ago. And all this is the very *purpose* of my existence." I felt him turn toward me in the dark. His body was very close to mine, and again I perceived that indescribable sensation of almost-touch, like a ghost's whisper passing through my hair. "My greatest purpose. At least… it *was*. Until there was *you*."

He took a deep breath. "Tell me, little thing. Are you familiar with the legends… of the Great Old Ones?"

My heart skipped a beat. "Yes! I mean… no, not really. Ms. Epistola is always going off about them in class. But she's a nutzoid, and she dresses like a cage dancer. Oh, and Vik—"

"Ms… *Epistola*." Riley enunciated the name with great care. I didn't like the sound of it upon his lips. "That is of interest, but to be placed aside in pursuit of more pressing concerns." I didn't think that Ms. Epistola was of any interest whatsoever, but I kept that thought to myself as Riley continued, "For now, know only this: the Great Old Ones are not legends, they are terrible *reality*. Once, they walked among the stars as giants. Now, many of them slumber beneath the stones, in the dark places, in the *spaces between spaces*. Many, but not all."

He paused for a moment, and I thought I could sense a

hint of hesitation about him. Riley, hesitant? What awful, deeply personal secret could he be about to share with ordinary me?

"We stand now beneath the stones, little one. *I* once walked among the stars, a giant. *I* once slumbered here, in a space between spaces. *I... am the Priest All-High of the Great Old Ones.*"

The words hit me with the force of a blow. I gaped in the dark. I was shattered, the awful weight of implication crushing me to a fine powder. Riley... a *priest?* "Does that mean... that you can't... you know, *be* with someone...?"

He sighed, a tired sound. I supposed that opening up to me like he was must have been taking a lot out of him. "No, that is not what it means. I am not that weak breed of priest, though there is a parallel. I am a true *conduit*. Between *your* world above... and a much greater power *below*. The prophecy proclaims that when the stars are de-aligned in peak celestial chaos, I am he who is to *call*, to rouse the Sleeping Beast and plunge your world into *mine*. To *negate*, gloriously. Absolutely. It is my ontological imperative."

"Wow..." I didn't know what else to say. "So are you... going to?"

He was silent for a long moment. I felt that he was examining me carefully in the impenetrable gloom. His intensity passed over me in palpable waves.

"Peak celestial chaos approaches, little one. The autumnal equinox has heralded a glorious harvest: the doom of all. My time to act draws nigh, and yet... no. I shall not." For a moment it seemed as though he would continue. But he was silent, and I felt like I had to know more.

"But... why?"

For a split second, I thought I could see his eyes, glittering green amid the black. But he did not speak. It was clear that he was unwilling to continue the thread of conversation, so I decided to pursue a more roundabout track.

"Okay, never mind. How about... if all of this stuff you're saying is true, why are you here?" *In my life.* "I mean, in Portsmouth? In *high school*, even? If you're really as old as you say you are, shouldn't you be in college at least by now?"

"It is... difficult to explain in such a way that your pitiful mind will comprehend. But I will try." He took a weary breath. "Each being in this vast multiverse is endowed with a destiny, irrefutable and inescapable. Mine, as foreseen by some long forgotten prophet, is to *call.* To rouse and unleash the Sleeping Beast that would destroy your world. My call can only be sounded, can only pierce the veil of the multiverse, during the time of celestial de-alignment. There have been such *Alignments* in aeons past when I have not sounded my call, for the signs were not in place and the time was not right. For then, I too slumbered. But truly, I believe that this approaching peak of chaos is now, at last, the time foreseen. For you see, young thing, there is more to the prophecy than just the doom of all... there is more. And never before have the proper signs and portents arisen. But now... I see signs. I see portents. I see... you."

"...Oh?" I was very glad that Riley could not see the look of complete bewilderment that must have been painted all over my face.

"Oh, yes. The prophecy alludes to a being who is not of the Great Old Ones, not of the Elder Gods, but one who shall arise possessing the power to prevent me from sounding my call. This... *Young One*, if you will... is to be a mortal."

He paused as if expecting something of me, but when there was nothing I could offer, he continued:

"When you appeared in my dream, I understood that you were—*are*—the mortal of prophecy."

I gasped. "Me!?"

"I came to Innsmouth in this human disguise—"

"You mean Portsmouth."

He shook his head. "You call it that now, but its true name is *Innsmouth*. Remember, young one, that words have power. None more so than names. Innsmouth is a center of great power and purpose more ancient than one as simple as you could imagine. Truly, it is fitting that I should meet my foil in Innsmouth."

"…Oh."

"If I may continue? I came to *Innsmouth* in order to hunt you, to watch you. I stalked you as the *p'cp'ynt'ri* stalks the *m'gn'thp*, to learn your secrets and discover your powers and likewise your points of weakness. Thereby I could but hope to be equipped to defeat you when the time came that you would stand before me as my nemesis."

I really did not like the sound of that. Me, Riley's nemesis? No, a thousand times no!

"But I don't have any powers!" I disputed. "I'm just a girl, you know? How could I possibly prevent you from doing anything you wished? By asking pretty please?"

There came that strange chuckle-choke sound again. I imagined that if I could see him, he'd be wearing his half-smile.

"It is no matter. Regardless of whatever powers you possess, lurking untapped within your body or spirit… I feel that my destiny—irrefutable, inescapable—has been refuted.

Escaped. How can I explain to your tiny mind the sudden change within me? With the sum of my being, I yearn to call, to bring ultimate undoing to this mortal plane. With all of my being... except my heart. Because *you* belong to this mortal plane, little one. And now, for that reason alone, I shall instead protect it."

"...Riley, I don't understand any of this."

"Yes... I know. Let us depart this place and seek further illumination in the light of day." With that, his footfalls began to move in the direction we'd come from. I did my best to follow blindly. Soon the dank, dim light of Riley's home began to creep back into my awareness, the strange shapes and twisted angles reiterating themselves. Yet somehow it was all no longer vile and horrifying, but instead imbued with subtle, abstract beauty. We arrived back at my stone chair, still encircled in the loops of rope. Which reminded me...

"Um, Riley?" I said, holding up my still-bound hands even as they continued to clutch the statuette. "Do you think you could undo this?"

Again, that indecipherable half-smile. "Oh, yes. Of course." The ebony blade reappeared. "But first you must do something for me. Please get on your knees."

"Um... okay, I guess." I carefully lowered myself, the strange rock harsh as gravel against the bare skin of my unbearably boney knees. He stepped close before me and again placed the flat of the blade against my upturned forehead.

"You and I are now of singular purpose," he said with great solemnity. "When we met in the realm of dreams, our destinies became entwined irrevocably. Thus do I hereby anoint you as my sacred charge and accept you as my burden, my albatross. I shall protect you always, for you are small and weak. And I am greater than you."

In that moment, I could not disagree. With another blindingly fast and careless motion, the rope around my wrists was severed—but I was bound more firmly than ever. As I gazed up into the otherworldly emeralds that were Riley's eyes, I recognized that I had been sleepwalking for sixteen years. Now, truly, I was awoken. I was in love.

"You will change your clothes," he said. He turned to walk, sharply as a shark swims, to one of the impossible pieces of furniture. "Those scraps you wear are unsuitable for roaming in the sun." And he was right—I was still wearing nothing but my purple bikini from the beach party.

Riley opened—or rather, *contorted*—something that must have been a drawer, or maybe a trunk, and produced several articles of clothing which I immediately recognized.

I gasped. "Hey! I left those in my locker on Friday! How did you get them?"

I expected that he would look embarrassed, or at the very least a bit flustered, but his expression didn't budge. He stated matter-of-factly, "I anticipated this eventuality."

"Well!" I gushed, immediately chastising myself for the childish display of girlish emotion. "That was sweet of you. But... do you mind?" I asked, not sure if I wanted him to mind or not. He just stared at me for a moment, and then turned his back. I was about to pull the clothes on over my bikini when I noticed that clean underwear was still stuffed in the leg of my jeans where I'd stashed it. At first I was elated to be able to get out of the cursed bathing suit until I realized they were the pink 'FLIRT' panties. Oh god, please say he hadn't noticed them! I changed as quickly as possible.

"Those guys on the boardwalk," I asked hesitantly as I finished hitching up the crisp pair of W.G. Ilman sequined jeans with the butterflies on the back pockets, fearful of rousing his protective impulses by reminding him of my self-disgrace. "What... happened to them?"

He was silent for a moment, as though searching for just the right words.

"The most merciful thing in your world, young one, is the inability of the human mind to correlate all of its contents." His voice was low and filled with a quality of subdued menace. "I unburdened them of that inability."

I didn't understand what that meant, and he did not elaborate.

"Okay, all done!" I said, knotting the last shoelace. Part of me wished that there were something identifiable as a mirror on the strange walls, but the rest of me was horrified at the thought of what I'd look like in it.

Riley turned to appraise me, his eyes moving up and down my body. I blushed at being examined so openly by the boy I loved. "Better?" I asked.

"Adequate. Now," he said, holding his hand out to me, "there is someone you must meet."

Surprised at my own boldness, I stepped forward and took his hand. His touch was electric. My heart was beating with such force that I was certain he must have been able to hear it. But he gave no indication, he simply turned and lead me around a corner-which-was-not-a-corner to go up a set of winding stairs that were surprising in their identifiably stair-shapedness.

"My purpose has changed," he said as if I might have forgotten that fact in the past two minutes. In truth, I kind of had. The feel of his hand around mine was far too distracting to focus on much else… But I made an effort, responding with what I hoped was a cognizant nod.

It seemed to work, because he continued, "But the Alignment continues to approach. The threat of chaos is still nigh." His grip on my hand clenched painfully as he glanced back over his shoulder at me. The look in his eyes made my heart flutter. "I will do anything—anything—to protect you, little one. Your world must not be destroyed. And to this end, we will now seek the advice of one whose knowledge and wisdom is further reaching than even my own."

What could that mean? I wondered, but was too distracted by how lithely he moved up the stairs to ask.

We climbed for what felt like many minutes, one of my hands in his the whole way as the other clutched the dream-statuette. But I didn't feel like I was climbing. I was light as air. I was in love, and I would follow Riley to the very ends of the universe, if only he would let me.

After the boat on the underground lake with this mysterious, impossibly alluring boy, I now knew what it must have been like to be Christine, spirited away by her Phantom to the dungeon of his black despair. I pressed the statuette to my heart. Very few girls ever got the chance to live out fantasies from their favorite books. And it had all happened without Riley even realizing. I was truly luckier than I ever dreamed I could possibly be.

As we ascended, our surroundings became decreasingly tenebrous. Almost without my noticing, the otherworldly stones of mostly stair-shape gave way to actual wooden stairs. Nebulous boundaries at the edge of sight became brick walls shedding ancient coats of no-color paint in long strips. By the last ten steps, I could almost believe we were coming up from a normal, everyday, run-of-the-mill basement.

At the top of the stairs was a fairly regular four-paneled wooden door. It was illuminated by a bare light bulb which hung from a very standard seven-foot ceiling.

"Prepare yourself," said Riley sternly as he turned the handle and drew me out into…

…the street across from a junk shop?

Chapter Ten
Chaos

THE SHOP SHARED AN OLD-TIMEY WOODEN STOREFRONT with a Blockbuster and a small bakery, and I realized we must have been just off Main Street. The big front windows were cluttered with velvet-covered displays of pendants and tarot card decks, ceremonial candles, books and sets of hand-carved dice. A hand-painted sign above the windows read *The Crawling Chaos.*

Riley crossed the street and pulled the door open, but then hesitated, watching me expectantly as I caught up to him, his fist clenched tight around the tarnished bronze handle. I started to ask him what was wrong when he swept his arm forward, beckoning me in. He was holding the door for me.

Blushing, I took a step into the darkened shop and sneezed. The sunlight streaming through the dingy front window showed a cloud of dust billowing around me with every step. I lifted my sweater over my nose and mouth, my eyes watering. I felt like I had stumbled into a crypt. Clearly nobody had been in this place in ages.

Something clattered behind me and I turned to see Riley pulling the door shut. Attached to the doorframe above his head was a set of chimes carved to look sort of like human rib bones, dangling from an unnervingly realistic skull. I turned away, creeped out by the hollow pits of its eyes staring down at me, and I tripped over a trunk hanging open in the aisle.

I shrieked and threw out my hands, but before I could smash to the floor, Riley's strong arms wrapped around my middle and set me upright. For a moment we stood still, so close I could smell the salt of the sea on him and feel his chest rise and fall with each breath.

"Thank you," I whispered.

His perfect fingers twisted through my hair and I felt my heart bursting in my chest. I wanted those fingers running down my face, around my cheeks, over my lips—

"NEIL?" Riley turned, calling down the aisle. An empty shudder rolled through me as his saltwater scent faded.

I stifled another sneeze. "I don't think anybody's here," I said uncertainly. The shelves and counters around us looked like they hadn't been disturbed in years. Dusty junk covered every surface. Hundreds of small, lacquered boxes carved with geometric designs filled one bookshelf and spilled onto a nearby table, where a dozen small wax dolls stood on hooks, each stuck with a dozen different pins. A magazine rack overflowed with old journals and books bound in leather and what looked like tree bark. The aisles were stuffed with furniture, dusty rolls of carpet, trunks and wardrobes that looked like holdovers from before the last century.

I stopped in front of a full-length mirror set into a gold frame. 'Y'tir'uce'sni' was carved into the frame over the glass. I was sure it meant something important, but it was nonsense to me. The thin film of dust over the mirror made my reflection blurry, turned my hair even frizzier than normal and somehow made my thighs bulge out wider than my hips. Behind my reflection, I could see Riley's perfectly-proportioned frame moving down the aisle. When I focused back on my own reflection, I saw the red splotch of a pimple about to form on my forehead. I clamped a hand over my mouth and jerked away from the glass, feeling around my hairline, but there was no lump to be found.

"He is here," Riley said grimly, taking me by the arm and starting down the aisle. "Do you not smell him?"

I stumbled after him, sucking air in through the sleeve of my sweater. We passed a shelf of multicolored orbs that appeared, through some trick of the light, to be floating a few inches above their clawed pedestals. "Smell what?" I asked, and then sneezed again. All I could smell was dust.

"YOU'RE IN THE WRONG STORE," a metallic voice boomed down the aisle, making me jump. Riley took a sharp right at the next intersection, following the sound. "THE PHARMACY IS TWO DOORS DOWN. GET AN INHALER. Oh." There was a brief clatter, and the voice turned normal, if a bit raspy. "Hey, Squidface! Why didn't you tell me you were dropping in?"

I turned the corner to find a low counter kiosk made of dark polished wood trimmed in bronze. A middle-aged, skinny man in a Chicago Bulls jersey and threadbare bathrobe sat behind the counter, an old-timey speaking horn at his elbow. He hunched over a cash register with a reserved, wild energy that made me think of a jungle cat. He grinned at Riley, and I noticed that his yellowed teeth, which held the end of a long black pipe, were sharpened to points. His eyes darted to me and back to Riley. "What have I told you about food in the shop, kiddo? I'm still cleaning offal out of the rafters from your sister's visit."

Riley's shoulders went rigid. *"D'svnknuu d'arr,"* he snapped. *"Y'gnthme'l dgn jgvn'skuth Fgnthul."* He grabbed my hand protectively. My stomach did a little loop-de-loop as his firm, strong fingers curled through mine.

The man straightened in his seat and appraised me with eyes like black holes. For a moment, his bearing seemed transformed into something regal and powerful, yet cruel. But I blinked, and the illusion was gone as he moved the pipe to the other side of his mouth and a faint puff of purple smoke curled up from the cup. It smelled a bit like lavender. Maybe that was the smell Riley had mentioned. He must have a nose like a bloodhound to have caught it from all the way across the shop.

"No kidding." The man's voice turned flat. "Looks just like the last one. Where do you dig these women up?"

The loop-de-loop in my stomach flipped into a nose dive and I jerked, ripping my hand from Riley's. He looked at me, startled. I quickly straightened my sweater, afraid to look him in the eye. "The last one?" I mumbled, my heart thudding in my ears.

"It was long ago," Riley said stiffly. "And a grave error."

Whose error? I wanted to ask, but my throat was clamped shut. Of course there would have been someone else. How could any woman not fall head over heels for that perfect face, that unkempt hair, that hint of an accent? The mirror showed it well enough. Next to him, I was frumpy, when there were so many more beautiful women in the world—

The man behind the counter cackled and pushed himself to his feet, grabbing a bronze-plated cane with a dragon's head carved into the top. He shuffled out from behind the counter with a soft-shoe rhythm—his swagger reminded me of the Cab Calloway videos Bree had once forced me to watch. A faded pair of moose slippers poked out from the bottoms of his jeans.

He took out his pipe and spread his arms in a bow. "Well, excuse me, madam. You'll have to forgive my nephew his past transgressions as well as his rudeness, because he should have introduced us by now. I am Nyarlathotep, but you can call me Neil."

Warmth crept back into my cheeks, along with a little smile at the gesture. "No trouble," I murmured, holding out my hand. Instead of shaking it though, he took my wrist and pressed it to his lips like a knight from legend, a crooked grin curling across his face as he caught my eye.

"Neil!" Riley nearly shouted, and he stepped between us, forcing Neil to drop my hand. "Her name is Andromeda." His voice lowered, but remained charged with tension. "And we have urgent matters to discuss."

"I'm not loaning you anymore money."

"It's about the coming Alignment," Riley said through gritted teeth. "And… the prophecy."

"Oh, that old shtick." Neil picked a dust rag up from the counter and started polishing a yellowed globe the size of a beach ball. "Does seem like a bad time to pick up a human squeeze, with the material world ending and all. But eh, *c'est la vie*, right?"

A thin, long-haired tortoiseshell cat jumped onto the counter with the jerky, tired motion of an old feline. I absently reached out a hand to pet it.

"Ah ah ah!" Neil tsked without looking up. "The Queen of Sheba does not tolerate the touch of mere mortals—no offense."

Before I could withdraw my hand, he passed the globe to me. "Hold this." I took it without thinking, and he proceeded to wipe an inch-thick layer of dust off the shelf.

"So you know about the prophecy?" I asked, shifting the globe around in my arms, trying to find a comfortable way to hold the thing. It must have weighed fifty pounds.

I thought I saw Neil roll his eyes. "Do I know about the... *Chica*. We go through this every decade or so. There's always some crazy bastard out there who smokes too much catnip and starts on a rant about the Elder Gods or the Jolly Green Giant here—" he threw a finger at Riley "—returning to Earth and making a mess of your little human lives whenever another Alignment comes along. Sooner or later one of them will hit the nail on the head."

"This prophecy is real," Riley said quietly. "And I do not wish it so."

"Eh? Two months ago you were jumping out of your chair for a chance to make some apocalypse happen." Neil turned, running the cloth over a ram's skull. My arms were starting to burn under the weight of the globe.

"You know how things change, Crawling Chaos," Riley whispered, and for a moment, I thought I heard the edge of a plea in his voice.

Neil looked from Riley, to me, and back. I opened my mouth to ask if I could set the globe down, but before I could get the words out, my arms collapsed and it fell to the wooden floor with the heavy, painful smack of a bowling ball dropped into the alley. I yelped and stumbled back before it could roll over and crush my toes.

Riley picked it up like it weighed nothing at all and studied the little continents painted on its surface, his green eyes soft at the edges, tender, as he traced the coast of New England with one perfectly manicured finger. "The Alignment approaches, and the prophecy is in motion," he said. "It cannot be allowed to bear fruit."

I glanced at Neil. His eyes went wide and he had stopped chewing on the edge of his pipe as he stared at Riley like he had sprouted tentacles.

"Well." Neil crouched behind the counter and came back up with a large tin divided into a dozen small compartments, each holding a different sort of dried leaf or seed. He quickly began stuffing a pinch of each sort into the cup of his pipe. "Well well well. You're serious."

"The Alignment's peak falls next Saturday," Riley said.

My mouth dropped open. That was in exactly one week! When he'd said it was coming soon, I hadn't realized there was so little time.

Riley continued, "And the veil between worlds is thin. If one of your..." he paused, as though the words were uncomfortable in his mouth, "*catnip-smoking bastards* summons me then, I am afraid I will not be able to resist my directives."

"It's not like you can read summoning instructions off the back of a cereal box," Neil muttered, adding an extra pinch of tiny dried flowers to his pipe for good measure. "These things take a lot of preparation. It's unlikely a human could complete the ritual. You need all sorts of stuff. Sanctified candles and charcoal made from burned rowan wood and a human sacrificed with a knife forged from a meteorite, and it has to be the right sort of meteorite—"

"Things any human could find in this very shop," Riley insisted.

"Well," Neil looked uncomfortable as he put the pipe to his lips again and struck a match on the counter. "I don't sell humans for sacrifice. Local ordinances. Cultists are industrious little buggers, though, they could probably find a hobo to sacrifice if they really wanted. But all the prep doesn't mean anything if they don't have the right books to read from."

Books to read from?

"What sort of books?" I asked uncomfortably.

"They're not easy to come by." Neil touched the match to his pipe, and sucked in a deep breath of the fragrant smoke that curled from the bowl. His shoulders immediately slumped in relief. "The first is the *Eldritch Grimoire*. There's only two copies left in the world, and I know where they both are."

"And the other is the *Necronomicon*," Riley supplied.

Neil nodded. "There aren't many copies of that left lying around, either."

Necronomicon. I slumped to the edge of a low counter, sitting between a stack of dusty papers and what looked like a human hand encased in a block of glass. "Oh," I said.

Riley turned to me, his beautifully carved jaw jutting in concern. "Oh?"

"Vik had one of those." My heart started to sink out of my chest and melt between the cracks in the floor. "And it was stolen a couple days ago."

"Cultists," Riley guessed. "Nobody else would have a reason to steal it."

Neil pursed his lips and exhaled a long stream of purplish smoke that twisted into a spiral shape before disappearing. "Well, at least the *Grimoires* are safe," he reassured me. "Nobody can bind your snookums against his will without it."

"Where are they?" Riley demanded. "We must be sure. We cannot take the chance that cultists will find one before the peak."

Neil puffed out a perfect ring of smoke. "One of them's locked in a vault in a ruined city at the bottom of the Atlantic, and it's been there since the day I threw Atlantis into the sea. Unless your cultists have a deep submersible vehicle, it's not going anywhere."

I looked up from my knees, startled. "Atlantis is real?"

"It was for a while. Then the King tried to backtrack on a deal he and I had, and—"

"Where is the second book?" Riley interrupted.

"Down in the Big Apple, locked up at Port Authority."

I jumped up from my seat, and Riley groaned. "It is sitting in a rental locker just a couple hundred miles away?"

"Would *you* think to look for an ancient eldritch artifact in a bus depot?" Neil puffed up defensively. "It'll be fine. Nobody but the three of us know it's there."

"Not good enough." Riley set his jaw, his eyes flashing dangerously. "The safest place for it is right here, with me or you, until the Alignment passes."

Neil sat back in his chair and sighed, exhaling a long puff

of smoke that clung to the likeness of a teardrop before vanishing. "If you insist. I guess I can make room for it in the shop safe. You'll have to go get it yourself, though. I've got a booster draft tonight."

"We will," Riley said, taking my arm with a gentle squeeze that made me feel all gooey inside. He met my gaze and I could only look into his green eyes for so long before the hammering in my chest became too much to bear. "We will find it, and keep it safe until the time of danger has passed. I will not be used to harm these humans." He brushed a strand of hair out of my face.

An abrupt clanging sound from behind the counter made me jump out of my trance. Neil dropped a set of car keys onto the wood in front of Riley. "Take Cleo," he said generously. "She hasn't been driven enough lately."

Riley snatched up the keys. "Which locker?"

Neil gave him the number. "Oh," he added as an afterthought as Riley took my hand and we ran for the shop exit. "I left a briefcase in there too, could you grab that for me?"

As the door swung shut behind me, I heard his fading call. "I mean it! Don't forget the case!"

Chapter Eleven
Cleo

RILEY LED ME TO A DETACHED GARAGE BEHIND NEIL'S shop. From the look of the building's faded sides and sunken roof, I expected a hoarder's delight and a total junker inside. But Riley opened the garage door in one graceful but powerful motion, and—

"*Oh wow*," I breathed, as I could feel my eyes growing wide.

Riley smirked at my wonder. "A 1967 Chevy Impala, in nearly perfect condition. It is my understanding that your kind covets these vehicles for their power and luring qualities," he said, and there was a slight mocking tone in his voice.

"Are you kidding me? I don't know anything about cars, but even I know that this is like, a dream car," I said, feeling a little defensive of Americana. "Where did Neil even get this? And has he *ever* driven it?"

"He took it from two brothers after cheating them in a game of sport he called 'billiards.' "

"Those brothers couldn't have been too happy about that," I commented, and feeling suddenly daring, I put my hand on the hood of the black beauty.

"The ensuing fallout was hardly anything one of our kind could not escape," he replied, "Neil insists he only intended to borrow it, that he'll give it back to them one day."

"Yeah, what's 'one day' when you're immortal," I shot back, and the sarcasm I felt surprised me. I looked at Riley, the Great One, beautiful, majestic, and unknowable. "We really are just ants to you," I whispered as my heart sank. "Just blips on screen."

Suddenly Riley was before me, and before I could protest my hands were in his. His touch sent a shock up my arms and down my spine, making my knees feel weak. I felt like I was nothing, and the tears began to well up in my eyes. It was all too much; things had been happening too fast and my brain couldn't handle the overload—

"Andromeda," he commanded, and my head snapped to attention, looking him in the eye although all I wanted was to hide my shame. "I am here now. And I will do everything in my power to see that no harm befalls you."

His hands tightened around mine, almost too tight, anchoring me back to reality, pulling me from wallowing in my self-pity. "*Everything*," he repeated with a wild fierceness. "Do you understand?"

I nodded dumbly. He let go of my hands, but as I was about to lift them to wipe the wetness from my eyes, he cupped my face, his thumbs gently wiping the tears away. I froze, the intimate gesture sending my heart into overdrive. I felt both burned and frozen, and my body begged... *more.* For a brief moment, he seemed to lean in as if... as if he would... *kiss me*—

But he blinked, and the moment was lost. His hands dropped to his sides as he stepped back, the pure marble god once more. I felt like a lost fool standing there.

All I ask of you, I thought, before looking away from him as I swallowed my hurricane of emotion. "I don't get it," I said instead. "Why can't we just 'magic door' to New York City." I waved my fingers for effect.

Riley frowned, but not in displeasure. He almost looked... embarrassed.

"I am... not as powerful as I was since I rescued you last night," he confessed, and it almost seemed to cause him pain. "I have not consumed sustenance as my kind must, and as such—"

Realization dawned on me. "You... you used up the last of your powers... for me?" I whispered.

"My uncle could sense my... weakness," he explained, his face growing dark. "I am surprised he said nothing."

This incredible being, this Great One, this beautiful boy in front of me, weakened, because of *me.* I wanted to say something, but couldn't find the words. Once again, I desperately wondered *why me*, the little girl living her silly little life. Nothing special, nothing worth fighting for. And yet, he thought I was. Why? What did I matter to him in the grand scheme of things?

"So... who's driving?" I asked, trying to force a lightness to my tone.

Riley looked at me—and to my shock, rolled his eyes! "I will be," he declared imperially, and he unlocked the passenger door, gesturing for me to get in.

My jaw dropped. "Wait a minute, you really won't let me drive this thing?" I protested as I slid into the seat. He closed my door and I watched him go around the long hood to the driver's side. I made another attempt as he took his seat, "This is a classic muscle car, when am I ever going to have the chance again?"

"You are an inexperienced driver, and we must make haste for the city of New York," he explained as he put the key into the ignition. "I must drive."

"But it's Saturday afternoon! There won't be any traffic on the highways or anything!" I argued.

"Do not argue with me, Andromeda," he ordered, his voice low and impossible to deny. He looked at me, and something in his eyes made my breath catch. "One day, I will teach you how to drive a car such as this," he promised softly.

I wanted to protest that I knew how to drive *thanks*, but that softness in his voice and face touched me instead. The thought that one day, just the two of us, Riley carefully but expertly instructing me as we made our way down some empty road—

I blushed. It would have been impossible to keep my eyes on the road with Riley sitting so temptingly close anyway. It was for the best if he drove.

"Okay, well, that's a promise then, mister," I said awkwardly instead.

"Put on your seatbelt. We are not leaving until I am certain you are secured," he ordered.

I blushed again, and grumbling, did as he said. He could make me feel like such a little girl.

The Impala roared to life, the power of the engine making my nerves tremble with delight. Now this was a car, not at all like the brick I was stuck with. Riley pulled out of the garage and down the driveway. At the front door of *The Crawling Chaos* stood Uncle Neil, looking all the stranger in the mid-morning Rhode Island sun. He put his pipe in his mouth and waved at us, almost cheekily.

We were on our way.

~*~*~*~

We went down the highways, zipping through Connecticut as if it didn't matter. It was an hour into our trip before I could unclench my hand from the door bar. Riley drove as if the hounds of hell were on our tails. I couldn't understand how we hadn't been pulled over yet, and I told Riley as much. He only grimly smiled and said, "I'm not completely powerless, little one."

We drove in relative silence. I had tried to turn on the radio, but there was nothing good to listen to, only the latest terrible pop songs and static. As we drove, my eyes drifted to Riley's profile. Like a thief, I stole glances at him, the opportunity to look too great a temptation to pass.

I thought I was being subtle, but then without turning to me Riley said, "Is there something you require?"

I stiffened, my face flushing red. "Um… no, nothing," I mumbled.

"You are bored," he suggested, eyes still on the road ahead.

"No, no it's not that, it's fine," I stammered. "I mean, it's not like this is a vacation or anything, we have a mission."

"A vacation?" he asked.

"Yeah, like, you know, a road trip. Just to see the sights," I explained. "I mean, we're not doing this for *fun*. This is to, like, save the world and stuff." I winced at my awkwardness.

Riley said nothing at first, and I thought that was it. I'd turned to look out my own window when his voice interrupted the silence. "And if this were a road trip?"

I looked back at him, surprised to hear him speak once more. "Do... do immortal being things not... go... exploring?" I asked, grimacing again at my failure at English.

"When we travel, it is with an end in sight. A purpose. A destiny," he declaimed.

"So, not for fun," I offered.

Suddenly, Riley stiffened, and my stomach sank. *Great, now you've said something stupid.*

"What my kind does for... fun," he began, his voice sounding pained. "I don't believe you would see it as such."

A black hole seemed to open between us, sucking out all the air. *Ants, remember?* I kicked myself mentally. "Oh," I said meekly instead.

"And if this were a road trip," he repeated after a moment. "What would you do?"

I racked my brain, trying to think of an answer while simultaneously trying to fathom why he cared. "Um, well... we'd go to see the sights. Like, we'd have a cool destination in mind. And while we travel, we'd listen to music. Or sing," I tried to explain.

Riley's mouth quirked into a small smile. "Sing?" he

repeated. "Then do so."

My mouth dropped open. "Sing?" I squeaked. "I... I can't sing!"

"You have vocal chords," he pointed out.

"I can't sing *well*," I countered, hugging myself.

"Sing for me... please?" he said, his eyes glancing at me for a moment.

My emotions were in a tumult. Was this how the ingénue Christine felt, the first time her Angel of Music, her Phantom of the Opera, commanded her? I felt unable to resist, even though I desperately wanted to.

"O-okay," I stuttered, but I knew exactly what to sing. "Um. This is from my favorite musical—*Phantom of the Opera*. It's... it's really beautiful."

And so I gave in, singing what I knew best—*Angel of Music* from *Phantom's* first act. To my own ears I sounded horrible, low and timid and shaky. I didn't dare look at Riley lest I catch sight of a mocking smirk on his lips. I finally made it to the end of the song, and taking a shaky breath, stopped, glad it was over.

I felt a tug on my elbow, and Riley's cool hand slithered its way into mine. I looked up at him in shock.

"That was surprisingly... beautiful," he admitted, his eyes ever on the road before us. "Do not doubt yourself, Andromeda."

"*Yeah, what he said.*"

I jumped in my seat, a small scream escaping past my lips. "Did... did the car just..."

From the radio, the sound of laughter pealed forth, a mix of merriment and mockery.

"*Neil,*" Riley growled, moving his hand back to the

steering wheel, leaving mine feeling empty and cold.

"*Neil?*" I repeated, and the voice only laughed again. "Is it... is it some kind of—"

"Yes, it is some kind of magic! The magic of *radio!*" Neil intoned, laying it on thick. "You mortals are a riot, you always forget your own technological advances."

I was mortified, and my face burned red at his teasing. "Look, it's been pretty insane ever since I met the both of you, so—"

"Touché, touché," Neil's disembodied voice said, and he sounded contrite. "Anyway, back to the business at hand! You're making good time, kids," he pointed out, "but you don't want to get there *too* quickly."

"The sooner we secure the *Grimoire*—" Riley began, but Neil interrupted him.

"Yeah, about that. Sorry, Squidpickle, but I forgot to mention. I've got a Spell of Dimensional Protection on that sucker. The portal is the locker door, but... the book's only there to grab at midnight."

"Which midnight?" Riley snapped.

"Which one do you think, Tentakins?" Neil shot back. "Local time, and on the dot too so don't be late about it. And don't forget that briefcase! Neil, out!"

Riley fell silent. I could feel the waves of disapproval rising from him, and I shrank back, trying to make myself even smaller. Neil's news had put him in a foul mood. I tried to distract myself with the world outside my window, despairing that Neil had interrupted... *whatever* that moment had been, when Riley's hand had been in mine.

It was a gorgeous autumn day with a bright blue cloudless

sky. The air that blew through our open windows was brisk but still warm. The traffic increased as we got closer to Manhattan, but Riley wove the Impala through the cars with an expert's touch, never having to brake suddenly or swerve madly. I was even beginning to enjoy our little 'road trip.' The silence within the car had grown companionable. Even though a part of me was still holding my breath, terrified of what being with Riley might do to me and unsure of what lay before us, I had eased into a sense of complacent confidence. I couldn't be one hundred percent certain, but my soul seemed to sigh, *yes… I trust him with my life.*

Before I knew it, the island of Manhattan rose in front of us, weighed down by an explosion of metal and glass, the spires of its monuments to the modern age reaching toward the sky. I had only moved to the East Coast a couple years ago, and hadn't yet had the opportunity to visit New York City. I stared out of my window as we drove down the West Side Highway, the Hudson River to my left, the metropolis to my right. I only wished I had my cell phone so I could take some pictures, but I knew they could never do the sight before me any justice. To finally see it—its ordered chaos laid out before us, its frightening heights compacted within the confines of the tiny island—was dizzying.

"There are so many humans," Riley muttered to himself as we waited at a red light. It was barely three hours since we'd left Portsmouth, and we had finally reached the New York Port Authority Bus Terminal at 8th Avenue and 42nd Street.

"No kidding," I replied, as I stared at the sea of bodies swimming across the street and down the sidewalks. How could there be so many people in one place? It made me feel tiny, insignificant. I sank into my seat; the sight of a pristine

'67 Chevy Impala was catching eyes, even in a city this frenetic. It made me nervous.

Riley made a right turn when the light changed, taking us away from the Port Authority. "Hey!" I said, twisting in my seat to watch the bus depot fade away. "Where are we—"

"We must wait until midnight," he reminded me as we continued driving south.

"But... we still have to hang around, don't we?"

"I will not risk losing you in the crowd," he interrupted, and his tone was final. "We will return at midnight to reclaim the *Grimoire*. The cultists who stole your friend's book do not know where Neil has hidden the *Grimoire*, nor would they know our purpose in coming here for it. There is no need for us to wait nearby until the appointed time."

I didn't really agree with him, but who was I to argue when it did make sense. And the thought that we were necessarily delayed in getting the *Grimoire* sent a warm feeling through my spine, straight down to my toes. As my brain caught up to my fuzzy butterfly-filled stomach, I realized—

We had a whole day to spend in New York City.

Together.

"This is our 'road trip,' " Riley said, and the use of 'our' made my heart skip a beat. "What shall we do first?"

Chapter Twelve
Cosmopolis

THE SOUNDS OF CLINKING GLASS, THE RINGING OF silverware and excited conversation surrounded us like a symphony. I sat upright, allowing it to wash over me and wishing the moment would never end.

"Andromeda—"

The voice that commanded my very soul reached my ears, drawing all of my attention to it. "You have barely consumed your cheesecake. Was it not as the waiter assured us it would be?" Riley's face darkened at the thought that our server may have lied to us.

"Oh no, no, I just... look at it, Riley, it's huge!" I protested, picking up my fork to poke at the giant slice of cheesecake before me. "I can barely eat another bite!"

It was hardly a surprise, considering the feast we had ordered. The appetizers of fruitwood smoked salmon with classic garniture and multi-grain bread, the jumbo lump crabcake served with smoked tomato piquillo aioli and salad. The main course of true Sardi's classics: spinach cannelloni au gratin for me, steak tartar for Riley.

Oh, if only Bree could see me now, sitting in Sardi's with the pre-theatre crowd. When we had first pulled up to the restaurant, I thought for sure getting a table would be impossible, but we were seated immediately upon Riley's command.

"Hmm… that is a shame, but I suppose I will allow it," Riley said with a hint of a smile. A careless wave of his hand, and our desserts were cleared from the table.

I flinched to see the barely touched cheesecake taken away—it felt so wasteful.

"Are you sure I can't tempt you with an aperitif?" Riley offered.

"A… a what?" I asked.

"An after-dinner libation."

"You mean… alcohol?" I grimaced at the thought. "Ugh, I never want to touch alcohol again as long as I *live*."

Riley's eyes narrowed. "*Good*," he said curtly. "I want you to never put yourself in such a situation again, and as you don't know your limits, it is best if you abstain."

Only then did I realize that he wasn't just teasing; it had been a test. I reddened at the memory of Friday's party—was it really only last night that those horrible guys had tried to take advantage of me? If I had been more responsible, if I hadn't been out there dressed in only that little bikini, drunk out of my mind, then—

The realization was a sobering one. Then *none of this* would have happened.

"Excuse me, Riley," I said, putting my cloth napkin on the

table.

Riley straightened in his seat, his eyes narrowing. "Where are you going?" he demanded, and his tone froze me in place.

"To... to the... little girls' room," I explained, feeling myself flush in embarrassment and hoping he would get the hint.

He relaxed and nodded. Still burning, I hurried to the restroom. It was frightening what Riley could do to me, making me feel so unsure and childlike. And yet—

The ladies' room was empty, and I went straight for the sink, turning on the faucet to let cold water run over my hands.

It had barely been a day, but the flood of memories of our time together felt like a lifetime. Chinatown and Little Italy, the crowds and the smells and the colors. Driving by Ground Zero and not knowing how to explain that dark day to an unknowing god. Being forced into a small SoHo boutique where Riley bought me the dress and shoes I was now wearing (a storm-blue sleeveless pencil skirt affair that made me look like an adult, high heels in a silver hue and a Kate Spade bag to compliment the lot). Even if he had let me, I couldn't bear to see the final price. I was sure it was more money than I could spend in a week, much less a single purchase.

"You can't wear *that* to dinner," he had purred, motioning to my jeans and sweater ensemble as the saleswoman handed me the newly purchased items. "Change here."

I'd wanted to protest, but the words just wouldn't come to my mind, and so I obeyed. I shoved my old clothes into the Kate Spade bag, the thought of my ratty things touching such an expensive bag making me queasy.

In the Sardi's ladies' room, I smoothed down the skirt, reveling in the feel of it under my hand. The fabric was delicious against my skin. The dress could hardly do much to help my pathetic figure, but the look in Riley's eye when I'd stepped out of the dressing room...

As much as I suddenly wanted to, I couldn't wash my face to cool it down—I was wearing makeup. *Me.* Wearing *makeup.* The result of a stop into Sephora, where a gorgeous redhead with a playful but no-nonsense manner gave me the royal treatment at Riley's request. They discussed what colors suited me best—they could have been talking another language entirely. "Not that she even needs any makeup," Riley had boasted, smiling at me as the woman laughed and agreed. I could only blush, but secretly, the complement set my heart aglow.

It felt only natural to explore 5th Avenue after that, taking in all the high-end designer stores that ran its length. I watched my reflection in the restroom mirror as my hand moved as if of its own volition to the silver Tiffany necklace I now wore. I felt like Cinderella. I only wished ruefully that this night would never end.

Sighing, I turned off the water and dried my hands. I had wasted enough time lost in thought. Riley was waiting. Besides, the night was far from over—it was only 7:35 p.m. I wondered what else the evening could possibly hold for us. Midnight seemed forever away.

I felt calm and confident as I walked out of the ladies' room. I kept my eyes on the floor, attempting to appear demure and sexy, while in actuality trying to make sure I didn't trip and end up looking like a total idiot in front of Riley. I got back to my seat, sat down, looked up and—

Riley was gone.

I could feel the blood drain from my face. Where could he have gone?

The theatre crowd had made their escape, and the restaurant was much quieter than even just five minutes before. An icy cold chill dripped down my spine. Had he left me there, all alone? Where was I supposed to go? I had no money, no phone, no way to get back home without him. The check was still on the table. Surreptitiously, I opened the little black folder; there was change. At least Riley had paid while I was in the restroom. Not that stiffing your—

The word stuck to my tongue, choking me. We had spent all day together, exploring and dining. He'd bought me clothes, for Pete's sake! But... a *date*? Why would someone as worldly and gorgeous as Riley ever consider me dateable? Had he done it out of pity? An apology for whisking me away to his other-dimensional abode? Perhaps, but it was impossible to think it could be anything more than that. Especially now, when from the best I could tell, he'd up and left me—

"Get your things, we mustn't be late."

Riley's cool, seductive voice snapped me out of my miserable reverie. I looked up at him, gaping dumbly as he leaned his forearms on the back of his chair, looking down upon me with both impatience and—

Affection?

"What's the rush, I thought we couldn't get the—*you know*—until midnight?" I said as I struggled to gather my bag.

"That is still the plan, yes. But curtain is at eight." And with a devilish smirk and a flourish, he produced two theatre tickets from the inner pocket of the blazer that fit him like a dream.

Two tickets to *The Phantom of the Opera*.

I gasped, my hands flying to my mouth in shock. "You must be joking!" I cried.

He blinked—suddenly the impossibly suave, unknowable creature was replaced, and his slight head cock made him seem like a confused little puppy. "Is this not pleasing to you?" he asked, stiffening as if preparing for a blow.

"Not pleasing? Riley are you kidding?" I yelled, and without thinking, I leapt forward, throwing my arms around him as if he were only Bree or Vik.

It was a mistake, a glorious, horrible mistake. My brain shut down as the proximity to him sent a wave of longing through me. My arms instinctively drew me closer to him, and the heady smell that was distinctly Riley—of fresh salt breezes and deep, murky seawater—filled my nostrils, setting my nerves on fire.

Only then did I realize that if I thought he had been stiff before, he was a plank of wood now. *Crap!* I panicked and threw myself away from him, my chest heaving as I did. "Crap, I'm... I'm so sorry, Riley, I just got so excited. I've always wanted to see *Phantom*," I babbled. "I just can't... I just can't believe you... remembered."

His nostrils flared, but he seemed to soften once there was distance between us. "Andromeda, you *just* mentioned your love of the thing this afternoon. I am old, but I am not senile," he droned, and I smiled sheepishly at him.

He checked the clock on the wall. "Now quickly, before we are late," he ordered.

But his bossy tone meant nothing to me, for as I passed

him, his hand gently touched upon the small of my back, and he guided me out of Sardi's and down the street to the Majestic Theatre. My emotions were so great, I later would barely remember that walk—was it short? Long? Straight? With turns? Nothing mattered. I was with Riley, and we were about to see *Phantom of the Opera.*

I didn't come back to my senses until we entered the Majestic Theatre. I was in awe—it truly lived up to its name. It felt lush, rich, just like I imagined the Paris Opera House would be. Riley, his hand still against my back, ushered me up the stairs, through the throng of people excited for a night of Broadway.

An usher stopped us on the mezzanine level and took our tickets. His eyes widened when he saw the seating assignment—I hadn't caught a glimpse of the row or seat, and his reaction made me curious.

"Right this way, sir, madam," he stammered, and we followed him up a few more stairs, down a hallway—

And to a door labeled '5.'

"Box Five," he said with an stutter.

Now it was my turn to be shocked. "Impossible!" I gasped once Riley opened the door and ushered me over the threshold. We were in a dimly lit room that only added to the majestic ambiance. A scarlet curtain separated us from our seats.

"This box was actually quite easy to procure," Riley said, and then added with an almost predatory smile, "for me."

I couldn't believe it. The perfect seats for the perfect show. I almost clapped my hands in delight.

"Shall we?" he said, his arm sweeping toward me.

"Please," I breathed, putting my hand in the crook of his

elbow.

By the time the cast was taking their final bows, I wanted to leap to my feet, wanted to applaud madly and yell *Bravi, bravi, bravissimi!* But somehow I managed to keep my cool. I did, however, clap until I thought my hands would fall off. I looked back at Riley; he had stayed seated and wasn't clapping, but there was a ghost of a smile on his face. But he wasn't looking at the stage. He was only staring at me.

In that moment, as we gazed at each other, the words almost escaped my lips in my euphoria. *I love you.* The thought sent a jolt of longing through me. My Great One. My Riley. My beautiful, frightening, unknowable, perfect Riley.

I knew then that I could never, would never love another like I loved Riley in that moment. That all else would only be a pale shadow of the reality before me. No matter what he might feel toward unworthy me, I would forever be his. Forever.

We sat in Box Five a few moments more, waiting for the audience to make their exit. "You enjoyed the show," he stated as the crowds finally started to disperse.

I struggled to find the words, and all seemed inadequate. "It was everything I ever wanted," I whispered, bringing my hands to my face in girlish wonderment.

Riley smiled, and standing, offered his hand. I placed my hand in his, and once I stood, found we were barely a foot apart. He towered over me; I had never felt safer.

"Come," he ordered.

I obeyed. We emerged into Times Square, Riley's hand once more against the small of my back. The crowds were much smaller than before, but there were still people hustling about, taking in the nightlife and the lights. I let the rush and excitement wash over me, the LED billboards painting the air around us in brilliant, bold sweeps. I leaned into Riley's protective touch. We were an island amidst the sea of humanity. I felt untouchable, like a ship sheltered in a cove, protected from the sea's rage.

We meandered around Times Square in a comforting silence, absorbing the sights and sounds. I wanted the night to never end. But then, just like Cinderella—

"It is time," Riley said. He took my hand and led me down 42nd Street toward the Port Authority Bus Terminal.

Midnight was almost upon us, and I couldn't shake the growing fear that I was about to lose everything.

Riley deftly wove us through the crowds with the same finesse he displayed in driving. I followed blindly, preparing myself mentally for what might lie ahead. What if we were late? What if there were cultists waiting for us? What if—?

"Desist," Riley ordered, but he threw me a small smile over his shoulder. "I can feel you worrying."

I nodded mutely and tried to keep up. My heels, while shockingly comfortable, were making it difficult to match the pace he was setting. I was relieved when the Port Authority finally loomed over us, a strangely ominous and dark structure after the wonderland that was Times Square. It looked more like a prison fortress than a bus terminal, and if it hadn't been for Riley's pull, I might have paused there in the street in a sudden lack of courage. Instead, I was dragged forward, and I took a deep breath to steel myself.

Inside the Port Authority was a deserted maze of stairs, ugly orange tiles and brown trim. I looked around, already disoriented and unable to determine where the lockers would even be located. The silence within the terminal was stark and oppressive compared to the streets just outside. My eye caught a glimpse of a clock—it was 11:45 p.m.

"Riley—" I began, but he shushed me.

"Not now," he growled, and he looked like an animal on the hunt. He glanced at me. "Don't look—but we are being followed."

My eyes widened, and I nearly did look over my shoulder.

"Don't," he ordered. "They are flanking us as we walk."

"Riley," I whispered, clutching his hand in fear. "What are we going to do?"

"They are cultists... They will not attack us until we have the book in hand," he predicted, continuing his brisk but steady gait.

"And then what?" I whispered.

"And then, I will keep you safe," he promised, his expression darkening.

We found the rental lockers, lined in identical rows. We only had seven minutes, but Riley pushed forward, not paying attention to any of the signs or numbers, seemingly guided by something else.

Out of the corner of my eye down one of the aisles, I caught sight of a black-robed figure. I gasped and turned away, clinging tighter to Riley, frightened. I didn't know how we'd get out of there with the book, much less—

"It is here," Riley said. I tightened my hand around his arm for one moment more before I released it to let him work.

It was number L1890, just another in a row of lockers. But a strange sort of energy seemed to be building within it. It set my teeth on edge and raised the hairs on my arms.

Riley placed his hand on the normal-looking combination

lock. "Aeons and aeons and he's still using the same combination," he muttered with a roll of his eyes, and then he looked at me. I glanced over my shoulder and my eyes found a clock on a nearby wall.

11:59 p.m.

"Whatever happens," Riley whispered, "you will do as I say." It wasn't a question, but an order that allowed no argument. I nodded.

The seconds passed with agonizing slowness as his hand poised upon the door, waiting for the appointed time. I tried to calm my breathing, tried to prepare myself for whatever might come next. I had to pull it together, if for nothing else, then for Riley.

The clock struck, its mighty chime echoing through the terminal. In a flash of movement, Riley had the lock off and the door open. He plunged his arm into the locker, as if reaching into unfathomable depths. He suddenly grimaced and gripped the locker edge desperately with his other hand. I nearly grabbed him as he abruptly surged back from the door, and then surged forward again as if to punch something inside. He then reached once more, as deeply as he could, into the locker. His eyes widened, and with a grunt, he pulled something out of it.

It was a brief case.

"*Neil*," he growled, and plunged his hand back into the locker. "Of *course* his accursed briefcase would come first."

Riley seemed to root around within the locker's depths, struggling to find the book.

"I have it!" he finally cried, and with a mighty pull, his hand emerged clutching a slim tome bound in ancient red leather. *The Eldrich Grimoire.*

"Close your eyes," Riley ordered as he shoved the book into my hands. "And get down!"

Going on pure instinct, I did as he commanded, clutching the *Grimoire* to my body as I sank to the ground.

I could hear the patter of running footsteps. A rough hand grabbed my arm—but before it could pull me to my feet or touch the book, a roar the likes of which I'd never heard rang through the locker room, making the metal shake. I could sense the lights flickering from behind my eyelids. In terror, I gathered the book even closer to myself as tears began to fall down my face uncontrollably.

The sounds of a desperate fight surrounded me. How many attackers there were, I could not tell. A body was slammed into the lockers to my left. The metallic crash shook me, and I felt the body hit the floor. A male voice began screaming in unimaginable pain.

"*Riley!*" I cried.

Another body fell, this time even closer to me. I wrapped myself tighter around the book, desperately squeezing my eyes shut. There was then a strange change in the air around me, the sensation of something—powering up. A wind seemed to rise from nowhere, whipping about me, trying to suck me in. The air seemed to scream, and I could swear its voice sounded—human.

The wind died as suddenly as it came. I did not dare open my eyes. In the dark silence, a hand grabbed my upper arm and I struggled against it, lashing out wildly.

"Run!" a voice at my ear said, and I nearly collapsed in relief. It was Riley.

"No, don't look, just run!"

He pulled me forward, and I struggled behind him in my

heels. I thought for sure I would fall, or drop the book, that we would get caught, that something terrible would happen—

The cool night air hit my face and I gulped it down gratefully, trying to wash away the violence that had filled the terminal.

"To the car," Riley ordered, and I hesitated.

"Those... those people that attacked us?" I whispered blindly.

"Cultists," he confirmed huskily.

"Can I open my eyes?" I meekly asked, afraid of the answer.

He paused. "Yes, now you can."

I did, and instantly sought him out. There he was, briefcase in hand and breathing heavily, but there was an ethereal glow about him. Even his eyes seemed to burn emerald in the yellow haze of 42nd Street at night.

"What happened back there?" I all but sobbed, clutching the book tighter.

Riley's eyes seemed to flare. In that moment I could almost have been frightened of him.

"The cultists are no more," he said. "My hunger is sated."

"You... you ate them?" I forced the words out of my mouth. It came out as a squeak even though the shock was finally subsiding.

He looked at me for a moment, and then let out a low laugh. He shook his head slowly. "I have consumed that part of them which held together their sanity. Their being."

Their souls, I realized. There was nothing I could say.

He stepped closer to me. "Does that frighten you?" he demanded. "Does it, *Christine?*" he taunted. He stared down at me, his face tortured but also… fierce.

Wild.

Beautiful.

I impulsively reached up and touched his arm.

"No," I grimly said. And it didn't.

Riley's eyes seemed to flash again, and he grasped me by the elbows to gaze deeply into my eyes.

My knees faltered. The evening was finally catching up to me.

"Whoa," I mumbled, my eyelids suddenly feeling impossibly heavy. "I think it's midnight for this Cinderella."

I sank into Riley's arms as the last of my adrenaline abandoned me. I gazed up at him, and in his expression I thought I again caught a glimpse of something almost like…

Affection.

"Sleep," he ordered. "I will care for you."

And so, I obeyed.

Chapter Thirteen

Changes

DREAMS... HAUNTED MY SLEEP.

I could feel the embrace of one strong and all-powerful, lifting me from harm.

I could feel the sweet vibration of the Impala's roar, my chariot to safety.

I could feel the strength of one holding me close, gravity fighting an elevator's pull.

I could feel the soft cocoon of bedding, welcoming me to Morpheus's embrace.

"Sleep," was Riley's whisper. "And be safe."

I obeyed.

~*~*~*~

A knock on wood brought me to my senses, and my eyelids fluttered.

Another knock, and my eyes flew open. They blindly searched my surroundings, confused by the nearly total darkness. I realized I was in an unfamiliar king-sized bed, the sheets tucked up to my chin.

Knock, knock, knock, came again, and on its wing, the cry of, "Room service!"

I forced myself up in the bed, throwing my legs over the side. A quick glance revealed that I was indecent. I was wearing only the hot pink 'FLIRT' panties and my old t-shirt. In what little light there was, I could make out the storm blue dress draped neatly over an armchair across the room.

Another knock on the door, and I began to panic.

"Room service!" the voice submissively declared again, and steeling myself, I stood. Room service? Was I in a hotel?

I scrambled through my memories of the night before, but I was at a loss to recall anything from after we found the book. Vague sense memories taunted me—the feeling of sliding my dress off and pulling on my t-shirt, of someone picking me up from a chair and placing me upon the softness of a cloud, hands tucking the cool sheets around me, fingers caressing my hair...

Where was Riley?

Knock, knock, knock!

"I'm not ready, please come back later!" I yelled at the door. The woman must have heard me, because a moment later I could make out the sound of a cart moving further down the hallway. I took a deep breath in shaky relief.

It was obvious to me now that I was in a hotel, but the thick drapes blocking out all light made it hard to determine what time it was. I walked to the window and ripped the curtains open—

I gasped.

The sun shone brilliantly in a bright blue sky, and spread long and vast before me, was Central Park.

"Holy crap," I whispered. Glancing at the stationery on the desk confirmed my suspicion.

I was in *the* Plaza Hotel.

"You are awake," Riley's cool voice said from behind me.

"*Riley!*" I shrieked as I whirled around. He stood in the doorway that led to the suite's sitting room. *Oh god!* I pulled the hem of my shirt down as far as it would go. *Why did I have to wear these panties?* "Don't look!" I demanded.

He cocked his head at me. "I don't understand—"

"Close your eyes!" I begged. I wanted to sink into the floor and die.

He actually did as I asked, crossing his arms over his chest as his perfect eyelids lowered. He was utterly beautiful in the morning light, his skin practically glowing. He looked like he had recently showered, his hair still damp. My fingers itched to run through his black locks, but I ran for the bathroom instead and grabbed one of the expensive towels, wrapping it around my waist.

"I don't understand what is wrong," Riley said, and he sounded annoyed.

"You can open your eyes. I wasn't decent," I explained, still red with embarrassment, but at least feeling like I was on more equal ground.

"You are wearing clothing, aren't you?" he pointed out.

"I'm... I'm in my *undies,*" I whispered, mortified.

"How are 'undies' different from the bathing attire you wore at the beach? Everyone could see you then. You might as well have been naked," he retorted.

My mouth clamped shut. He was right. The memory of that night and what could have happened immediately brought tears back to my eyes. Crap, when did I totally lose all control over my emotions? When did I become such a *girl?*

"I am sorry," Riley apologized politely. "I have caused you discomfort." I thought he might come over to me then, to comfort me like he had last night, but he did not move. It took a moment, but then the impact of his stiff reaction hit me almost like a blow. I felt alone, lost. So much for Cinderella's night at the ball—it was time to face reality again. I wiped the wetness from my eyes, and stood up straight.

"You should shower and dress," he suggested, and he took a seat in the armchair, making no move toward me, his gaze distant. His obvious lack of attention stung me. But rather than say anything to risk revealing the sudden shakiness of my voice, I merely nodded and went back into the bathroom, closing the door behind me.

What is going on? I thought as I turned on the shower, slid off my clothes and climbed in. The lavish room quickly filled with steam—there was no need to wait on old pipes to grumble and get to work in the Plaza Hotel.

Yesterday Riley had been so... attentive. I winced as the disinterested expression he was probably still wearing in the next room flashed before my mind's eye. I worked the hotel shampoo into my hair—it smelled like vanilla, rich and creamy. *He took me to see Phantom for Pete's sake! He bought me a dress and a necklace and—he acted as if he were my... my...*

"Boyfriend," I muttered, letting the water rinse the suds away. I washed my body and conditioned my hair, rushing to get cleaned up. I turned off the shower and wrapped my wet hair in a thick towel, putting on a luxurious white bathrobe. I needed answers. I needed to no longer feel confused and alone and insignificant. I needed to get to the bottom of this. I opened the bathroom door—

Riley was gone again.

My heart sank to my toes.

"There is clothing for you on the bed," his voice rang from the sitting room beyond the doorway. "Dress yourself, and then come in here."

My heart leapt back up. I put a trembling hand to my chest. How was I ever going to survive like this?

On the bed was a new pair of jeans, fresh underthings and a new light sweater. I had the uncomfortable realization that Riley obviously knew all my sizes as the items fit like a dream. I sighed as I examined the result in the mirror. I looked like plain old me once more, and I glanced at the dress and heels still draped over the chair.

Pull it together, Cinderella, I snapped at myself, and sighing again, dried my hair as best as I could, brushing it with the comb from the hotel complimentary package. I put my hair up in a messy bun—it was useless to try any other kind of style—tied my shoes and entered the sitting room.

It was a beautiful suite, light and airy. I felt like I could live there, high above the city's rush in my own little world. Riley was gazing out the vast window beside where he sat at a table, a white cloth set with a breakfast spread. My stomach growled, but I froze; Riley looked impossibly gorgeous, and my heart broke at the thought of ruining the moment by launching into the thoughts that had plagued me through my shower. I would give up all the Plaza suites in the world if I could just be worthy of this boy for the rest of my life.

He sensed my presence and looked up—my breath caught in my throat. "Eat," he ordered, nodding at the chair across from him. I stumbled toward the table and plopped down.

My eyes couldn't believe the feast before me: eggs, sausage, bacon and potatoes, toast and pancakes, juice and fruit and coffee, all served on silver flatware. I felt like an impostor masquerading as a queen.

Riley didn't move, didn't so much as blink. He only stared at me, his face blank. I cleared my throat nervously. The thought then hit me. "The book... the briefcase..."

"They are both safe," Riley said.

I bit my lip as I glanced back to the bedroom doorway. "There's only one bed," I observed. "Where... where did you sleep?"

"I found accommodations," he said, finally shifting in his seat, running a hand through his still-damp hair. "After last night... the space within these walls would not have been suitable for me. I needed..." he looked at me, his eyes glowing with emerald fire, "more."

I gulped. *Last night...* I remembered what he'd done to those cultists.

"Eat," he repeated.

I noticed there was no place setting on his side of the table. "What about you?" I asked.

He shook his head. "After last night," he said in an almost dreamily contented tone, "I have no need."

"So then... all this breakfast is just for me?" I asked.

He stared at me intently, and a long pause followed before he leaned back with widened eyes and flared nostrils and said, "Please, don't concern yourself with my needs. Enjoy your own sustenance."

I piled my plate with the eggs, fruit and pancakes. Riley's gaze followed my movements as I made myself a cup of tea—peppermint, what a comforting relief after everything that had happened. It almost felt like a tether to reality.

Riley's eyes narrowed as I started on some potatoes. "Does the meat not please you?" he demanded.

"Of course it doesn't," I replied. "I'm a vegetarian."

Riley shook his head. "I don't understand—yesterday, you ate meat."

I recalled our dinner at Sardi's, and smiled indulgently. "That was fish, silly, that doesn't count."

Riley blinked at me slowly, then shook his head again. "Flesh is flesh. It never ceases to amaze me, the rules you humans will implement to justify your inconsistencies."

The insult made me flinch. We were a fickle species, weren't we? Hypocrites, the lot of us. I looked down at my food, and tried to concentrate on eating.

"Does what I say bother you?" he asked.

I couldn't speak. I only shrugged, hoping he would drop it.

"Do not let it. It merely amuses me. I marvel at it," he confessed, and I looked up. His beautiful face held nothing but earnestness.

I managed to clean my plate, but there was no way I could finish all the food on the table, even excluding the meat. Once again, I felt guilty at the waste. Riley didn't seem to notice, and told me to gather my things.

I tried to keep my face from falling. "We need to be getting back to Portsmouth, after all," I said, but I was unable to hide the dejection in my voice.

"This saddens you," Riley noted. He was staring out the window again.

I shrugged as I packed my clothes. It hurt to have to fold the dress and put it in the bag. I just knew it would wrinkle. *I guess sometimes there's no way to avoid having to crumple up something so beautiful...*

"It's just, I've never been to this city before." I tried to sound nonchalant. "There's still so much I'd love to see and do..."

"There is no need to rush away," Riley said offhandedly. My head whipped around to look at him, and he looked back at me. Cool and distant and framed by the sun's golden rays, he looked every inch a god-figure handing down decrees to lesser beings. "The day is still young."

Though his face appeared unchanging, he lowered his voice and it came out as a seductive purr, "I want you to enjoy yourself."

I didn't need to be told twice. The idea that this Cinderella might get a second chance at the ball was too great to resist, and I was packed and ready in the next thirty seconds. Riley opened the door for me, and with a slight bow, motioned me to lead the way. I practically tripped out of the room and toward the elevator in my excitement to get back into the streets, but a part of me was hyper-aware of the physical distance between us. Riley seemed to be keeping himself at arm's length from me, and the idea that he was doing it consciously made me ack. In the elevator, I racked my brain, wondering if it was something I had done, but nothing came to mind. Unless—

We'd only come to New York to get the book so that he

could make sure I was safe. And now that was done. The cultists were no more. My safety was assured. Why would he want to waste any more time on me? Offering me one more day on the town was just his way of pitying me.

The idea depressed me, and I hardly noticed the splendor of the Plaza's lobby as we passed through it. We exited the building, but I paused when we emerged—before us was a pure white open-topped carriage with plush red velvet seats, drawn by a beautiful white horse. I smiled but rolled my eyes, until Riley walked before me, and opened the carriage door.

"After you, Andromeda, my princess," he said softly.

What else was I supposed to do?

I got into the carriage, and he followed, sitting across from me, careful to not let our knees touch. The driver took his seat, and with a "giddup," our second day in New York City began.

Not a date, of course, I told myself, even though the thought made my heart ache. But as I gazed at Riley I promised myself that whatever the day was, I would cherish it.

~*~*~*~

We left New York around 5:00 p.m., driving up the I-278 from Brooklyn on our way back to I-95. I leaned my head against Cleo's window, closing my eyes as I allowed the day's memories to wash over me.

Riley and I had taken the white carriage through all of Central Park, riding high above all the other tourists and New Yorkers. We ate lunch at Tavern on the Green—well, I had eaten. Riley once again only watched, not hungry. We collected Cleo from the Plaza's parking lot, but stopped off long enough in the West Village to pick up Magnolia cupcakes. I'd wanted to try one ever since Bree was always raving about how 'wicked delicious' they were.

"I need to know what all the fuss is about," I'd teased Riley as I handed him one. "One for you and one for me."

"Must I?" he asked, eying the pale green frosting with suspicion.

"You said you wanted me to enjoy myself!" I protested. "I promise you won't regret it."

He looked at me with one part indulgence, one part annoyance. He did, however, peel the paper off the cupcake, lift it to his perfect lips and take a bite.

From the way his eyes brightened and the unmistakable pleasure that bloomed over his face, I'd known I was right. If only I knew somehow that the cupcake wasn't the only thing he wouldn't regret about our day together...

I sighed as I shifted in my seat. He was so infuriatingly hard to understand. All day I'd felt so frustrated, unable to read him or his emotions, feeling like I'd been cut off from him. And yet, he had driven me around, taken me to see everything I wished, bought me all those clothes and food and had put up with me for far longer than he'd needed to.

What was going on in that magnificent mind of his? It would be easy for me to believe he was phoning it in, just going through the motions. That's what it felt like, but why would he even bother? It must have been obvious to him my... interest... in him. Was he just trying to let me down gently?

But then that meant he cared... didn't it? It was a small consolation.

He hadn't touched me once since last night. The memory of how he'd held me in his arms, making me feel warm and safe, made my insides churn.

Don't you see, I chastised myself. *He may have some feelings for you… but why should he? Think of how it must seem to him. You're nothing compared to him. How would you feel if you had feelings for an ant? Admit it. He likes you, but it's like liking… a puppy! He can't love you, not like you… like you… love him.*

Do you think just because you got the book and saved the day that now it'll all just work out and you'll be all boyfriend and girlfriend? As if he'd ever see you that way! You shouldn't be getting this attached to him. He's just going to hurt you.

I could feel a tear forming in the corner of my eye. I tried to hold it back. It had been such a perfect weekend…

I must have fallen asleep, because a feather-like touch on my cheek woke me. I looked around blearily. Riley was still driving, both hands on the wheel, and night had fallen.

"We have arrived," he said. "I will drop you off at your home before I take the *Grimoire* to Neil."

"I'll come with you to Neil's," I offered, sitting up as I rubbed my eyes.

"No. You will go home." He looked at me, and there almost seemed to be… regret in his face. "You have… school in the morning."

"You do too!" I countered, but I knew there was no point in arguing with him. His mind was made up.

We had the book, and the threat of apocalypse was halted in its tracks.

The world was safe. I was safe.

He had no more reason to keep me with him.

"No, it's fine." I bit back my growing resentment. "Just drop me off." Within my chest, I could feel my heart twist in pain.

"I will see you tomorrow. In the school," he offered.

"Yeah, sure," I muttered.

A sudden desire came over me then. A desire to just out and say everything that was on my heart and in my mind. To confess, to lay myself bare before him and let him destroy me emotionally if he must, but to just *end* the horrid 'will he won't he' nonsense and get a straight answer—

But just as I was building up the words to lay down, we turned the corner onto my street, and my jaw dropped.

In front of my house was a police cruiser.

"Oh crap," I whispered. I looked at Riley.

"My parents called the cops."

Chapter Forteen

Castigated

I'D NEVER BEEN SO GROUNDED IN MY *LIFE.*

"Mom, it wasn't that—"

"Not a phone call all weekend. *All weekend.* And then we find out Bridget hasn't seen you since Friday!" Mom had yelled, her face red with anger and splotchy from tears. I'd never seen her so upset before, and it freaked me out. I looked to my dad for support, but he just stared at me, pale as a ghost.

"Mom, stop overreacting—"

"We thought you were dead!" she screamed.

"I'm sixteen, I forgot to call, I don't know why you're acting like this!" I yelled back.

She just stared at me, her eyes nearly bugging out of her face.

And that's when the grounding happened. No internet. No friends. No movies or TV—I was surprised she didn't take away book privileges while she was at it. Home immediately after school, and I had to call as soon as I got out so she could time me. I was a prisoner in my own house.

I wasn't stupid though—yes, I had to tell them I'd spent the weekend with Riley, but I wasn't crazy enough to reveal we spent the whole time in New York City. Not that it helped—no more Riley *ever* was the law now, and not even me completely dissolving into utterly distraught tears and running up to my room in abject misery would change their minds.

My only consolation was that I would at least still see him 'in the school.' I clung desperately to his promise like a lifeline.

When I woke up the next morning after falling asleep from sobbing my heart out, things were still tense in the house. Mom made Dad to drive me to school, but he could barely talk to me. I'd never felt so low before, so rejected by my own parents.

How could I explain to them what had happened? They would never understand.

"Aren't you going to wish me a good day at school?" I asked Dad, breaking the awful silence as he pulled up in front of the school.

He bowed his head, bringing his hands into his lap. We sat there in horrible silence for a long minute.

I opened the door awkwardly. "Have a good day," I offered, grimacing at how fake it sounded.

"Andi—" he said suddenly, looking up at me. I cringed at the look of misery on his face. "Andi, I just… just… be safe, sweetie. Please?"

I nodded and closed the door. Oh god, why did he have to

guilt me like that? Riley and I *had* to go to New York—not that I'd ever be able to explain that to Dad—but couldn't he see how bad I felt about everything?

I stared at the facade of my school, dread creeping up on me. How would Riley treat me today? I took a shaky breath and walked inside, pushing past the flocks of students lingering in the halls.

I instantly knew how terrible the day would be when I walked into the half-filled English classroom. Riley's desk was still empty, but Bree was in hers. I slid into my seat next to her, but something made me hesitant to catch her attention. With good reason too, because when she turned and saw me, her face whitened.

"What the hell, Andi?" she hissed, her words harsh even though her expression was tinged with confusion and worry. "My parents almost freaking *killed* me when your mom called asking where you were. Your folks thought you were with me the whole weekend, why didn't you—"

But then Mrs. Phillips walked into the classroom.

"Not now," I whispered, pleading with her. My eyes were glued to the door as students continued to dart inside.

Bree stiffened—I shrank in my seat, desperate to avoid a Bridget Fifan Third Degree Special. She seemed torn between continuing her tirade and shutting up, but she pursed her lips in the end. "Lunch," she ordered, and then turned around in her seat, the hunch in her shoulders cutting off any retort I might have made.

The motion stung me. Of all people, I thought Bree would at least try to understand before she just turned away from me like that. I felt my own anger grow. How *dare* she interrogate me, judge me! If it hadn't been for her, I wouldn't have gone to that stupid college party in the first place. This was all her fault! Nothing would have happened if it hadn't been for Bree!

"Nothing would have happened," I whispered under my breath, and the thought sent me reeling. Once more, I realized—there would have been no rescue, no road trip, no Riley.

Where was Riley?

The bell rang, and Mrs. Phillips closed the door. "Good morning, class. Take your seats," she began.

Riley's empty desk seemed a gaping wound to me.

He never showed up for English. He wasn't in French, either. I spent all of snack break, scanning the halls for him. By Marine Biology, I was a mess. I realized then that I didn't even have his number to try and call him. He'd never given it to me... Or asked for mine. Perhaps that should have tipped me off.

But still, part of me couldn't help but be terrified. What if something had happened to him? What if some other cultists had waylaid him before he got the book to Neil's? What if he—

What if now, with his mission complete, he had no more need to attend Portsmouth High?

Had no more need to... see me?

We had saved the *Grimoire*, stopped the doom of the world as I knew it. It was over. Done. Why would he bother coming back to school? He was done *with me*. And the world as I knew it felt more doomed than ever it could have been before.

"Miss Slate!" Ms. Epistola's voice snapped at me. I jerked out of my despair, and looked up at her, disoriented.

"If my class is that uninteresting to you, please, don't hesitate to take a trip down to the principal's office," she sneered scornfully.

"Sorry," I mumbled, stealing a glance at Bree and Vik. They both looked at me with confusion and... concern. I wanted to cry.

I don't know how I made it through the rest of Bio—Ms. Epistola focused particularly on harassing me after my slipup. My chest felt like it was cracking under the strain. When the bell rang, I leapt up, just trying to get my things and get away—it was lunch time, I could just hide somewhere and—

"Not so fast," Bree said at my ear, grabbing me by the arm. Vik stood behind her, looking concerned but remaining silent and not making a move. "We need to talk."

Bree put her weight into it and pushed, pulled and shoved me into an empty classroom across the hall. Just outside the door, the corridors were filled with the rest of the school excitedly making their way to the cafeteria. Soon enough though, the hallway fell silent, and I stared at Bree and Vik before me.

"You could have just asked, Bree," I snapped, rubbing my arm. I felt cornered.

Bree looked at me strangely, but then took a deep breath and rubbed her face. "I'm... I'm sorry, look, I just wanted to talk."

"Well, here I am," I snapped again. I could feel myself wanting to lash out at my two friends like a trapped animal. I tried to restrain myself, but my fears and worries about Riley had run me to the edge of sanity.

Bree seemed kicked off-balance by my aggressiveness, and she took another deep breath. "Look, I'm sorry if I came off rough, but Andi, we were wicked freaked out over you last night. I… I was so scared."

"I was too," Vik interjected, daring to look at me, but then quickly averting his eyes.

"Look," Bree said, "just—don't disappear like that again, okay? I… we just need to know you're safe."

"I already got this speech from my parents, Bree. I really don't appreciate it again from you," I said coldly. "If I wanted more guilt, I would have just stayed at home."

Bree stared at me as if I were some kind of strange, dangerous creature. Good. Let perfect Bree with all her perfect advice and perfect sense finally see that maybe her understanding of life wasn't so perfect after all. What did she know, anyway? I had *seen* things, experienced them, things she couldn't even ever hope to comprehend or believe.

"What happened?" she asked, leaning against a desk with her arms crossed. "It's just… when your mom called, and it hit me that I hadn't heard from you since the party, I just got so… so scared that something had happened to you and—" She took an abrupt trembling breath, "and it was all my fault!" Her eyes were beginning to look wet.

"So sorry if I got you in trouble, Bree," I sneered. How like her to be looking out for herself when I was the one that could have been dead—or worse!

"It's not that! I just… where *were* you?" she begged.

I took a deep breath. Did I trust her? I looked to Vik, standing behind her like a faithful hound, ready to jump in if she tag-teamed him, a strange faraway look in his eyes. Did I trust either of them?

I took a slow breath. "I was with Riley," I said. My voice came out surprisingly calm and level.

Vik took a sudden step back, knocking into the desk behind him, and Bree's jaw dropped. "The whole weekend?" she asked.

"Yeah," I said, feeling defiant. "I was feeling... spontaneous. Just like *you're* always telling me I should be," I countered, unable to resist the jab.

Bree's face fell. "Didn't you think of calling your parents? Me? Anyone?"

I honestly hadn't. Not once, all weekend. The thought surprised me. "No," I said, my voice coming out more shaky than I wanted it to. "I left my phone at home... and I just got so... so caught up in the weekend... I just... I just—I just wish Riley were here!" I gasped, and a tear slipped down my face.

Bree, kind dependable Bree, turned on me then. "Andi, that's so not like you!" she said, straightening up. "I mean, yeah you're slow to respond to texts and stuff, but a whole weekend!?"

"I wasn't thinking!" I wailed, back on the defensive. "Look, it was really sudden, and there was so much to do in New York, and—"

Uh oh.

"Wait, *New York?*" Bree demanded.

"New York!?" Vik echoed almost simultaneously.

I took a deep breath. "Riley took me to New York City," I confessed.

Bree went from victim to listener to attack dog in mere seconds. "Oh my god, Andi!" she cried, "I thought you just meant you were like, at Riley's place all weekend... *doing stuff.*"

Behind her, Vik blanched. But before he could say

anything, Bree went on.

"But instead, he took you to New York City? And *you didn't tell anyone*? What if he was a creeper? Or a murderer!"

"You're the one who was defending him last week!" I yelled back, stung by her words. She didn't know Riley like I did! He wasn't any of those things!

"That was before he made you an idiot!" she yelled back.

Vik had turned away and was leaning against a desk.

The silence hung heavy between us.

"Andi, please," Bree said after a minute. "You just met Riley, what, two weeks ago? And all of a sudden you're running off with him, *leaving the state*, for a whole weekend without telling anyone? This isn't like you. That guy's just... he's just bad news. You have to—"

"You should go get lunch," I cut her off, cold as ice. "You know how cranky you get if you don't eat."

Vik twisted around and looked at the both of us in shock. Bree just flinched, and turned to leave. But she couldn't go without one last parting shot. "Andi, please, just don't... get so wrapped up some guy that you can't... can't see what trouble you could—"

"Riley is the last one to get me in trouble, *Bree,*" I snarled, remembering Friday night. "I'm a big girl, I can handle Riley."

Bree left. I was alone with Vik.

"So what, now I'll get it from you, too?" I shot at him.

He lifted his hands in a helpless gesture. "Look, Andi, I know Bree didn't... she was just so worried about you, she was a real mess yesterday," he tried to explain. "I was too..."

"Don't," I snapped. I felt cold, alone... betrayed.

"Hey, we're still your friends," Vik said. He crossed the space between us, putting a hand on my shoulder.

I couldn't help it then. The tears I'd been holding back all morning, deep inside me, welled up. Vik's brotherly arm moved around me comfortingly and I plopped my head defeatedly against his shoulder.

"She just doesn't understand! I... I just—" and I couldn't say it. *I love him!* I wanted to scream it to the heavens.

Vik gave me a reassuring pat, but was otherwise still until I managed to regain some semblance of control, and then he pulled back to look down at me. "So... What did you guys do in New York City, anyway?" he asked, his tone artificially light.

I sniffled, but smiled. "You have no idea, Vik!" It suddenly occurred to me—if anyone could appreciate it all, could truly comprehend, Vik could. "Vik... it's all true!"

He looked startled. "What's true?" he asked warily.

"All that Elder Gods stuff Ms. Epistola goes on about! The Great Old Ones, your book, the one that got stolen! Riley..." I couldn't tell him Riley *was* a Great One, but... "Riley... knows!" I squeaked. "That's why we had to go to New York. We had to go and get this other ancient book so that his uncle—Riley's uncle Neil has this shop, *The Crawling Chaos?* It's right off Main Street and you would love it, Vik, it's so full of creepy artifacts and stuff—but Neil sent us to New York for this book so that he could hide it away from these... these *cultists* that were after it. They wanted to bring about the end of the world, Vik! But we stopped them. Me and Riley! I was so scared—they came after us in the Port Authority but we got away! Riley saved me..."

I sighed, the bittersweet memory stinging my heart. "He

took me to see *Phantom*."

Vik was staring down at me as if I had three heads.

"Please, I'm not crazy, Vik!" I cried, grasping his hands. "You believe me, right?"

Vik's fingers immediately wrapped around mine, and he leaned in close, looking deep into my eyes. I could see how much he cared for me. Good old Vik. I'd never lose him.

"Andi..." For a moment, he seemed at a loss for words, but then he shook his head as if to clear it. "It's all so much, but... Scarlett's been showing me things, and... no," he said, abruptly squeezing my hands. "You aren't crazy."

I could have wept, I was so relieved. Instead, I threw my arms around him, hugging him hard. "Thank you, Vik," I whispered.

He seemed to melt against me. His voice was low, but he sounded relieved as he answered, "Don't mention it." A moment later, though, he worked himself away from me to study my face as if he were trying to make up his mind about something. He tucked a strand of my hair back behind my ear before he spoke again. "But seriously, Andi... Riley?"

I nodded.

Vik took a deep breath. "I don't know what to think of him being connected to all this," he confessed. "I'm worried about you. If he's telling you the truth—"

"Of course he is!" I laughed.

"Then this is some dark stuff." Vik's warm gaze poured into mine, making something strange twist in my stomach. "You have to keep yourself safe, Andi."

"You don't know him, Vik." I took a step back. "Riley only wants to protect me. He would never hurt me."

At least not physically... It was true I'd been in incomparable anguish all day over him. Oh god, where was he? Would I ever see him again? Was everything really and truly over? I couldn't hold back a fresh sob. "I just... I just wish he were here."

Vik's jaw set. "Where is he?"

"I don't know!" I confessed. "Gone. Forever, for all I know. I don't even have his number..."

Vik's expression seemed so soften and he exhaled a weary sigh. "Andi... I hate to see you so upset like this."

I tried to say something—that it wasn't Riley's fault, that I only had myself to blame for getting so attached to him when I should have known better—but I couldn't make the words happen.

"Forget him," Vik snapped. "A jerk like that who would drag you around and then just disappear? You don't need him."

"I can't forget him," I whimpered.

Vik studied me for a moment and then shook his head, as if he had finally made up his mind. "Oh, come on now," he said in a softer tone. "It'll be a piece of cake to get your mind off that guy. There are plenty of other things to focus on, to look forward to."

"Nothing that matters."

"Aw, c'mon, sure. This is Portsmouth! The greatest town in America. We've got boats. And apple trees. And... there's the Pumpkin Festival this weekend?" he offered, obviously trying to lighten the mood. And I couldn't help it, I laughed.

He smiled at me and gave the sides of my arms a reassuring rub.

"You can't be serious," I said.

"Oh, I am very serious about pumpkins," he said, arching a serious eyebrow at me. "Pumpkin pie, pumpkin bread, pumpkin carving... the Pumpkin Ball...?"

"...Vik," I began, an uneasy feeling creeping into my stomach.

"You know what I think?" he said quickly, as if in a rush to get the words out. "We should go together."

I blinked. "To the Pumpkin Ball?"

"Sure," he shrugged, but his tone sounded oddly expectant.

"We go everywhere together," I countered.

"Well, maybe we should go as... non-friends," he said. "Like. Together."

The open and warm expression on his face made my stomach twist. He looked so hopeful, so... vulnerable. I couldn't take it.

"We can't, Vik," I whispered.

"Why not?" he asked.

"We're just friends," I said, unable to meet his gaze.

"But that's just it, Andi." He took a deep breath and stepped up to me, taking me by the arms, his grasp gentle but firm. "I was thinking that maybe... maybe it's time we thought about being more?"

"Vik..." I winced and had to look down.

"Hey, look, I mean it when I say I hate seeing you so upset. Maybe I could keep you from feeling that way? We always have a good time together, don't we? We could make something a lot more exciting out of the Portsmouth Pumpkin Ball if we went... together."

My breath caught and I shook my head as I took a step

back, slipping out of his grasp.

"What, am I not good enough?" I could tell he was only half joking.

I shook my head quickly. "No, of course not."

"Well, why not then?"

"Because… Vik," I bit my lip hard, and then it burst out of me, impossible to deny, "Because, I love Riley!"

When I finally worked up the courage to lift my eyes again, Vik looked… alien. There was a strange harshness to his face, but it was mixed with unmistakable heartbreaking pain.

"I… I've got to go," he said, and he turned quickly to make for the door.

"Vik, please—"

"No. No, I get it. It's cool." He lifted his hands in a dismissive gesture, trying way too hard to look casual, even as he refused to meet my eyes. "I just remembered I've got stuff to get done. Scarlett's putting me through the wringer. I mean, she's a great tutor and all, but a total tyrant. Yeah. I've got to… I've got to be prepared."

The slamming of the door echoed to the bottom of my being.

I was truly alone.

Chapter Fifteen

Confusion

I WENT STRAIGHT HOME AFTER SCHOOL, BECAUSE WHEN my mom says Super Grounded, I know she means it.

"I'm here," I said glumly as I entered the house.

There was a flurry of activity in the kitchen, and I could hear Mom talking on the phone. Dumping my backpack by the driftwood bench in the foyer, I went to investigate.

"Susan, you don't understand, *this is a bad time for me*—" she was saying. She caught a glimpse of me, and her lips thinned. Great. I was still in the doghouse. I tiptoed to the fridge, feeling like a thief in my own home.

Susan on the other end of the line seemed adamant though. Mom sighed. "You owe me more than you know. No. No I'll explain when I get there," she said, stealing a glance at me. "Yeah. Yeah, fine. See you soon."

She hung up, and then just stood there for a minute. She tended to do that when she had to do something she really didn't want to.

"Something up?" I finally asked, mustering my courage.

She looked up at me, and she seemed to soften. "Dad won't be home until later, but Susan just called—she needs me to do an emergency fill for a lecture tonight."

"Oh," I said.

Mom looked me square in the eye. "We still need to talk about this weekend," she pointed out. "But right now, I need to know that you will do as I say. No going out. No TV. No friends over. I need to trust you this time, Andi."

Not even an 'Andromeda,' but an 'Andi.' She was seriously trying to get on my good side.

"Done," I said. Why even bother explaining to her that I had nowhere to go and no friends left?

"This isn't over," she warned.

"I know," I mumbled.

She eyed me warily, but seemed to feel it would have to do. "Okay then. I have to leave now if I'm going to get there on time," she said, reaching for her bag and keys. "Dinner's in the fridge. Do your homework. Dad or I will call to check up on you. Just. *Please*, Andi," she begged, and I knew what she was asking.

"I'm sorry, Mom," I whispered. "I'll be good, promise."

"Okay." She hesitated, but then leaned close and kissed me on the forehead. "Be good," she repeated.

And then she was off.

The house's silence instantly seemed to shout at me. It was horrible. I was all alone. I had nowhere to go. Vik hated me now, Bree thought I was crazy and Riley was gone.

Gone... An icy claw squeezed my heart at the thought.

The buzzing of my phone distracted me. I practically leapt

upon it, but found it was only a text from Dad explaining how he was at the aquarium for an opening exhibit reception and wouldn't be back until after midnight. Great. Another nail in my proverbial coffin. I stuffed the phone deep into my backpack. *Thanks Dad. Just what I need.* I was facing an entire evening of microwaved leftovers and not even the obnoxious parental watchdog eyes to distract me from the growing blackness gnawing away at my soul.

Where was Riley?

Did he go back to his weird house where nothing made sense? Was he even still on this planet? Was he even still in this dimension? The sheer magnitude of how truly far apart I could be from him almost bent me double right there in the hallway. I choked back a dry sob and clenched my teeth.

It's your own fault, I berated myself. I should have known better. I shouldn't have let myself get so lost in his perfect features, his perfect body, his perfect everything.

I will do anything—anything—to protect you...

His words slithered through my memory like silk pulled along exquisite marble. *Anything...* But now that he'd done it, he was gone. Just like that. Of course he was gone. Why on Earth would he stay? For me? Ha! Who was I kidding? I was nothing, an ant. A speck. Utterly insignificant, compared to what mattered in his unfathomable world.

Upstairs, I changed out of my school clothes and pulled on a teal spaghetti-strap tank top and my little blue and green plaid drawstring shorts. If I couldn't be happy, I could at least be coordinated. I decided to distract myself with one of the less-desirable portions of my hygiene regimen. The weekly epilation ritual. At least it would kill part of the evening. I slipped into my flip flops and trudged to my claustrophobic bathroom at the end of the hall.

I sighed when I saw myself in the mirror. My eyes were so red. I looked like I'd been crying for hours, even though I had yet to shed a tear since I got home. I could feel them, though, tickling the back my throat, threatening to rise again at any moment like rebellious mutineers. *Of course* Riley would just be done with me after we stopped the cultists. I knew it yesterday, and I'd been right. I hiccupped and my upper lip quivered.

No! No. I would not cry. Not anymore. I was not worthy to cry over him. The mere fact that I dared to even entertain the notion that he might have even *considered* staying was an insult to him! I would not debase him that way with my stupid tears. I chomped them back as I twisted my hair up into a sloppy bun and plopped down on the cold porcelain edge of the antique tub.

As I smoothed the Nair over my legs, I tried to think of the homework I should have been doing instead. The lab report Ms. Epistola assigned…

My expression clouded as I thought of it. It wasn't due until Friday, but she'd assigned it a week earlier than Mr. Cho's syllabus had stated. I don't know how Vik looked up to her so much. She didn't know what she was doing at all. Maybe if she spent less time dolling herself up like a trollop, she'd be better prepared for class. Half the time she didn't even talk about science, and when she did, she clearly got everything she said out of *Marine Biology For Dummies*. I would know, I'd read it. My parents thought it was a decent intro to their precious field. But decent or not, Ms. Epistola had no place stepping into wise old Mr. Cho's shoes as often as she did. If she really was an adjunct at the university and so chummy with Vik's folks, then my parents had to at least know who she was. Maybe they could talk to the school board about her. And while they were at it, talk to Vik's parents about letting her 'tutor' him.

I winced as I thought of Vik... He'd given me the silent treatment for the rest of the day after lunch, but even if he really did hate me now, I still had his best interests at heart. The Scarlett woman had to go. I would definitely have to tell my parents everything about what had been going on with that trashy phony... whenever they got home.

The sudden remembrance that I was alone for the night immediately undid all the good my anti-Epistola internal venting had wrought. I slumped with a deep sigh and dug the heels of my palms into my stinging eyes.

Riley. My Great One.

No. No, no, NO! Don't degrade his perfect flawless memory with tears. Love him enough to let him go. That's what my beloved Phantom did for the only one he ever loved. That's what I would do for Riley. And do it with the dignity Riley deserved from pathetic, immaterial me. It was the greatest thing I had left to offer. It was kind of funny, really. I had dared to dream that I might be Christine in the situation. But if all the sadness of the world was in anyone's eyes right now, it was in mine.

I cleaned the white goop off my now-smooth legs and wandered out of the bathroom like a blind person.

When I got back to my room, I found Riley sprawled across my bed, using my laptop.

I yelped, practically jumping out of my skin.

He looked up at me with a slow languid movement, and I felt the old familiar fluttering awaken in my chest when our eyes met. My mouth must have been hanging down to my knees.

He rolled over and propped himself up on one elbow, his dark blue t-shirt twisting slightly around his lithe body. I was too shocked that he was there at all to mind the enigmatic smile that tugged at the corners of his lips as he looked me over. It had been less than twenty-four hours since we last parted, but after a day like today, it felt like eons, and I couldn't get enough of just *looking* at him.

Riley Bay here. Really here.

Riley Bay on my unmade bed… touching the part of the sheets that touched me when I slept… late afternoon sunlight from the bay window streaming over him. The effect was almost angelic.

My breath escaped me softly. "*Oh…*"

Riley slid off the bed, but stayed next to it and I noticed that his tousled hair was damp. I didn't think it was raining outside. Had he just had a shower? I blushed at the place my thoughts started to go and I quickly looked down. The computer on the bed caught my eye and I noticed that he had my AOL account open.

I contained a gasp. "Were you reading my email?" I felt my cheeks begin to grow hot. What did he see in there?

He ran a hand over the top of the screen and just smiled at me.

"That… that… you can't do that!" I stammered breathlessly.

"Why not?" he asked, cocking his head to one side, a piece of his raven hair falling across his alabaster forehead.

"Because it's just… that's not cool. You can't just read someone's private email without their permission." I sucked in a deep breath. "I know you're technically like a primordial cosmic being or whatever, but here on Earth we... we... well, we have certain rules!"

"This is a law?"

"Well, no..." My cheeks were on fire then, and my heart was beating a mile a minute. Had I gotten any instant messages while he was on? Did he see my email to Vik from last week where I expounded at length on what a jerk I thought Riley was? Was he pissed? He didn't look pissed. He almost looked... amused.

"But it's a privacy thing, you know?" I bleated in a pathetic attempt to explain.

"But I want to know everything there is to know about you," he said.

My heart skipped a beat. If my face was red before, it was positively glowing now.

He took a step toward me. I felt my knees go buttery. "*Everything*," he repeated, his voice a husky whisper.

Above his chiseled cheekbones, his celestial eyes burned into mine and I realized I'd stopped breathing. I tried to say something, anything, but words were beyond me. I nodded slowly, dumbly. It hit me distantly that this was the first time I'd ever had a boy in my room.

But he wasn't a boy. He was so much more... The gravitas of it slammed into me like the sky falling. How could this amazing being, who by all rights shouldn't even notice I existed, care enough to want to find out everything there was to know about *me*? I could never understand it.

He lifted a finger, a flawless finger, and twirled it into one of the wispy tendrils of hair that hung loose from my bun. The back of his hand almost brushed my cheek. So close...

My breath caught.

"I thought you were gone for good," I barely whispered.

He paused and his mouth opened slightly as if he were at a loss for words. Then he blinked and shook his head, chuckling under his breath. "You truly do not understand, do you?" He smirked as if enjoying a private joke, and gave my hair a gentle tug. If I tilted my face a fraction of an inch, it would be leaning against his hand... but I didn't dare.

"I like this," he said, looking at my messy bun.

I blushed. I looked a fright and I knew it. I put a hand to the side of my hair and turned away. For the first time since I came into the room, I remembered I was wearing only the tiny shorts and tank top. Crap, caught indecent again! Oh god, where was my robe?

"But I would like it better wet."

I froze. Did I hear him right? I turned back to him slowly. "Did you say... wet?"

He grinned, his eyes sparkling, and then he caught me by the hand. "Come," he said.

I was too distracted by the fact that my entire body had turned into complete jelly to protest as he drew me from the room. He was back! And he was... happy! And he was holding my hand! After the two days of stiff emotions and no physical contact at all, it absolutely undid me. To be smiled upon and touched by Riley, the boy of my very dreams! But oh god, where was he taking me?

"My parents..." I protested lamely as he took me downstairs toward the front door. How does one explain Super Grounded to a multidimensional godlike creature?

If he heard me, he ignored it, and I was thankful I still had my flip flops on as he hustled me outside. I stumbled on the front porch steps though, and immediately forgot about my prison sentence when I saw what was in the driveway. A pristine BMW Roadster, so black and shiny that its sleek paint seemed to absorb all light around it into an unfathomable dimension. The convertible top was down, revealing two blood-red leather seats, and the tires were so clean, it looked as if it had never been off the lot.

"Is... is that your car?" I stammered. If I thought Cleo had been impressive, nothing could have prepared me for this fierce machine.

Riley strode to its side and opened the chiseled-cut passenger door for me. It took me a moment to make my legs work, but he waited without answering, only a patient smile on his face.

What would my parents have thought if they saw this parked so brazenly in our driveway? But something told me that Riley knew they would not be home. Either knew, or did not care. Because no measure of boldness was too much for him when it came to what he wanted.

And what he wanted right now, was me.

My heart skipped too many beats. Oh god, how was I still even alive at this rate?

I hesitated at the door and he laughed, pressing a hand against the small of my back to usher me in. I settled into the seat with chagrin. I felt like I was bringing the Blue Book value down just by touching it.

"Where did you get this?" I asked as he circled the glossy hood to his side.

"I bought it."

I blinked. When? And how? It looked brand new. But I didn't ask. Where did he keep it, I wondered. Didn't he live in that labyrinthine underground lair of his? I didn't exactly remember a garage down there. And it certainly hadn't been in Neil's garage. For that matter, where did Riley get the designer clothes he was always wearing? I never saw him in the same thing twice. As he slipped into the driver's seat, I admired his slim-fit navy blue Hermès t-shirt and dark Armani jeans. I couldn't exactly imagine him crawling the Portsmouth Galleria mall with the other teenagers. Maybe he did all his shopping online? But where did he have his packages delivered?

I burned with questions, but was too distracted by the way he ran his long slender fingers back through his still-damp hair to ask. I buckled my seatbelt obediently before he even had to mention it, and watched him flip on a pair of impenetrable sunglasses as he backed us out of my driveway. Oh god, how was it possible that he still looked so alluring even with his astonishing eyes completely covered?

I was grateful I'd had so much time to get used to his driving style over the past two days, as the power of the Beamer's modern engine let him take his ferocity behind the wheel to the next level. I practiced my Zen breathing and respectfully kept my mouth shut, only lifting a hand to shield my eyes against the myriad light of the setting sun beyond the windshield. It was a wonderfully warm evening, but the strong breeze through the open top as we picked up speed made me shiver.

Riley responded immediately, reaching behind his seat to pull out his slim leather jacket. "Put this on."

I slid into it gratefully, for both the warmth and the chance to hide the shame of my lack of decent clothing. The buttery material felt so supple wrapped around me, like a second skin. I snuggled into it and inhaled its rich fragrance. Mingled with the leather smells were the fresh scents of the ocean. Of Riley. I would never take it off!

"Where are we going?" I managed to ask as my heartbeat finally began to regain control of itself.

"There is something I want to show you. Something I want to share with you."

I felt shivers despite the warmth of the jacket. He wanted to share with me! It didn't matter where we were going. I would follow him anywhere. How could I even begin to tell him of the anguish today had been when I thought he was gone forever? Did I dare even try? As I was contemplating it, I shifted in my seat and my leg bumped into a shopping bag on the floor down by my feet. It felt like there was something hard and heavy inside.

"What's this?" I asked.

"That is for you," he said without looking at me. Or maybe he was. It was impossible to see his eyes through the dark shades. The thought that he could be looking at me without me even knowing it sent exciting chills across my flesh.

"For me?" I gasped in amazement.

"For you. A token." He hesitated and then added in a tone that made him sound almost unsure of himself. "A gift."

He'd bought me a present? My heart started racing again. "What is it?" I asked, brushing my fingers over the paper handles of the bag.

He chuckled and shook his head, his hands twisting the black leather of the steering wheel. "Foolish little thing."

I felt my cheeks grow hot. Of course, it was a stupid question. I would find out when I opened it. How he could tolerate me when I said such things, let alone like me enough to bring me a present, I could never understand.

I pulled the bag up into my lap. It was heavier than I expected. I reached inside and drew out a black leather-bound book with gilt edges. "Oh…" I breathed. The texture of it felt so rich, almost like it could be alive. There was nothing written on it, so I turned it over and realized I'd had it backward. The front was embossed in filigreed gold leaf and the flourishing script read *Le Fantome de l'Opera, Gaston Leroux.*

"Oh Riley!" I exclaimed. "It's beautiful!" I gingerly cracked open the cover and my eyes skimmed the French text on the first pages. My favorite book in its original language!

"It is not as simple as you might suspect to find a French book in this land of yours. It took me all day."

I looked up at him, too amazed for words. So was that why he wasn't in school? Because he was hunting down this book for me? *For me…* Truly, I did not deserve such thoughtfulness.

"But why?" I asked, cowed. "You didn't have to do this. It was my fault my old book got ruined…"

"No!" he snapped, the anger in his voice impossible to mistake.

My hands clutched the book and I peeped up at him. His jaw was clenched for a moment and he shook his head sternly. I saw his hands tighten on the wheel, his knuckles paling.

But when he spoke again, his voice was softer, though his tone was grave. "No. It was my fault, little one. I never should have allowed you to place yourself in that situation. I was a fool to think I could stand to see you come to harm. I was near enough to prevent it, but I did not. It was I who failed to protect you from yourself."

He turned his face to me and swept the sunglasses up over his hair. His eyes were soft, beseeching. A look I'd never seen him give anyone but me. He reached across and laid his fingertips tenderly over mine on the book. "This is the least I could do."

I exhaled deeply, feeling my heart flutter. "I love it," I whispered. I looked back down, turning through the pages, admiring an illustration plate of the Phantom and Christine singing 'Don Juan Triumphant' on the Paris Opera stage. I tried to translate the caption at the bottom of the image using my learnings from two years of Monsieur Cousteau's French classes, but it was hard going. I let out a wistful sigh. "I just wish my French was better, so that I could really read it properly… as it's meant to be read."

Riley's attention was back on the road, but I saw the corners of his lips twitch in smirk. "I could offer you my services as a tutor."

I felt my face grow hot again. If I blushed anymore today, I was going to start getting light headed from all the blood rushing up and down inside of me! My thoughts immediately drifted off into a fantasyland of after-school hours spent with Riley, alone, learning French from his lips… reading *Phantom* together. I couldn't picture anything closer to heaven!

I knew I should answer him somehow, but what does one say in the face of such a dream come true?

"It's perfect," I managed. And it was. The perfect gift from the perfect boy.

I hadn't even realized he'd noticed what book it was that Travis stole before he rescued me. But of course he'd noticed. Riley noticed everything about me. How he could know my very soul so well when we'd only met two weeks ago was a mystery that the selfish, secretly indulgent part of me hoped I could somehow spend the rest of my days figuring out with him.

I was so lost on my dreamcloud of paradise, that I didn't realize where he'd driven us until we got there.

He had brought me back to the beach.

Chapter Sixteen

Cleansed

RILEY PULLED THE BMW OFF THE ROAD AND BROUGHT it to a stop at a rocky outcropping that overlooked the ocean. The rocks circled off on either side to create a small cove. It was a section of the beach I'd never been to before, and from the looks of it, neither had many other people. Somehow in the vicinity of Portsmouth, we had discovered a swatch of unadulterated nature. And despite my particular predispositions, even I had to admit the scenery was absolutely beautiful. A moment later, I noticed a narrow path between the rocks that led down to the sandy strip where the low waves crested quietly in the shelter of the cove.

Was this what Riley wanted to show me? But I'd seen the ocean countless times. He had to know that. No, he must have had something more in mind.

My entire body tensed. "Riley?"

"Hmm…?"

His distracted tone made me pull my eyes from the darkening waters below as the last of the dusk faded into night. He was leaning forward in his seat, his strong chin propped on the steering wheel, his bright green gaze seeming to pierce the windshield straight through to the ocean.

The look of pure serenity on his beautiful face took my breath away and I forgot what I was going to say.

A moment later, he seemed to snap back to reality and he turned to me with a smile, his eyes sparkling. "Come."

He was out of the car before I had a chance to react. "Your bathing attire is in the glove box," he said as he moved toward the rocky edge.

I blinked. "Wait. What? You can't mean we're going swimming."

Looking at the ocean was one thing, but going *into* it? *That* was what he wanted to share with me? The one thing I could never sanely do? I pulled his jacket tighter around myself and tried to shrink down and disappear into the leather seat.

After less than a minute, though, he was leaning over my side of the car, opening the glove box. He withdrew a cloth bag that he dropped in my lap. He then opened my door and stared at me expectantly. I did not budge. I knew I should, I knew I was behaving atrociously when he'd been so sweet to me, but I simply could not move, paralyzed in my seat.

"I... I can't swim," I managed to stammer.

He laughed softly under his breath and reached across me to undo my seatbelt, and then he lifted me from the car and put me on my feet with an effortless strength I was too startled by to even consider resisting.

I bit my lip. "But... but it's dark out now! It's not safe.

Night is when the sharks come out." I didn't know if that was exactly true, but it seemed plausible. Why risk it?

He stared down at me as if I were speaking gibberish and then he burst out laughing. I felt my face grow hot.

"Sharks, little one?"

"There might be," I muttered, looking down at the slinky bag clutched between my hands, unable to meet his eyes when he was clearly so amused at my expense.

He was still laughing and shook his head, putting a hand to his side as if he'd given himself a stitch. "Sharks…"

I set my jaw and looked up at him indignantly. "Besides," I said, "there's nowhere for me to change."

He smiled and lifted his hands as if to gesture to the entirety of the newly fallen night around us as he took a step back from me. "Oh, Andromeda, there is *everywhere to change*."

My eyes widened in shock, but before I could respond to his cryptic words, he turned from me, pulling off his shirt as he went back to the rocks. He dropped the shirt absently on the ground behind him, and ignoring the path, he jumped down. For a moment I couldn't see him, but then he reappeared on the sand below by the water's edge. His jeans were replaced by the same deep green swim trunks he'd worn at Jerrid's party. Or maybe they were different ones. I couldn't see them well enough to tell, and I was too distracted by the way the moonlight defined the muscles of his back to spend much time being bewildered by how quickly he'd changed.

I felt drawn to the edge as if there were a string connecting us as he strode out into the dark water. And then he gracefully dove beneath a cresting wave and disappeared under the reflection of the emerging stars. I gasped and waited for him to surface, but when he didn't after a minute, I wondered if I should start to worry. What was he doing? Would he be okay down there? How long could he hold his breath? Oh god, what if a shark got him!

I went back to the car and quickly fumbled into my bathing suit. It was the bikini I'd forgotten I'd left behind at his strange home. I thought I'd never wear it again, but alone with Riley, I suddenly didn't feel as opposed to the idea. So thoughtful of him to remember to bring it back for me. There really was no one around, but I felt so wrong changing out in the open. I did my best to stay hidden behind the car door until I was done, and then I ran down the path toward the water.

"Riley?" I called. He was nowhere to be seen.

I held my breath and listened, my eyes scanning the mirror-like expanse that filled the almost circular cove, but there was no sign of him at all. The only sound was the gentle washing of the low waves on the shore. I went all the way down, but stopped at the edge of where they reached, keeping my feet dry.

"Riley?" I called again, unable to prevent a note of hysteria from rising in my voice. Oh god, I couldn't lose him now. Not after everything! But what could I do? I gaped at the waves that moved in and out like the breathing sides of a slumbering creature. I curled up my toes as one almost reached me, as if the ocean were enacting the dream-state version of its usual sinister efforts to try to hook me by the ankle and drag me under.

But gentle waves or not, I couldn't go in after Riley. How could I even begin to try to find him below the black water?

The cove wasn't very large, but the far side of it opened up to the vast expanse of the monster of the Atlantic. Could he have gone all the way out there so quickly? As fast as he moved, anything was possible. But why would he abandon me here?

"Riley?" I whimpered.

Part of me wanted to sink down onto the sand and weep, but I was frozen in place by all the horrible possibilities rampaging through my mind.

After another minute of cursing my hopeless ineptitude, I noticed a change out in the water beyond the egress of the cove. It looked like it was swelling up, as if a giant wave were building from nowhere, like a huge ship was somehow sinking in reverse. I gasped and scurried back on the sand, but I could not take my eyes off it. I thought I saw dark, jagged shapes break the surface, but I couldn't begin to wrap my mind around what they could be, and then they were gone as quickly as they'd appeared.

The swell sank, but the wave it caused broke and crashed mightily before me. I winced, covering my eyes against the spray. When I looked up again, Riley was in the center of the cove, striding toward me out of the waist-deep water.

He seemed entirely unaffected by the waves that crested against the back of his legs as he approached the shore. I reached out to him, and he took one of my hands, circling me to stand at my back. He put his other hand on my shoulder. It was wet, but his touch was warm, and when I shivered as he ran his fingers down my arm to clasp my wrist, it had nothing to do with temperature.

I felt a drop of water land on my shoulder as he spoke at my ear. "There is nothing out there for you to fear,

Andromeda. Not with me."

I turned my head to try to look at him, but he would not let me, pressing me back so that I was forced to face the ocean. I wanted to object. There was very much to fear! A litany of terrors hovered at my lips, but I held my tongue. The experience seemed to mean so much to him. How dare I allow my own weakness to spoil what had been such a perfect evening so far? Save for the past few minutes when we were apart, at least...

"I couldn't help it," I said apologetically. "Please don't ever do that again. Don't leave me alone, not with the water."

He laughed softly and I felt the damp pressure of his face against the side of my hair. "You weren't alone. I am here. I will always be with you. Simple creature, do you still not comprehend? I cannot bear that you be unprotected." He turned me to face him and slid his arms around my waist, a wry smile on his lips. "And from what I've come to know of you, I think we can both agree that you have far more to fear from yourself than you do from the depths of the sea."

I wasn't so sure of that, but as I found myself becoming lost in his verdigris gaze, I more than ever wanted to believe he could be right.

"You have only had human experiences in the water. It must be wretched to be as limited as you are." He released me and took me by the hand, turning back to the ocean. "Come, I wish to show you but a taste of what it is like to be me."

As he drew me to the edge, I felt I wasn't afraid. With Riley, I was comfortable. Safe.

I took a sharp breath when the first wave washed over my foot. It wasn't as cold as I expected, but the tingling of the foam that brushed my ankles made my flesh crawl. I went rigid.

"Riley," I gasped. "I can't!" My breath started to come more rapidly. Another wave washed past my legs. I swore I felt something skitter across my toes. I yelped and turned to try to run back up the beach, but Riley held my wrist in a firm grip and I couldn't move more than a few steps. I whimpered as my knees began to shake.

He laughed and stepped toward me. For a moment I thought he was going to follow me back onto the dry sand, but then he swept me off my feet and into his arms. He held me cradled against his chest, just like he had when he'd carried me out of the dark alley on Friday, except this time there was no material of his shirt between us. I knew trying to squirm out of his extraordinary grip would be useless, but moreover, when he held me that way, I suddenly felt I didn't want to be anywhere else. He began to wade out further, carrying me over the place where the waves broke, and I stared in fixed dread as the water level rose closer and closer.

He paused a few yards out, just before the water was high enough to touch me, and I exhaled in relief. Around us, the almost placid glassy surface reflected the starry sky as if the cosmos were below as well as above us, and when I looked out past the rocks, I couldn't tell where the horizon fell. If not for the rocks, I could have imagined we were floating in the very center of space.

Riley turned his face down to me so that his lips brushed my ear. I was too distracted by the sparkling sensation that shot across my skin from his touch to fully take in the implication of the words he whispered until it was too late:

"Take a deep breath."

I did, and not a moment too soon as he plunged into the water, bringing me with him. We must have been on the edge of a drop-off, because it felt like he dove down fathoms in mere seconds, propelling us deeply with strong strokes that I couldn't understand considering that his arms remained wrapped firmly around me. It didn't even feel like he was kicking.

And I was too swept up by glorious *sensation* to be afraid. The way Riley held me against his body as we moved through the water made me feel safer than I'd ever felt in my life.

I don't know how long we stayed under. I could see nothing, though I knew not if my eyes were open or closed. And yet somehow, without sight, I was aware of cyclopean shapes that weren't shapes rising and falling around us. They were accompanied by monolithic sounds that were of a frequency I couldn't hear, and yet I somehow perceived as if with a new sense I'd never before been capable of tapping into. I felt no stinging from the salt, no pain from the pressure despite how deep we must have been, no burning of my lungs to breathe. I felt nothing at all beyond the pure, perfect bliss of sharing the timeless, spaceless moments with Riley, and absolute *elation* in the power of his command over the element that surrounded us.

When we finally surfaced, it felt like the world must have ended and begun again afresh. The cove surrounding us looked the same, but it was as if the pattern of the stars above had become entirely new. Riley set me on my feet. The waviness of the sand made me wobble, and I caught onto him for support. The water around us lapped at my elbows.

I took a few slow breaths, trying to process the experience we'd just shared, but it felt so tenuous to me, like a vaguely remembered dream that was already slipping from my grasp.

Riley brushed some of my wet hair from my face, and then ran his fingers through it to pluck out the elastic that had pretty much given up on holding onto its former bun. He smiled as he pulled the wet strands down over my shoulders. "Yes, I like this better."

I blushed. I must have looked like a drowned rat. His own hair curled darkly around his flawless ears, and the moonlight reflecting off the water defined his chiseled features even more perfectly than I thought could be possible.

"So you really aren't going to leave?" I breathed.

He cupped my face in his hand. "How could I?"

"But what will this mean? Will you just keep going to high school? Pretending to be human? Pretending to live a normal life?" *Will you be my boyfriend?*

I didn't dare ask. It was more than I was worthy of to even have him here in this moment.

"I will go where you go," he said, his voice a warm balm over every insecurity I'd ever suffered. "If that is high school, it makes little difference to me. Anywhere."

Anywhere... Even if it was only around this boring little town where I languished. Suddenly my days would have color and meaning, no matter how mundane the activities. With Riley beside me, nothing would seem mundane again.

Anywhere...

"There's this..." I hesitated, "this... thing coming up this weekend." I searched his eyes, then glanced down with chagrin. "It's stupid really. I have to go, my parents make me do it every year. But I mean, everyone goes."

"Then I will go."

"But you don't even know what it is yet."

"It matters not."

Could he really mean it? As I met his eyes again, I could tell that he did. He was *with me* now.

"Well, it's the Annual Portsmouth Pumpkin Festival," I yammered awkwardly. "There's... well, there's pumpkins. But a lot of other stuff too." I chewed on my lip for a moment, then looked up at him again. "And there's this dance. The Pumpkin Ball." I took a quick breath. "It's really stupid, I know."

He caught my chin in his fingertips and tilted his face close to mine, commanding me to look into his eyes. "I don't think it is. It could not be, if you will be there."

I felt ready to turn to goo under his gaze. I shook my head just faintly, afraid he would let go if I moved too much. "How can this be real?" I whispered. "I mean you... you... where you come from. Your world. It is so beyond everything I've ever known. And you would... you would take me to the Pumpkin Ball?"

"Try and stop me."

The gooey feeling flushed to my extremities. "But what is it like?" I queried. "Where you come from. I wish I could know. How do things look there?" I let my eyes drift from his face, following the trails of water that dripped from his hair and ran down the sculpted marble magnificence of his chest. "Did you always look like this?"

"This human form of mine is but a mask," he said. "It has little use beyond this earthly plane you inhabit. I thought it appropriate for my initial purpose in coming here."

A mask... like the one my beloved Phantom wore. The Phantom who Riley was so very like, whether he realized it or not...

Riley continued, "I could hardly take my place in your high school in my true form."

I blinked and pulled my eyes back up to his face. "Why not?"

He chuckled and tilted his head back to look at the stars. "I wouldn't exactly fit in."

Considering he looked a thousand times more gorgeous than any of the other boys in my class, he didn't exactly fit in as it was, but I was too intrigued to mention it.

"Will you show me?"

"No." His head snapped down to look at me with narrowed eyes, and his hands squeezed the sides of my arms roughly. "No, little one. I am not for eyes such as yours."

I felt like I'd been slapped. He'd shared so much with me, I wanted to know more! I wanted to know it all. I wanted to love him completely.

He must have been able to tell that I meant to protest, because he shook his head firmly. "Your imagination would not be able to cope with seeing one of my kind in his true horrible majesty."

"I can handle it," I said. I *loved* him, though I hadn't been brave enough to tell him so yet. But it was true nonetheless. And that love gave me the power to do anything where he was concerned. I was standing in the middle of the ocean with him, for Pete's sake! With Riley, I was able to conquer my greatest fear. I wanted to know him fully, as he really was.

His midnight eyebrows knit in an expression I could almost call dismay. He was quiet for a moment as he studied my face, and then he shook his head again, a sad look in his emerald eyes. "Can't you understand that I only refuse for your protection? Beholding my true form would drive you to madness. Why would you ask such a thing of me?"

Just like Psyche and her Cupid. Just like Christine and her Phantom. I was safe so long as I did not touch his mask… Would there ever be anything I could do that would make Riley realize that I was different from the others? Would he allow me to be?

I sighed in resignation, for now. "You said that you wanted to know everything about me. Well, I want to know everything about you too." Surely he could understand that much, at least.

"I have already told you of myself," he replied guardedly.

"No, there has to be more. So much more! What about your life before your came to Portsmouth? Before you… slumbered? You said you walked among the stars, but what about other times when you were here on Earth? Have you used this… human form before?" I felt my eyes drifting downward again and caught myself with a blush. I quickly diverted the subject. "And what about… Do you have any other friends? What about your family?"

He seemed to relax, his hands sliding down to rest against the sides of my waist under the water. "My family?" He shook his head with a softly bemused laugh.

"Well, I've met your uncle. And he mentioned your sister. What's she like?"

"Aside from my uncle, I have not had contact with most of my family in many a strange aeon. Most of them slumber, and dream. Waiting… waiting for the day I awaken them with my call."

"You mean the day of the Alignment…" I looked up at the stars. I'd never seen them appear so multitudinous and glittering before. It was like they had bloomed into an explosion of wonder just to make this night more magical for me and Riley. I wondered what he saw when he looked at them. Could he see the Alignment happening up there? So close to drawing to completion?

"The Alignment's peak is an hour of great power," he mused. "When the cosmic pull will be strong and chaos will beg to burst forth."

"And that's going to happen on Saturday," I said. Five days from now. The same day as the Pumpkin Festival. Such a seemingly innocent day... I felt a warmth blossom within me as I remembered that Riley would be taking me to the Pumpkin Ball...

"But I will resist that pull of chaos should it come."

Because of me... For me... Something he'd desired for more lifetimes than I could even imagine, something that meant so much to him. He would give it up, *all for me*...

"But what about your family?" I queried. "Will they be mad at you for not going through with it?"

"There will be nothing to go through with. We have secured the *Eldritch Grimoire* in my uncle's keeping. The cultists that attacked us are no more. And if there are any other cultists about, they will not have what they need to attempt to take advantage of the chaotic pull. There is no one who can summon me to the call."

"But hypothetically speaking. Would you family disapprove? Considering you're defying your original destiny and all, I mean?" *Would they disapprove of me?*

"Those who slumber would continue to slumber. And those who are awake..." I felt Riley's grip on my waist tighten painfully and a dark look came into his eyes. "Let them just *try* to compel me to do otherwise."

A thrill rushed through me at the thought of how fiercely he would protect me. Risking their disapproval. Putting me over even his own kin. But I didn't like seeing him troubled, so I tried to steer the conversation back to my curiosities. "So who is awake now? Besides Neil and your sister, I mean."

Riley's expression seemed to soften as he thought of his family. "There are several... My grandfather and a few cousins."

Cousins? Would I be able to meet them? The thought of a being as miraculously amazing as Riley having something so incredibly normal as extended family made me suddenly feel I loved him all the more. How that could even be possible at this point, I couldn't begin to comprehend. I was *gone* for him. And that was the greatest truth I knew. I was wholly, utterly his, and I wanted to be part of every aspect of his existence. So many questions! Where to even begin?

I settled for, "What are their names?"

He chuckled indulgently. "In her human form, my sister calls herself Chloe. My grandfather is more traditional... but I doubt you would be able to pronounce their true names."

I pouted, immediately indignant. I recalled how natural saying the alien words from the *Necronomicon* had felt that day in the school's arts garden. But that had been like pronouncing them in a trance. I tried to remember some of the phrases from the book. The one Riley had repeated to me two days ago in his home...

Ch'ftaghu shugg Cthulhu! Thr'ghlfnaw.

In my mind's memory, I could hear Riley's voice phonating the ethereal syllables so clearly, but when I took a moment to mouth them to myself under my breath, they stumbled all over my tongue in an awkward jumble.

Riley's eyes widened. "What was that?" he whispered, leaning closer to me.

Crap! I blushed and shook my head. He was right, his heavenly language was beyond my mortal tongue.

He took my chin in his strong hand, making me meet his eyes. "No, I heard you. Say it again. Andromeda. Tiny thing. Speak my name... My true name."

I felt all the color drain from my face and a fluttery feeling overtook me, and not in a good way. I couldn't move my face from his grip, but I had to lower my eyes.

"Say it." It was a command, but there was a gentleness to it as well, almost making it sound like a plea at the same time.

I swallowed thickly and took a shallow breath. "Tha-thoo-loo," I muttered inanely.

He blinked and then a moment later, laughter burst from him. "Oh, the human tongue is a source of infinite amusement to me!"

I tried to twist away, to pull back from him, but he held me tightly.

"But no, little one." He smirked. "Not quite."

I scowled and set my jaw. There just weren't enough vowels. I couldn't wrap my mouth around all the consonants. But I had done it before. It had to be possible. I closed my eyes and tried to remember the feeling of him... his true name... in my mouth, on my lips, on my tongue.

I tilted my face up and looked him boldly in the eye. I took a deep breath, and... "*Cthulhu!*"

And then horror... horror!

Before my very eyes I saw, as if in sudden slow motion, a droplet of saliva fly forth from my mouth. Time at once became a crawl, and there was nothing that I could do to stop the drop from arcing through the air, crossing the close distance between us, and landing squarely on Riley's upper lip.

I gasped, immediately clamping a hand over my mouth. I knew I should apologize. Oh god! But I was entirely tongue-tied.

My legs at once began to shake under me. I wanted to sink right to the bottom of the ocean and die of shame. I would never look at him again. This was it. It was over.

Riley blinked, and for an excruciating moment, did absolutely nothing. And then he released me and took a step back. His mouth opened as if he would speak, and then... and then... very slowly, he licked his lips, catching the drop on the tip of his tongue and making it disappear. His eyes seemed to blaze then, and the heat that was devouring my cheeks grew into an inferno. But at the same time... there was something about the way he moved his tongue that spread a sweeter warmth through my entire body.

My knees failed me, and I floundered in the water, but something kept me from falling, some pressure against me that I was too abstracted to try to comprehend.

When Riley spoke, the burning in his eyes belied the calmness of his tone, "I can think of a better way for you to share your saliva with me."

And then I felt the invisible pressure against me slither around my back and pull me toward him, like I was being drawn by some telepathic power. That same whispery smoke feeling that had graced me before, as if the night shadows had become solid and taken it upon themselves to gather me to Riley. And then his arm was around me again, his hand caressing the curve of my waist. He tilted my chin up to his with his other hand, and I felt enveloped in a cocoon of his protection. Just like it had been when we'd flown underwater. So safe, so perfect.

Riley ran his tongue over his lips again, and then before I could draw a breath, his mouth was on mine.

I couldn't describe the feeling of Riley's kiss in a million years. There weren't enough words. Not English words anyway. Maybe it could have been described in Riley's eldritch language, if one had a million years to try. But at the same time, it felt like the kiss lasted far longer than that.

My eyes were closed, but I could swear saw the stars spinning wildly above us. Electricity coursed through my entire body, making it feel as though my hair stood on end. The water fell out from beneath us, the sky shot up into the heavens, and Riley and I were alone together in a space between spaces, a dimension between worlds.

Suddenly I comprehended completely what he'd meant when he described walking among the stars. Together, we were soaring, locked in each other's embrace—but at the same time we were submerged beneath the deepest part of the ocean, in a copious cavern in the center of the world where everything was molten, like the quicksilver that was racing through my veins, sizzling every last fiber of my being... a being that extended beyond my physical self in ways I'd never imagined—through time, though the very fabric of inconsequentiality.

And in that single, perfect, wonderful moment, I *understood*. I fully understood what Riley meant when he'd said that the human mind couldn't fathom his greatness, because suddenly—*suddenly*—I could.

I fathomed it.

But unlike the terror of madness that had gripped the other mortals who'd caught the merest glimpses of his glory, Riley was there with me, holding me together, making the impossible possible.

And for the first time ever in my feeble, minute, paltry, insignificant existence... I felt entirely complete.

Chapter Seventeen

Complications

I AWOKE WITH A MIND BRIMMING WITH MEMORIES (THE swimming, the talking, Riley's sculpted body glistening in the moonlight, the soft look in his eyes that I'd always hoped for but never dared to expect), but I was certain it all couldn't have been anything more than another sweet dream mocking my hollow life. Such things didn't happen to people in the real world, and certainly not to me. And so, when that little crack of sunlight spilled through my window, I rolled out of bed sluggishly, wistfully certain it was a Tuesday morning like any other.

My morning shower was like a sudden jolt of lightning. Something about the warmth of the water cleared my head, and it hit me—my life had changed. Subtly, minorly, almost undetectably, I was a different person than before. The old Andi Slate was no more. Last night hadn't been a dream. Overcoming my fear of sea, being held in Riley's strong

arms, getting pulled into that divine kiss that shook the sky—
it had been a dream *fulfilled*.

Heartened by the thought, I became a little more daring
than usual as I dressed for school. A chartreuse tank top—
glittery, even? Today, it was possible. Black short shorts and
sandals? Well, why not? I could make it work. Today I felt
like I could wear a yellow fedora with a pink flamingo feather
stuck in the brim and still feel good about it. Riley would see
it for what it really was: me being me. And the more *me* I
was, the more he'd love it.

Dad noticed something was up the moment I climbed into
his car for the ride to school.

"Someone's in a good mood," he offered cautiously.

A good mood? Just 'a good mood' didn't begin to do it
justice. More like a state of utter bliss. I played it cool,
though, and just shrugged. "I guess."

"Well, I'm happy you're feeling better, honey."

I nodded absently. My mind was elsewhere. I was just a
car ride away from seeing Riley again, after all.

I told myself that I had no fears of him being absent from
school this time. Not after how obviously difficult it had been
for him to part with me last night before my parents got
home. Like removing suction cups. It had been excruciating
for me as well, but I knew if my folks found out I'd had a
boy over, much less left the house with him, they would have
made my life all the more unbearable.

I'd made sure Riley had taken my number, though when
I'd asked for his, he only vaguely suggested that there were
better ways to call him. I wasn't sure how I could manage
that without a number, but the sudden realization that his
digits would be stored in my phone if he'd called or texted

since last night, had me diving into my backpack to dig it out.

But when I found it, there was only an unread text from Bree, time-stamped 7:42 p.m. yesterday:

'What did u do to Vik???'

My mouth fell open. I texted back furiously, 'Me??????'

Her reply came almost immediately: 'nm'

I glowered down at the phone, but before I could think of a suitable retort, another text from her came through: 'r u ok?'

I frowned in uncertainty. I was more than okay! I was better than I'd ever been in my *life*. But did Bree deserve to know that after the way she'd treated me? I considered for a few moments before I answered, 'I'm fine.'

Again, her response was immediate: 'Sorry bout yesterday :(:(:(Buy u lunch???'

And just like that, our fight was over. I had my best friend back, and Riley and I would be together again in mere minutes. I smiled serenely out the car window at what I knew was going to be a gorgeous day.

Riley was waiting at the desk beside mine in English class and the sight of him almost made my heart stop and start over again once more. But he looked… different than usual. There was something hidden behind his halo of perfection, behind his infinite, emerald green gaze. Lurking in his eyes was the look of someone taking a few nervous steps into a foreign land after only having observed it from afar.

When he saw me, a cocky smile lit up his face. It was overwhelming. I forced myself to return his gaze instead of looking away as undeniable feelings of unworthiness sprang up in me. For a moment, I wondered if it would all crumble away like the dilapidated stone ruins of my long-ago dream.

Would Riley's shining smile twist down into the disgusted grimace he always used to wear?

"Andromeda," he greeted me softly, his voice still somehow managing to come from all around me. Heads began to turn—was the new boy, the hot boy, really talking to *Andi Slate* like that? Andi the outcast, the ugly duckling, the scaredy-cat? Instantly the whispers began.

"Oh, hi Riley," I said meekly, returning his smile. I took a deep breath and sat beside him, acutely aware of the eyes around the classroom following me and the fingers already hitting the cell phones, beginning a text-storm of gossip that would follow me for the rest of the day.

"You look cold," said Riley during a lull in class as Mrs. Phillips left to take an important phone call. "Are you alright, milady?"

Milady. He'd just called me 'milady,' and in public! "I'm okay," I said, which was the understatement of the eon. If I was shaking, it was only from how thrilled I felt. Though maybe it *was* a little cold in the room.

"I guess it's kind of chilly," I admitted. Whether it was true or not didn't matter. Only seeing the look of concern on Riley's face did.

"Here," he replied immediately as he slipped lithely out of his jacket. "I do not truly have need for such a garment. Wear it," he commanded.

I could almost hear the clack-clack of texting gossipers hitting a fever pitch.

An hour later, French class proved just as strange and wonderful. "Now, let us go over zis week's vocabulary," said Monsieur Cousteau. "We are reviewing ze—how do you say, ze 'infinitive verbs.' Now, let us begin with the word 'aimer.'

What does eet mean?"

It was as if Riley wanted to answer without words—our desks were so close together that he didn't even have to scoot nearer to put his arm around me. I tensed, surprised, and I blushed. *Aimer*, I thought, rejoicing in his strong arm wrapping me in a protective half-embrace.

To love.

~*~*~*~

To my chagrin, Riley was summoned to the vice principal's office during our break after second period. He'd skipped school yesterday, after all.

"I will abide by their foolish human rules," he said with irritation as we parted, "if it will prevent any future complications... though I would much rather remain with you."

Even being separated from him for a short time threatened to yank me right back out of my newfound ecstasy, but at least I didn't have to spend snack break alone.

Bree's face lit up when she saw me. "Andi!" She rushed over, taking a huge bite out of a Pop-Tart and staring me down like a detective about to grill a suspect. "I've been stuck at emergency play practice the past couple hours—"

"Emergency play practice?" I echoed. "There's *emergency play practice?*"

"You've never seen how wicked bad a play can go, have you?" asked Bree.

I shook my head.

"Consider yourself lucky," she said darkly. "Anyway, apparently you've been having *quite* the morning, yourself."

It was a tiny bit embarrassing—I'd been focusing so intensely on Riley that I hadn't even noticed Bree's absence from my first two classes. As long as I didn't bring it up, she didn't have to know.

"So... *what* the heck is going on?" she asked, and I could sense her caution. "Yesterday, you're crying your eyes out, but now I've been hearing about jackets and arms and great romantic timing in French class all morning, and everyone's asking *me* about it, but I don't want to say a single word until I've heard the whole thing from you. So...?"

She lifted questioning red eyebrows at me. What could I say? I'm sure I blushed.

"So, wait... so you and Riley... you guys are... dating?" she asked, detective Bree on the case.

I couldn't help it. I beamed.

Bree gave a short, shocked laugh. "Wow," she said. "I mean... well, if you're happy, then that's great!" She gave a sincere shrug. "But seriously, Andi, don't take any crap from him," she warned, but there was playfulness to her words. "You are way more important than any old Riley Bay, so if he acts up, you send him to me!"

Oh, Bree, sweet, dependable, loyal Bree. If only she knew just how much more important old Riley Bay was than insignificant Andi Slate. But I nodded, and despite it all, I just couldn't stop smiling.

"So, are you going to *tell me* what happened?" she asked, finishing off her second Pop-Tart.

"Well," I said, but stopped myself. I had to be careful about the way I explained everything. As infected by my happiness as Bree seemed to be, I knew how much Riley had fallen in her estimation after New York, and how weirdly worried she could get about me. So no bringing up the prophecy that had brought us together, or stuff like the fact that I was now dating an ancient godlike superbeing in human form. Probably not the most comforting things to tell Bree. Instead, I opened with, "You know how I'm afraid of the ocean?"

Bree nodded.

"We went swimming," I said meekly, my face flushing at the memory. "He took me to the beach. And while I was with him, I... well, we went swimming."

Bree gaped at me. Closed her mouth. Gaped again, then decided to take a sip of pop. "You're serious, aren't you?" she said finally, looking floored. "You? In the ocean?"

I grinned.

"Andi, that's... *wow!*" She laughed, sounding relieved. "Wait. Swimming or... 'swimming?' "she asked with an eyebrow waggle that made me scream and laugh, a flush rushing to my face. Anything that might have been left from the strange rift between us was closed. It was so good to have my good old Bree back.

"Swimming-swimming!" I whispered, exasperated but endeared.

She laughed, but studied me for a moment, wonderment in her eyes. "I don't know, if he seriously got you over your hydrophobia, he's something else... I don't suppose he's actually some kind of angel?" she teased.

I looked away quickly but couldn't stop grinning. Close, Bree, but no cigar.

The bell shrieked before she could press me for more, and I sighed heavily in reply. It was time for my least favorite class of the day. I'd long given up hope that Mr. Cho would return to rescue third period any time soon. The best I could wish for was the principal realizing the epic levels of Ms. Epistola's awfulness and kicking her vapid butt to the curb before she wrecked our GPAs for all eternity.

And of course I was right, when we arrived, Mr. Cho wasn't there.

But neither was Ms. Epistola.

And for that matter, neither was Vik.

It took me a few minutes to realize anything was amiss while I was distracted by my reunion with Riley at our desks, but Bree's lingering look at Vik's empty seat beside her told me enough.

No Epistola *and* no Vik with no explanation? Bree must have been wondering the same thing that was in my mind: was there a connection here? There had to be, with how much Ms. Epistola had wormed her way into Vik's life. Riley, too, looked as though he were in deep contemplation.

Without a teacher, the classroom erupted into chaos. The principal, Mr. Pence, showed up and tried to disperse the bedlam of our unwatched class. "Everyone," he shouted futilely into the cacophony of gossip, games and texting, "remain quiet! A lack of teacher is no reason to act like undisciplined delinquents!"

There was no response, and after five minutes, Mr. Pence surrendered to the classroom's madness, started up *Finding Nemo* and slammed the door, presumably leaving to pour himself a hard drink and wonder how he got stuck with a post at Portsmouth High.

"You know," said Bree wryly as we watched CGI sharks darting after two tiny CGI fish, "I think I'm learning more about marine biology from this movie than I have from Ms. Epistola all year."

~*~*~*~

"Why wouldn't Vik show up?" I asked. It was lunch, and we were sitting at our usual spot in the cafeteria. Riley sat where Vik usually did, looking confident and at ease as always despite the occasional cautious glance from Bree.

Bree shook her head. "I don't know for sure. He's been acting a little weird the past couple weeks. It could be—"

"Ms. Epistola didn't show up either," I broke in intelligently.

"I noticed," said Bree, her voice tightening a little. Beside me, Riley said nothing. He was watching us with what appeared to be only mild interest. Bree continued, "I know you hate her, Andi, and I get that. Whatever else you think she is, she's a terrible teacher. When she's not rehashing stuff we already know, she's going on about Great Old Ones and all that loopy stuff."

Riley perked up suddenly. An intense green fire seemed to ignite in his eyes.

Bree continued, oblivious, "…but I think something else could be going on too. With Vik, I mean." She hesitated as if unsure whether she should continue and then sighed down at her pizza. "He was wicked upset yesterday. I tried to talk to him after school, but I couldn't get much out of him. He wouldn't even look at me, and then he just ran off to go to tutoring."

With Epistola. It was all I could do to keep from gagging.

"Andi," Bree said, her voice small. "What happened

between the two of you?"

The fire in Riley's eyes roared, flashing bright with alien power. "The two of you?" he repeated.

"Nothing happened," I answered quickly.

Bree shot Riley a look, but then focused back on me. "*Something* must have happened to make him blow me off and then not even come to school today."

"Well, it's not my fault!" I scoffed.

Bree shook her head slowly, her gaze falling again. "I just… I've never seen him so upset before."

I tried to ignore the faint twisting feeling that returned to my stomach at the memory, and I heaved a sigh. "He asked me out," I confessed. I felt Riley's entire frame tense at my side and I rushed to add, "I told him no."

"That boy," Riley said slowly, his words dripping with displeasure, "sounds presumptuous to me. Perhaps even disrespectful to you."

"No, he's my friend," I insisted. "And I think he only did it because he's all mixed up right now. Like some kind of cry for help." I shook my head and put a pleading hand over Riley's. "Honestly, I think he's in trouble. With Epistola. She's messing with his head. He's been spending way too much time with her. And he had tutoring with her last night and now they're both not here? What if she's done something?"

Riley didn't look convinced, his eyes remaining narrowed and his hand stiff under my fingers. "What is the worst this teacher could do to the boy?" he asked dismissively.

"You should call him," Bree interrupted suddenly, swallowing a spoonful of applesauce. I'd almost forgotten she was there. "I tried like three times last night, but he wouldn't pick up. But maybe he'd answer for you? I mean, he could just be sick. But if you really think he could be in trouble..." She shot Riley a cold stare. "Andi's right. We don't know. Something could've happened to him."

But no matter whose cell phone we used—mine or Bree's (Riley just stared at me when I asked for his)—Vik's phone only went straight to voicemail. The three of us sat there mostly quiet for the rest of lunch as all the other students laughed and talked or asked each other out to the Pumpkin Ball, stammering and blushing. High school went on, a carefree bubble around us, even as a deep stifling fog lingered over our table.

Before we knew it, the bell was ringing again, calling us to the next little slice of school.

"Andi," Bree said, before we parted ways in the hall. "We need to find him, alright? We need to find Vik as soon as we can. Ask your parents to talk to his." She lowered her voice to a whisper. "And if you can get your boyfriend to help..."

"If it's important to Andromeda," said Riley on my other side, not even acknowledging Bree's furtiveness, "then I will do so." As thrilled as the sentiment made me, there was something distant about his tone that had me suspecting his mind was elsewhere.

"Good," Bree replied. "I'll try swinging by his place after school, alright? I'll see you guys in Algebra 2, but call me after you talk to your parents tonight and tell me what you find out. Okay?"

"Right," I said. Bree gave me a curt nod and went off to Economics, leaving me and Riley in the hall.

I moved to continue to class, but when I realized Riley

wasn't following me, I turned back in confusion. He seemed to be in his own little world. His flawless face was wearing an expression of deep concentration.

"The boy is gone," he muttered, remaining stock still. "And this is the same boy who possessed the *Necronomicon?*"

I frowned. "But it got stolen."

He didn't seem to hear me, his eyes smoldering as he went on. "He is on intimate terms with this teacher, who you say has spoken of my brethren…"

The word 'intimate' almost made me gag, but before I could protest I noticed that all the other students had cleared out of the hall.

"Riley, we need to get to History," I urged.

"History?" he laughed, a low rumbling sound under his breath that felt like it came from all sides of me. "Don't you see, little one? It is all coming together."

"What is?" I inquired.

"The cultists in New York," Riley reminded me. "I could not help but wonder why they would ambush us. Yet if this woman speaks of my family—of the Great Old Ones—and the Alignment approaches… No, it is too much for simple coincidence. She may not be a mere scholar."

"What are you saying?" I knew he was right on the money about Ms. Epistola possibly having nefarious connections, but I wasn't sure what to think of what that implied about Vik.

Riley shook his head. "It is too soon to say anything definitive about her. Perhaps… yes, that would be our best option." Riley grasped my hand. "We must go to my uncle at once. He will have means to unveil answers."

The tone in Riley's voice bothered me. Did I detect a

quiver of uncertainty? But with him holding my hand, I felt as though nothing could go wrong. That was, until Mr. Dunleavy stepped out into the hall and chastised us with a sharp, "Children? Will you be joining us any time before the next ice age sets in?"

Riley's hand tightened painfully around mine, but I shot him a pleading look. "We can go after school," I muttered under my breath.

Everyone was staring at me as we trudged into the classroom. At first I flushed with embarrassment, assuming they were doing it simply because we were late, but then I realized it was because Riley was still holding my hand. What did they all think had kept the two of us so long after the bell rang? I flushed with something else then—a feeling entirely new to me.

Joyful pride.

Chapter Eighteen

Crystal

TWO OF THE SHELVES IN *THE CRAWLING CHAOS* HAD been shoved to the walls to make room for a set of folding tables and chairs. Neil had produced an old-fashioned reel projector from the briefcase Riley and I got in New York. It sat on the end of the table, directed at a white sheet tacked to the wall. The Queen of Sheba was curled beside it as if she thought the projector needed her protection, the tip of her tail flicking warningly.

Riley and Neil hunched over the counter, murmuring to each other in their strange language. I presumed they were talking about cultists and the Alignment and stuff that an insignificant mortal like me couldn't understand. But I didn't care, my mind was elsewhere.

I sat at the table, trying to ignore how the cat was staring at me as I flipped through a leather-bound diary I'd found on the magazine rack. I wondered how Neil expected to sell it when there was a giant hole right through the center and it was just pages and pages about some kid's crappy life in an orphanage, and it definitely wasn't doing a good job of keeping my mind off Vik.

Crap. Vik. Why had he skipped school? Could Bree be right? Was it because of what happened yesterday? Was he mad about me and Riley? I was sixteen years old. Didn't I have the right to date somebody without constantly being judged and harassed for it? I'd told Vik for years that we were just friends. That's it—friends. Who I dated was none of his business. There was no good reason for him to get all bent out of shape about it, like he was my father or something.

I glanced over the book to see Riley leaning against the counter, his lean, defined body lithe and casual at the same time. I didn't see how anybody could protest me spending time with such a gorgeous creature. Any real, good friend would be happy for me.

Maybe Vik wasn't as good a friend as I thought.

Or maybe he was in some sort of trouble after all. Vik was a total nerd; I'd never known him to miss a day of school.

As if he could sense my eyes on him, Riley glanced up and met my gaze. "What is wrong, young one?" he asked quietly, interrupting Neil.

I blushed and folded my arms. "Sorry," I muttered. "I just—I'm worried about Vik."

"Who now?" Neil tapped the end of his pipe.

"My friend," I said, the word almost catching in my throat, though I wasn't sure why.

"This the kid who thought it would be cute to let cultists steal his *Necronomicon*?"

"The same," Riley answered for me, his expression

clouding over with dark warning.

I sighed. "But you don't understand. He's been acting weird for days. I just—I wish that I knew he was okay. That he's not angry at me. He's been so edgy and defensive lately. Especially about his stupid *tutor*."

Riley said something to Neil I couldn't understand, and Neil's eyes lit up.

"How close would you say you are to this kid?" Neil asked.

"I've known him all my life."

"Awesome." Neil stood and walked to the edge of the table, rubbing his hands together and grinning.

"Awesome?" I was confused.

"Yes. Been wanting to try this baby out." He patted the projector affectionately and then shooed the cat off the table. "Want to check in on your friend?"

"What do you mean?" I asked.

"This is Crystal," he said, introducing me to the projector. "Crystal, Andi. Andi, Crystal."

When I only stared at him, Neil rolled his eyes and continued. "Grab the crank and think about whatever—or whoever—it is you wanna see. If your connection is strong enough, Crystal will find it for you. Wanna check in on your friend?"

Behind me, Riley gave a disapproving snort. "Waste of time. The boy will be fine. We should be focusing on the cultists."

"Well, none of us have intimate connections to any cultists, now do we?" Neil countered.

I almost wanted to agree with Riley, but then I hesitated, remembering the resentment in Vik's expression as he stormed away from me, and I felt sick. What if he was still upset? I needed to know. I couldn't stand the anxiety.

Riley's annoyance softened into indulgent resignation as he saw my face. "Very well," he begrudged, flicking off the lights. "But let us make this quick."

I wrapped my hand around the crank of the projector.

"Think about finding your friend," Neil instructed, adjusting the lens. "His name, his face, his personality, as you're turning the crank. Give it a go."

It's worth a try, I thought, and pushed the crank. It made a clattering sound as it moved, and a light came on inside the machine. A glowing, flickering box appeared on the sheet on the wall. As I turned the handle, I thought about Vik's house, the Bollywood music playing in his kitchen as we snacked on naan together, his cute, bright smile, his faint accent, the way he loved his Vespa, the way he defended yoga as manly... Vik, my friend. We were still friends, right?

Colors and images flickered across the sheet.

"Slow down," Neil said. "I think we've got it. Is that him?"

A slender frame faded onto the screen, and I recognized the figure, the sweater vest and white shirt. It was Vik. I saw him like I was standing right there next to him. He stood at the edge of a platform in some kind of darkened cavern, his arms crossed as he studied the space. As he turned, I saw a sea of empty seats filling the space behind him and I realized he was standing in an old, dimly-lit theatre. Dark figures milled around the edge of the stage, melting in an out of the shadows as they worked at something just out of sight.

Across the stage, a white sheet covered a tall rectangular box standing almost like an upright coffin. Next to it, a gnarled leather tome sat open on a wooden podium. Letters and geometric designs were drawn onto the stage around the podium, radiating outward like a star. I recognized the book.

The Necronomicon.

I heard Riley gasp.

But it didn't make any sense. Vik said the book had been stolen. He wouldn't have lied to me, and if he'd just found it again, why was he standing there like he was waiting for something to happen?

But it was more than the book that made a cold ball of anxiety tighten in my stomach. The black-robed figures. The runes, the book, the murmuring. Somehow, all of it reminded me of what had happened in New York City. Could these be… *cultists?* What did they want? Why was Vik with them? And where was this theatre? If Vik was there, it couldn't be far from Portsmouth. *Innsmouth.*

So much for this boring place where I lived being a town of no consequence.

The sheet over the tall coffin box rustled, and a woman stepped into view, her long, smooth legs peeking out from the slit in her pencil skirt as she stood, graceful and confident in her black pumps.

Ms. Epistola!

Anger flashed through me. What was she doing there? Why was she hanging out in a dark creepy theatre with a student after school hours? Wasn't that totally unprofessional or something?

"There." A smile curved over her full red lips as she reached out and ran one perfectly-manicured finger down Vik's cheek. For a moment, Vik's lower lip quivered. "You see," she went on, her voice husky, "Everything is ready. You have it?"

Vik fumbled as he slipped a towel-wrapped bundle out from under his arms and passed it to her. "Here," he murmured. "I have it."

Ms. Epistola graced him with a smile that would have melted steel, and he nearly tripped over his own feet. Typical, stupid boy. Show him a pretty face and his brain totally turns off.

Then Ms. Epistola pulled the towel away from the bundle, and my heart plunged to the soles of my feet. Sitting comfortably in her hands was a slender, red-leather bound book.

The Eldritch Grimoire.

"NYARLATHOTEP!" Riley's roar shook the foundations of the shop.

I threw my arms over my head, cowering away from the rage, my heart thudding in my ears, my eyes glued to the screen. Vik had the *Grimoire!* Where had he gotten it? What was Epistola going to do with it?

"Keep your pants on," Neil grumbled to Riley, though somewhere in the back of my mind, I thought I heard a note of concern in his voice. "We'll figure this out."

"My darling!" Epistola cried, delighted with the gift Vik had given her, like she hadn't expected it at all. "You lovely, thoughtful boy!"

She leaned forward and, cradling the *Grimoire* to her cleavage with one hand, ran a finger up Vik's throat. At her praise, his eyes lit up and he leaned forward, as if entranced by her scent.

"Soon," she murmured in his ear, "we will command the gods themselves."

She kissed him. Parted her red lips over his, and before I could even identify the sour empty feeling crawling around inside my stomach, she was sucking on his face as if she were Bree and he was last of the milkshake in the bottom of the cup.

And he was kissing her back.

"No!" The word burst from my chest, Riley and Neil stopped bickering and stared at me. I gaped at the screen, watching Vik's eyes fall closed as Epistola painted his mouth with her lipstick.

A strange rumbling feeling sparked inside me, making my head hurt, tasting like bile in the back of my throat.

That bitch.

That grease-painted *bitch.*

My fingers clenched at the table so hard they were starting to go cold. I sucked at the air, trying to catch my breath.

"Oy..." Neil's bony hand closed over my shoulder and in one sharp motion, he turned me from the screen, ripping my eyes from the horror. "Breathe." He shoved a paper bag into my trembling hands, but I wasn't paying attention to him. Riley stood a few feet behind Neil. He had gone silent at my outburst and now he was staring at me, his face stoic but his green eyes on fire with—with what? Rage? Fear?

My heart started beating again, thrumming like a bumblebee's wings in my chest.

"Am I not enough for you?" Riley's voice came soft. A thrill of fear shot down my spine.

"Riley—"

"Am I so inadequate that you must cry after other humans as well?"

"No." Tears stung at my eyes. "No, Riley. It's not like

that. He's just a friend. Please believe me." I reached out for him, brushed my fingers over his hand but he jerked away from my touch.

"I have no use for disloyalty!"

A curling darkness filled my chest. I could barely breathe. My mouth opened but no sound came out.

"*Sgn 'wahl! Sha 'shogg! Throd! Cthulhu 'ai!*"

All eyes fell back to the screen.

Scarlett Epistola stood at the podium, the *Eldritch Grimoire* open in her hands. Black-robed acolytes formed a circle around her, chanting softly. Candles flickered over the chalk design on the floor.

"*Uln Cthulhu! Wgah 'n ya!*"

Slowly, Riley sank into a folding chair. His gaze was fixed on the screen, enraptured. His fingers wrapped over the edge of the table.

"Oh boy." Neil took a step away from us.

"Riley?" I asked. My fingers reached out to him, but something held me back. "Riley what—"

"They... they call me," he rasped, all anger drained from his face.

Shock overwhelmed me. After everything we had done to prevent it, it was happening anyway.

We had failed.

"No!" I cried, falling to my knees at his feet. His eyes only grew unfocused and distant. *No!*

"Don't go," I pleaded.

"*Cthulhu tf nngu 'g nrar 'thlotn sz 'kz 'sy.*"

"They call me," he said again, his face ashen with strain. "I must answer."

"Don't." I touched his hand.

His eyes shot to my offending fingers and for a moment I wanted to draw away, then he looked into my face, and the confusion, the anger and fear and helplessness written in his eyes froze me to my spot.

The cultists' chant rose to a boom. "*Cthulhu dr'arn 'tgnthet gn hk tur.*"

Pain flickered across Riley's face. "They pull at me," he pleaded. "The call is strong. I must answer."

Tears ran rivulets down my face. "No. You can't. You won't. I—I won't allow it."

"Little one." He lurched forward, nearly falling into my arms as another arcane cry echoed around the room. His strong arms enveloped me, his fingers tangled through my hair, his seawater scent became my world. He let out a gurgling sound that might have been a laugh—or a sob. "You would not allow me? You would command me to stay? Just as soon command the sun to rise in the west and the moon to fall to earth—you are nothing to we who walk the stars."

"I'm not commanding you," I cried, "I could never! I'm asking you. Begging you. Riley... I..."

And what was it for me then, to give the final thing I'd been holding back for as long as I had known it in my own heart? I was nothing without him. What was my own pain, my own pride in the face of losing him?

"*I love you,*" I breathed.

His arms tightened and I struggled for air as Epistola let out another summoning cry, her voice wavering and desperate. "*Dead Cthulhu!*" she wailed. "*Mad Priest, great dreamer, the time is nigh – answer your slaves!*"

Dark spots appeared at the corners of my vision. With every exhale, Riley's arms tightened around me until my ribs ached. I cleaved to him in turn, my hands clenching the fabric of his shirt. I held on, even as my head spun and breathing became nearly impossible. I held one thought that kept me clinging to consciousness, one phrase that I clung to like a life preserver in a storm. "I love you. I love you, I love you, I love you."

And then he answered, words that sounded like heaven in my ears.

"I know."

He squeezed me tighter. I felt my muscles go slack, my chest convulse and still. Before the darkness swallowed my vision entirely, I heard him speak once more. His voice boomed through me, reverberated through the shop, stretched across time and space and echoed through eternity to find Epistola.

"*I am not to be summoned and made a slave to meaningless human whim!*"

On the screen, the chanters fell silent. Epistola froze, her eyes wide as she listened for the voice of her god.

"*Leave me be, or be devoured and forgotten!*"

Riley's arms opened, and I collapsed to the floor, my lungs on fire as I sucked at the air, my head screaming with pain.

"Great Cthulhu," Epistola whispered. "Dead Cthulhu. The time is nigh—the prophecies of old—for years have I labored for your glorious return—for years have I been your loyal slave—"

Silence welled through the theatre as they listened for an answer.

Riley angrily twisted away from the screen, running his hands through his black hair. "Slaves do not summon their masters," he muttered, but his voice carried no further than the shop walls. "And humans do not presume to control *me*. I am the Great Priest. Where my feet fall, you are crushed like ants."

Epistola and the cultists listened, but heard nothing.

A slow clap echoed through the shop.

I lifted my spinning head and cringed deeply. Neil sat in a beat-up La-Z-Boy in the corner, cradling a swirled blue pipe between two fingers as he watched us. White smoke curled through the glass tubing and formed the word 'encore' above his head.

"Bravo," he said. "You just defied occult convention with the power of *love*. Excellent show."

Riley spun on him. "You old fool. They have the *Grimoire*—where do you suppose they found that?"

Neil's clap slowed to a stop and he regarded Riley, the storm clouds in his eyes veiling something darker, something that jolted through me like lightning on a clear day.

"I like you, kid," he said. "But watch your tone with me."

"Apologies," Riley gritted. "Where did they get the *Grimoire*?"

Back on the screen, the cultists had begun to murmur dissent. Epistola flicked her fingers through the pages of the *Grimoire*, her eyes on fire with rage.

Neil puffed on his pipe and frowned. He leaned over the side of his chair to nudge the cat's litter-box aside with the tip of his cane, and then seemed disappointed to find nothing beneath it but dusty floor and a dead cockroach. "Okay, so… there was a kid poking around in here this morning while I was busy in the back," he shrugged. "I told you, you should have left it in the bus depot."

Riley closed his eyes. "You stored an *Eldritch Grimoire* in a box of feces."

"It seemed somehow appropriate. But hey, the danger's passed." Neil nodded to the screen. "You've resisted the summons through the sheer awesome power of love. Good job." He tapped distractedly at his pipe. "Of course, suppose it didn't hurt that she jumped the gun, performing a summoning ceremony before the Alignment reached full power..."

"Cthulhu has abandoned us!" One of the cultists shouted, and we turned to watch the screen again.

Epistola's eyes snapped up to the speaker.

"Cthulhu has found our leader unworthy," another agreed. "Perhaps it would please the Great Priest if we were to sacrifice her to his glory."

"Comrades," she said sharply, her eyes glittering with anger and—maybe—panic? "It is not Cthulhu who has found us unworthy. We have never faltered in our faith. We have never failed in our devotion. We have read the portents, we have remained vigilant. It is we who have found *him* unworthy!"

A wondering murmur spread through the cultists.

"Yes!" she said, snapping the *Grimoire* shut and stepping away from the podium. "The Alignment is at hand, and Dead Cthulhu stays dreaming! It is he who has neglected his duties. We have not failed him—he has failed the Elder Gods! We have all read the texts, we have all glimpsed the mad truths of the universe, and we know that They will return, They must return. If Cthulhu will not summon them..." Her voice fell into a deadly whisper, and her followers leaned forward to hear. "Then *we* will."

A gasp rippled through the group. Epistola smiled again, now that she was back in charge, her white teeth flashing. "Oh, yes. Destiny cannot be waylaid by a lazy priest. We will do what must be done. At the hour of Alignment, at the time of destiny… we will awaken… Azathoth." She looked around the shocked, silent faces of her followers, and whispered, "*Azathoth C'ndwfl'nasdfe.*"

And again.

"*Azathoth C'ndwfl'nasdfe.*"

And then, one by one, the rest of them, even ashen-faced Vik, joined in the chant.

"*Azathoth C'nd dsfaldn!*"

"*Azathoth C'ndwfl'nasdfe!*"

Riley jammed a finger onto Crystal's switch, and the image went dead.

Silence filled the shop.

The pain in my chest had begun to fade, but my ribs still ached with every deep breath I took. I lifted my head from the table and blinked slowly, waiting for the dizziness to end.

"Is that bad?" I asked blearily.

I wasn't sure if Riley heard me. "It is not possible," he growled at the screen. "*Humans* could not awaken Azathoth. Not without me. Not without my call."

"Well…" Neil mused.

Riley turned on him. "It is not possible!"

Neil lifted his hands defensively. "I just watched Cthulhu drop his aeons-old imperative and defy his inherent essence and calling because a human teenager batted her eyes and said 'please.' We're throwing all sorts of convention out the window today."

"Humans cannot awaken Azathoth!"

"If you say so." Neil took another drag on his pipe. "It's a long shot, anyway. If she didn't have the power to force you into anything, she won't hold a candle to him."

Riley's shoulders slumped in relief. "Exactly."

"Would it be very bad?" I asked again.

"It would be very bad, little one," Riley said, staring at the empty white sheet. "If it were possible."

His tone concerned me, but I wasn't sure how bad it could be. Riley had been strong enough to resist the summoning. He was still here, with me. He had forgiven me. Nothing could be so bad anymore.

"She's certainly a determined woman," Neil observed. "I'll bet someone pissed her off real good. Hell hath no fury and all that."

"You sound as if you admire this insignificant insect," Riley accused.

Neil shrugged. "It takes chutzpah to give Cthulhu the finger and call out Azathoth. Crazy, crazy chutzpah. She reminds me of this Egyptian queen I once—"

"Who's Az... Aza...?" I asked.

"God." Neil reached under the counter and pulled out a pair of tweezers, which he used to pluck at the herbs in the bowl of his pipe. "If God were a sleeping, blathering idiot and all of you four-dimensional critters were just figments of his dreams." He took a drag. "Also, my dad."

"You're Jesus?" I shifted my weight uncomfortably. So much talk of priests and God and stuff—I didn't like to think about it. It was all too meta for me.

Neil choked. "*Riley*," he said through his coughs as he waves the smoke from his face. "This one's a keeper."

229

"We cannot allow her to summon Azathoth on the day of Alignment," Riley said, bringing us back to business with a deadly serious tone. "If Azathoth awakens, his dream will end."

He looked at me, and I felt myself drowning in the sea of his eyes. Drowning in a good way, that made me shiver from my head to my toes.

"And if his dream ends," Riley said, "so will you."

Chapter Nineteen
Crushed

RILEY REMAINED SILENT AND MOROSE FOR A LONG TIME as the sun set through the shop windows. Neil prattled on about "the last time" something like this had happened, something about an ox-head and a squirming primordial mass called *Brr'tth'ythya*. I hardly listened to him, my attention fixed on Riley's perfect face. He seemed cut out of stone, distracted, upset even. I was worried too, worried about Vik in the clutches of that succubus, but Riley didn't need to know that. Why was he still so upset, anyway? We had defeated the monster, the monster inside him. The major crisis had been averted.

Hadn't it?

Neil took a long drag on his tie-dyed blue pipe. "I gotta tell you, I never get these cultists," he said. "It seems like whenever something pops up that they don't understand or can't explain, their first impulse is to worship it. What is that?

I will never understand you mortals." His eyes shone golden like the Egyptian desert. "Gotta admire that girl's tenacity, though, I'll tell you that."

"Indeed," said Riley. It was the first word he'd spoken in almost an hour.

"Are you okay, Riley?" I asked, moving closer to him. He didn't move, didn't even acknowledge me.

Neil leaned forward, examining him. "I've got some of the old 'Chaotic Abomination' in the back if you need to, eh, calm your nerves." He winked at Riley, and then looked at me. "I'd actually be kind of curious what it might do to you. I've never tested it on humans, *per se*, but there was this one time about a hundred years ago, I knew this Serbian scientist guy, and there was this old pulp fiction writer he liked to screw with, *huge* racist that guy, so one day he says to me—"

"I think that's enough for today, Neil," said Riley, standing up. "I think, for Andromeda, that is enough in general."

For some reason his words were like ice-water coursing through my veins. What did he mean by that? Doubly worrisome was the fact that Neil seemed to catch his meaning. "Ha, I figured that might be the case."

"What do you mean?" I asked. "What's going on?"

"Don't worry about it, my little cream puff," said Neil, standing up and ruffling my hair. "It's not your fault you're in way over your head."

"Neil—" Riley warned.

"I'm just saying," Neil continued, bowing apologetically to my Great One, "you're the one being deliberately vague, I'm just being the adult here and reminding her not to worry her pretty little head about it."

"Worry my pretty little head about what?" I asked, staving off tears. "What's he talking about, Riley? You resisted the call. You *said* there was nothing they could do now. They can't wake up Azerath."

"Azathoth," corrected Neil. "And no, they can't. We think. We surmise." He started chortling. "I don't actually know. Honestly, I'm just the errand boy. Or at least I *was* up until—"

"We must depart," said Riley. His gaze was now on me. Cold. Hungry, even. But for what? His eyes were so deep, so verdant, I couldn't read him.

Where was the softness I'd seen in him earlier? The soul who had responded so readily, so openly, when I had told him those three terrifying, deadly words:

I love you.

I swallowed. Something was wrong. Something was very wrong.

"Alright," Neil said. "But you tell me if you need any of the old 'Abomination,' if you catch my drift. Calm the old nerves. Her too, I'm curious to see." He gestured to me. "You know. Chemical reactions and such."

Riley didn't speak another word to him, instead he only grabbed my arm coldly, firmly, and dragged me out of the shop back to his black BMW. "Get in the car," he said.

I obeyed. It was the last thing he said for the entire ride.

I was consumed with worry, confusion. I had been overwhelmed during the cultist ritual, but of one thing I was sure: that I loved him, that I had said it out loud, and that he reciprocated. I knew he did. I *felt* it. It was as though my connection to him—our synchronicity—gave me special insight into the greater machinations of the universe, a sixth sense that no human had ever felt before or would again, because no human had a connection like I did with a Great One.

The thought chilled me; as I watched the trees go by in darkness, I started to wonder, perhaps no human had ever had such a connection with a Great One, because no human *could*.

But no, that couldn't be the case. Not after *all this*. Not after everything we had been through together. Not after him taking human form, rising from the deep to find me, to confront me, the only living human that could stop his dark destiny. Not after finding out today that, as the human of prophecy, I would stop him in the most unexpected of ways: *I was born to make him feel love.*

That was my power.

That was my life's purpose.

When Riley pulled up to my house's driveway, he finally broke the silence. "Get out," he said.

I obeyed.

The air seemed cooler as I stepped out of the Beamer, the autumn chill finally descending upon our small New England town. It felt so calm, so familiar, so *normal* that I could almost forget that I stood in the presence of the Great Priest.

"My time with you has been pleasant," he said. His voice was strained. "But I must depart."

I looked at him. I knew something was terribly wrong. "When will I see you again?"

His face grew hard. "I cannot say."

"You cannot say?" I demanded. "After all we've been through? After *Phantom?*"

Riley took a deep breath, and his cool green eyes found my mud grey ones. His eyes were like a knife in my heart. "Please tell me what's going on," I whimpered.

He stayed silent, and looked forward.

"I... you've opened my eyes so much," I said. "There is so much more of the universe that I understand now. Because... because of you."

"And so much you will never understand." I caught a sneer as he said it, and it pierced my heart like an arrow.

I put my hand to my chest, as though holding it would keep my heart from spilling out all over the place. "What... what are you saying?"

His lips spread into a thin line. He stayed silent. I started to get irritated.

"Tell me what's going on!" I demanded. "If there's something wrong with me, or if there's some other woman in the picture, I have a right to know!"

"I am merely stating facts, little tiny one," he said. He turned to face me, seeming to strain with the effort. "Facts that I have, until now, kept to myself for your own protection: You are less than an ant, far less than insignificant. You are but a figment of a dream, nothing more."

My lip quivered. "I don't care!" I spat, surprising myself. "It doesn't change anything! It doesn't change the nature of existence! It doesn't change the fact that *I love you!*"

"No, it doesn't," he said, averting his eyes from me coolly. "It doesn't change your understanding of love. But through all of this, I have been reminded of one thing. You are temporal. You are but a speck, a passing fancy. We may have stopped one insignificant human's plan, but it does not stop the inevitable; one day, Azathoth will wake, and Azathoth's dream *will* end. And with it, all of this. The ocean, the land, the sky, the sea, the stars, all of creation. And most of all, so will you."

I shook my head furiously, refusing to believe him. "But you said—"

"I said a great many things, puny one!" Riley bellowed, turning the full glare of his eyes back on me. Somehow, he seemed to me hundreds of feet tall, despite retaining his human form and size. I cowered before his might. "All of them," he continued, "in the service of a greater purpose."

I could feel my heart shattering. Did I still even have a heart? It felt broken, obliterated, evaporated, gone with the sanity of so many minds destroyed by the Great Cthulhu. And yet the thought of his callous disregard for the human mind, his power, only comforted me. No, I still wanted him. I still loved him, and I didn't believe him.

"I don't believe you!" I cried. "Why resist your call, then? Why resist your greater purpose, to summon your... your brethren or fellow doomsdayers or whatever? Why resist your call if you didn't have some reason to stop the apocalypse?" My voice became small, meek, like the voice of a mouse. "You said the reason was me."

"The reason, as I have stated before, is because I am The Towering Death and the Bringer of Doom. For epochs have I walked among the stars, devouring souls and destroying galaxies. Countless are the souls of those driven mad by the greatness of my true form, countless are the worshippers I have devoured to provide me with only the barest iota of nourishment. I am the Great Priest, and your ilk is naught but minor sustenance before me. Human souls are but snacks that feed the furnace of my burning rage. I am *not*, I repeat, *not* in the service of those who worship me, for those who worship me are beneath my notice, *as it should be.*"

His last words cut me even deeper; it was as though he meant them specifically for me. "Riley…"

"That they are even aware of my existence is mere runoff of my own greatness, that my dreams enter theirs. As they have with *you*, you pitiful, trivial creature."

I gasped, what tiny bits of unshattered heart I'd retained left me to scatter far across the universe. I was gone, hollow, screaming. *Tortured.*

Was this what it was to be driven mad by Great Cthulhu?

"Riley," I gulped. "Please… you don't mean this… I… *I love you.*"

"You cannot comprehend me, paltry, diminutive one," he growled. "Therefore, you *cannot* love me. And that is why I cannot go out with you."

"I can, and I do!" I cried. I fell to my knees, hands clasped before me, tears streaming in rivers down my face. "Please, just give me a chance! I can be worthy of you!"

"You are human. You, as with all the others, would be only driven mad by my true form. You cannot be with me because what I truly am would destroy your mind. I have always known this."

"Then why toy with me?" I sobbed. "Why all the games? The trip to New York? *Phantom* in Box Five? Swimming through the depths together? What about all you said to me about… about seeing Earth, seeing all of humanity as insignificant, but now knowing that even tiny things could be beautiful? You said… you said I had changed you! You said I *meant* something to you! That *I* was the reason that you didn't want to see the Earth destroyed anymore! That you have... a reason... a reason to..." I broke down.

"What has been weeks to you, diminutive being, were less than seconds to me," Riley said quietly. "To me, the time was nothing. As you are nothing."

"But... but what about the Pumpkin Ball?"

He turned from me. I thought for a moment I saw a tear slide down his cheek. "I... I cannot take you to the Pumpkin Ball."

I felt as though the hollow place in my chest where my heart used to be filled with acid. All I knew was pain.

"Soon, again, I will sleep, dead and dreaming until the stars once more are in perfect alignment, wherein I will awaken to fulfill my true duty." He stood up straight, his gaze to the cosmos. "My true duty. I cannot be your boyfriend, insignificant mortal."

"Then go ahead and do it now!" I wept. "Go ahead and kill me. Destroy the world. My life is nothing without you, do you hear me? It began with you, and it will end with you!"

"You have fulfilled your purpose, my Lilliputian child," he said. "You have fulfilled the prophecy, thereby postponing Azathoth's awakening. Now is not the time. I cannot do it now."

I grabbed his grey FUBU t-shirt. "Then devour me!" I begged. "I can't live now, not without you! You can't possibly just leave now, leave me in this pain! Devour me so my life will at least serve *some* purpose to you!"

"*Pain!*" he snapped, jerking away from me, making me fall. "Speak not to me of pain, infinitesimal mortal. You are too trifling to understand the immensity of all the word can imply. You know *nothing* of pain, do you understand? *Nothing!*"

"That's not true!" I yelled, sprawled out on the driveway, the agony burrowing through my veins preventing me from even getting to my knees. "If you have a shred of mercy in you, drive me mad like you have so many others! Consume my sanity! Or just go ahead and devour me whole! Whatever it is you do! But don't *leave* me!"

"I must, itty-bitty one. I must return to the city of R'lyeh. I must sleep. The time is not yet right, but soon it will be, and all will end. And you with it. I cannot waste any more time here, nor is it fair of me to pain you or endanger you any more than I have. I..." He turned from me again. "I am sorry."

"Please, drive me mad, kill me," I pleaded. "Anything, I beg of you, just don't *leave* me!"

I was crying openly, heaving onto the driveway, my fingers grasping at the strings of his Ray Ban shoes. "You can't leave me..."

"I can, and I must," he said. "I cannot expect your four-dimensional, microscopic mind to comprehend it."

My mind. I hated it. Deep down I knew he was right, though. I was nothing next to him. But that understanding didn't fill the gaping void that now resided in my chest, the place where my heart used to be...

"I would have you do me one favor," he said, his voice barely above a whisper.

With great effort, I pulled myself to my knees on the pavement, looking up at him, my face wet with tears. His was stoic, cold, like the deepest part of the ocean.

"I would ask you… that you not do anything heedless or foolhardy," he said. "I would ask that you not endanger yourself, in ways such as exposing yourself to those cultists, or standing in traffic, or hurling your tiny body from a high place with intent to harm it." He squatted down before me. Even in his human form, he made me feel insignificant. Limited. "Can you do this for me, inconsequential mortal? Can you promise me this?"

I pressed my hand to my chest, to the gaping abyss. I tried to speak, but only sobs came out. "Please," I whimpered. "Just kill me. My life is nothing without you. Drive me mad. Let me be your sustenance. Eat my soul. You're… you're tearing me apart!"

I could see the hunger in his eyes. He wanted to do it. I hoped he would. "I don't think you would find that experience enjoyable," he said.

"I don't care!" I sobbed. "I don't want to live… Just eat my soul, Great One. *Eat my soul!*"

"Pah! Your puny soul wouldn't satisfy me. If I feasted on you, I would have to devour dozens more to even come close to feeling sated! Would you want all of those lives on your conscience?"

"I don't care! I love you!"

Riley stepped back. "You are too insignificant a being on which to expend the effort. And if you value your planet, perhaps you might consider staying alive for the sake of your *loved ones.*"

Love? Love had betrayed me. I was unworthy of love. I could do nothing but sob.

Riley sighed deeply, expelling air into the night. "And

consider that in order for the prophecy to remain fulfilled, this world may yet need you alive, unharmed." He stood back up. "Do me the one favor I have asked, infinitesimal child. Simply keep yourself from harm. Consume not of the Tylenol in excess, nor look for trouble in bars frequented by bikers or gang members, nor leap from any bridges. You may yet be needed." He stepped into the car, leaving me prostrate on the cement. He closed the door. "For... the prophecy."

I heard the powerful engine turn. Watched as the car pulled smoothly out of the driveway. I waited, flat on the concrete, waited for him to stop the car. Waited for him to take it all back, to say it was all an elaborate lie. A test of my loyalty, perhaps.

But deep down, I knew it wasn't true. There was only one truth.

I was not worthy of him.

I was now forever alone.

Chapter Twenty
Captured

I RAN TO THE CURB, DUMBSTRUCK AS I STARED AFTER THE BMW's rapidly departing taillights. They shrank to barely discernible pinpricks in the night, then turned a corner and were gone.

Gone.

I collapsed once more to the pavement, head in hands, and I wept. I wept until there was nothing left in me but an iron ball of unrelenting emptiness. I wept until I thought I would die. But to my chagrin, I was still very much alive. Alive in a world without my great love. A life unworthy of the word.

After a while, I suppose I regained an outward semblance of composure, but I remained all turmoil inside; my empty chest wanted to scream, my body wanted to shake, my soul wanted to evaporate to nothingness. But I knew I couldn't just lie on the curb in front of my house forever. My parents would find me eventually, and I couldn't let them see. They would never understand.

I pulled myself shakily to my feet with the help of our mailbox. It was tackily decorated with swirls of sea-green paint, 'Slate' spelled out in scavenged seashells. The sight of it filled me with a spasm of disgust that briefly overwhelmed the crushing hollowness in my bones and somehow gave me the strength to push away.

I turned to look at the house. The front windows were dark, but that didn't mean my parents weren't home yet. They could be in the basement, looking at slides of dissected sharks, or in Mom's darkroom developing their latest monochrome photos of beach detritus. If they were there, they would surely hear me come in when the seashell wind chime next to the front door tinkled, as it did at every faint movement within two blocks. I could not bear to deal with their petty reproaches, not now.

Perhaps never again.

Leaving my backpack in the driveway, I pointed myself in an arbitrary direction and started to run. When I could run no further, I jogged. When I could jog no further, I walked with shuffling, indecisive steps. There wasn't a lot of town to get lost in, but I managed to lose myself helplessly in most of it.

I wandered like a child through the dark streets for hours, with no direction or purpose. Why should I walk with purpose? My existence was purposeless. If everything I'd learned over the past few days was true, the world could still possibly end by Saturday. Black chaos was poised to wash over the universe and submerge everything I knew. Riley denied it, but Neil thought it could be possible. So much for that prophecy…

But possible or not, I could hardly bring myself to care. For me, the universe had already ended. The black had already consumed me. Riley, my beloved, my Great One, deemed me unworthy to bask in his light. And *of course* he had! How had I been so stupid to believe it ever could have ended up being otherwise? How had I dared to consider myself, my *ordinary* plain boring vanilla-frozen-yogurt self, worthy of his attention? Let alone his affection?

Stupid, stupid girl, I said to myself with each catatonic footfall. *Stupid, stupid girl.*

I passed endless dark storefronts, each one catching my pale, slight, insignificant reflection. The sight of it disgusted me. I stood for a long time in front of Henrietta's, staring at the exact point in space where Riley and I had first spoken to each other. I imagined all the things we would never do, the joys we would never share. I wandered so long and so carelessly that I didn't notice when the buildings became sparse, the sidewalks and lawns giving way to sandy patches of ammophila grass.

In my state of shattered delirium, I had wandered all the way back to the beach.

Where was the cove Riley had taken me to last night? I was overwhelmed by the sudden desire to find it again, but I didn't know which direction to go. I burned to return to the place where I'd gone down with him, beneath the waves. Where he'd held me, and lent me his strength, and allowed me to conquer my greatest fear. I remembered, with the vividness of concrete reality, the hardness of him, the warmth of his body in the cool water, the movement of his muscles against mine.

My knees wanted to buckle, but I denied them their wish.

Why should they be satisfied, if I couldn't be? I did not know where the cove was, but the ocean before me now was the same one that had filled it. I began to walk toward the water.

I would never see Riley's true face. We would never share in each other's true, innermost secrets. I would never feel his arms around me again.

Oh god... I couldn't go on, knowing that he was out there, living his insupposable life, walking in spaces between spaces, experiencing things the likes of which no mortal had ever experienced. Without *me*.

I reached the tideline, my toes inches from the ocean's invading touch. My hand reached instinctively for the necklace at my throat. I hadn't removed it since Riley clasped it around my neck that dreamlike day in New York. It seemed forever ago. I undid it, the silver chain pooling into my hand. My eyes dully examined the little heart-shaped pendant. 'Please return to Tiffany & Co,' it read hopefully.

With a rending sob, I threw the necklace into the surf, as far as my sick rage would send it. The black waters swallowed the heart, and it was no more.

No... more...

Salty mist scoured my face, my eyes. I hardly noticed. It was all so clear now. I'd known my whole life, somehow, that it would all end beneath the waves. I'd dreamed of it since before I could remember. All I had to do was close my eyes, take a deep breath, and then one step, and then another, and just keep walking...

And it made sense. Ultimately, wasn't *death* everyone's greatest fear? I had feared the sea since childhood because I knew in my bones that my death would be a wet one. But now... I feared the water—feared death—*less* than I feared living out an empty, hollow, meaningless existence separated from my one great love.

The Atlantic spread vast and violent before me; beneath it was the place where I had been closest to Riley. The place where I could be closest to the memory of him. It was all that was left for me.

"You can do this," I told myself. I gazed into the churning black water, shot through with silver ripples of reflected moon rays, and I stifled a rising tide of revulsion. The ocean seemed to gaze back at me with dark intent.

"You can do this."

But I never got the opportunity to find out if I really could, for at that moment, something was pulled roughly over my head.

A burlap sack, reeking of old potatoes, jerked tight against my face. I tried to scream, but was stifled by something wet and sour with chemicals pressed over my mouth and nose. As I began to descend into chemically-induced delirium, I felt hands all over me, lifting me, carrying me, dropping me crudely into the seat of some vehicle. Several male voices spoke rapidly in a language which was decidedly not English. Just before consciousness too abandoned me, with my last desperate ounce of discernment, I recognized one of the voices.

The hole where my heart used to be, which moments ago I'd thought incapable of growing any wider, gouged out new depths.

It was Vik.

And then, blackness.

~*~*~*~

I slowly became aware of a foggy form of consciousness. My head was pounding, my whole body ached, and though I was standing upright, I couldn't move. The bag over my head stank of dirt, potatoes, my own stale breath and whatever had been used to knock me out. The sounds of purposeful activity surrounded me: rapid footsteps, a jumble of voices, brief snatches of indecipherable words. Once or twice I heard the dull scraping of a heavy object pushed across rough floor. Somewhere, a stereo was blaring uptempo flamenco music, as though setting the pace of the unknowable labors performed around me.

As the clouds lifted from my mind, I recognized the cold, heavy weight of chains all over me. I felt firmly affixed to some kind of vertical metal apparatus, my hands locked behind my back and a hunk of metal pressed directly between my shoulder blades, under my upper arms. The position was very unnatural, and very painful.

A brief sweet memory fluttered over me: lying in a gently rocking boat, my eyes softly covered and my hands bound with luxuriant silk. The recollection brought to mind a pair of impossibly green eyes, but they were quickly replaced by a pair of receding red taillights. A low moan escaped my lips.

All the sounds of activity abruptly ceased. I felt many pairs of hostile eyes upon me. The stereo clicked off, and I heard the sharp, deliberate *tap tap tap* of approaching stilettos. And then, *she* spoke.

"You're awake." It was Ms. Epistola, her voice moist as red velvet cake. The sound of her made me shiver with revulsion.

It was obvious I'd been kidnapped by her apocalypse cult. But why? What could she want with *me*? She'd seduced Vik to her side, but surely they couldn't think *I* would ever join them.

A memory stirred in my mind: Neil listing the items required for a summoning ritual, including a human sacrifice... *Oh god*, they didn't want me to *join* them. But Neil said they could find a hobo off the street! Why abduct *me*?

She's already ruined my oldest friend, I thought, and I recalled how she'd antagonized me in class yesterday... Did she have some personal vendetta against me? Well, the feeling was mutual. So we finally understood each other.

I wanted to reply to her with some cutting *bon mot*, some spontaneous display of wit to wound her to the bone. Alas, my well of wit was shallow and my tongue felt swollen and lethargic. All that came out was another low moan. My mouth was so dry...

"It was terribly difficult," Epistola replied, "fastening a thing as flimsy as you to that hand-truck. No curves for the chains to cling to." She laughed maniacally, and her collection of cultists quickly joined in. It was an old familiar sensation; everyone laughing at defenseless Andi Slate.

I worked my mouth desperately, trying to generate enough moisture to speak. Finally, I was able to muster two croaking syllables: "You *bitch*."

Another burst of histrionic laughter. Then *tap tap tap* as she stepped right up to me, took my head in her hands and tilted my face upward. She tore the sack harshly away, snatching some of my hair with it. I bit back a yelp.

Epistola's face hovered before me, her deeply-shaded eyes peering into mine, her red-painted lips forming a grotesque mockery of a friendly smile. I saw nothing in her gaze that reminded me of a human being, and I itched to look away. Unfortunately, her grip on my face was too severe to let me turn my head, and I could only glance downward.

The sight of her body was not a terrific improvement over her eyes. She was no longer wearing the clothes I'd seen on the screen. Instead, she was dressed up like an absurd video game trollop, all red leather straps and chrome buckles that revealed vast expanses of bare skin. The tops of her thigh-high red boots were shaped like flames, and they tapered down to preposterously tall needle-like heels.

"My dear irksome girl," she purred. "What did you call me? No, don't cringe away. I am not insulted. It's as apt a description of me as any. Such is the inevitable fate of one so unjustly scorned." She stroked my hair gently with her vile hands, and an expression of... concern played across her face. Almost sincere, but it did not reach her eyes. "It would seem, judging from the situation my minions rescued you from earlier this evening, that you too have experienced scorn?" Her vindictive smile returned. "Such a pity you won't live to suffer from it as I have, you *little meddler.*"

She slapped me hard across the face. Had I not been secured to the hand-truck, I would have toppled to the ground, such was the force of the scorn behind her blow. Tears of shock welled up in my eyes, but I refused to give her the satisfaction of crying out. I wanted to meet her gaze, to stare back levelly in bold defiance. But as I trembled within from the pain, I couldn't bring myself to do it, and so I looked away, trying to focus on my surroundings instead.

I recognized the large dark space of the theatre I'd seen on Crystal's screen. An odd smell of ancient dust mixed with stale popcorn filled the air. Thick, black tapers atop tall, ornate candelabra stood at deliberate intervals around me and provided dim, flickering illumination. At the boundaries of my peripheral vision I could make out the heavy red curtains, fluttering softly. As my eyes finished growing accustomed to the candlelight, I counted twelve tall hooded figures in long, dark robes. They arranged themselves around Epistola in a semicircle, their faces hidden beneath heavy hoods.

"It's fortunate you awoke when you did, Miss Slate." She stepped back a few paces, presenting me with a full view of her comic book fantasy outfit. She struck a little runway model pose. "I've only just donned my ceremonial garb. How do you like it?"

"You…" I struggled again to use my arid tongue, "…look like a streetwalker." Despite my vulnerable position, saying it to her face felt good. The pleasure was fleeting.

She stuck out one hip and crossed her arms, sassily. "Oh, you hopeless little nobody. Glass houses much?" She looked me up and down with derision.

"What…?" With great discomfort, I tilted my head on my stiff neck to look down my front. "Oh, come *on*…"

I couldn't see much of what I was 'wearing,' but what I could make out was even less substantial than the jumble of straps wrapped around Epistola. It was matte black, accentuating the stark whiteness of my very bare legs and midsection. I quaked internally at the thought of what the *back* of the garment must look like. The mess of chains crisscrossing me certainly didn't do my body any favors either.

"Yes, I share your misgivings, Miss Slate," Epistola droned. "Such a garment is manufactured to be worn by those of post-pubescence. It is our misfortune that we must make do with you. You too have been placed in ceremonial garb. As have we all."

She gestured grandly to the shadowy figures around her. As one, they stepped a pace closer. They were covered from the chin down, making Epistola's comparison somewhat specious, but their faces had become visible. I was still fuzzy from getting knocked out, but I could see they were all young and male. Each of them wore a blank, dumb expression beneath the heavy hood. Each set of eyes was locked unwaveringly upon her.

And then, among them, I saw Vik. The memory of the horrendous projection I'd watched in Neil's shop slammed into me like getting hit by a truck. With a sinking feeling, it also occurred to me that *someone* had to have changed my clothes. *Seen me naked.* For a moment I didn't know whether to puke or be comforted by the thought that it at least might have been Vik.

Episotla followed my gaze, and licked her lips. "Oh, yes. My precious Vivek." She sashayed her way over and leaned up against him sultrily. Throwing back his hood, she caressed his face, her vibrantly mocking eyes never leaving mine. Meanwhile, the dull eyes of the robed men never left her. Vik's eyes never left her.

"Vivek is my favorite, you know. My spicy little samosa. We've taught each other *so much.* He is a man now." She winked at me before turning to kiss him sloppily, expansively. Her fingers curled through his hair, moved over his chest. But then, *his* fingers were in *her* hair, moving hungrily over *her* body. I could hear them panting, pawing, squelching. Though I'd seen a similar performance on the screen, it was considerably more painful in person.

"Vik, no!" I screamed. The tears I'd been restraining finally escaped to pour down my face. "This isn't you, it isn't, *it isn't you!*"

"No?" said Vik, and I was so surprised that I gasped. He was glaring at me with great intensity, momentarily seeming to forget the half-dressed bag of compromised morals hanging off him. He disentangled himself from her, and strode forward until we were face to face. He was all clenched muscle and coiled tension, the fury in his expression twisting him into something unrecognizable. "Is it so hard to believe that after years of watching you with eyes for no other, receiving in return nothing but... but..."

He sputtered for a moment, unable to find the word.

"Scorn?" Epistola suggested behind him.

"Yes!" It was almost a shriek. "Scorn! Nothing but years and years of *scorn!* Is it so surprising that I would finally turn elsewhere? Somewhere where it isn't always 'Do me a favor, Vik!' Or 'Take notes for me in class, Vik, while I go do whatever!' Or 'Why don't you have a girlfriend, Vik, you're such a nice guy!' Or 'Maybe girls would like you, Vik, if you played a macho sport instead of yoga!' " He turned from me, and began to pace in a tight circle like a caged Bengal tiger. He seemed to address the surrounding shadows as much as me.

" 'We're just so close, Vik, I love you like a brother!' *A brother!* Or how about 'You're *such* a nice guy, Vik, but oh that *Riley* is so dreamy and mysterious, Vik!' 'I'm completely and utterly and *deliberately* blind to your feelings, Vik!'

"Well, *Andi,* being a nice guy never got me anywhere—"

He stomped back up to me, putting his face right in mine. For a moment, I thought he was going to hit me. Instead, he hissed, low and cold:

"So no more Mr. Nice Guy."

The effect was worse than if he'd hit me. For a long moment he just stared at me, breathing as though he'd fled from a bear, as if he were ready to tear down some great structure, brick by brick. Looking at him then, from my position of utter helplessness, it was impossible not to realize how strong Vik's taut and muscular body must be. For the first time in my life, he appeared to me as something other than just my childhood best friend, my confidante, my surefire source for complete-yet-concise notes from skipped classes. Somehow along the way... Vik *had* become a man. And I had missed it. I couldn't let him get swallowed up by Epistola.

"Vik, please!" I gasped. "You have to see through this! She has you under some kind of spell! Look around you!"

I gestured as best I could with my head, indicating the darkness, the robes, the candles, Epistola's general quality of absurd overcompensation.

"You've been tricked, or brainwashed, or hypnotized, or *something!* You would never say any of these things to me in your right mind! Please, you have to remember!" I stared at him, trying to make him feel all my own raging emotions, trying to break through the wall that had risen between us, the poison that had turned my Vik against me.

He remained silent, unblinking... but, did I detect a softening around his eyes, a twitching at the corner of his mouth?

"Enough of this adolescent prattle!" interrupted Episotla. Whatever real or imagined clarity had hinted in Vik's face immediately disappeared. He once again took on the slack expression of total passivity. He pulled his hood back up over his hair and rejoined the formation of zombies around their floozy queen.

"The time rapidly approaches, my minions of doom!" she proclaimed theatrically, holding up her ostentatiously naked wrist to her face. "I do believe it's time we revealed the whole plot to our dowdy leading lady, so that she might act her role to the very *best* of her ability." Another condescending wink in my direction. "Minions! *Let there be light!*"

The space was suddenly flooded with illumination, a painful shock to my darkness-accustomed eyes. I squeezed them shut, and in my exhausted fear, I couldn't contain a scream. This precipitated another wave of disdainful laughter from my captors.

I slowly opened my eyes and went through another dizzy period of acclimation. Crystal's projection had not done justice to the size of the theatre; there were several levels of floor seats and three balconies towering above. I imagined the place could fit four thousand people, and all the gaping empty chairs before me were especially unnerving.

Hanging a hundred feet above the orchestra pit was a giant crystal chandelier that held a thousand blazing electric candles.

"You're admiring our chandelier, are you, dear?" Epistola susurrated. "My little joke. I've seen you reading that melodramatic tripe you so love between classes. Now, it's true that Eldritch magic is more effective in the gloaming, but I couldn't resist mocking you, just a little. There shall be no lonely hero coming to spirit you offstage during your performance tonight."

Of course there won't be, I thought miserably. I was but a meager asteroid adrift in an uncaring universe, now utterly beneath the notice of one such as Riley. And even if he could notice whatever Epistola had planned for me tonight, he would not care. He had no reason to waste any more attention on a low harlot like her. He had resisted her summoning, she was defeated, that was that.

He was done with all of us. He was done with *me*. I slumped in defeat as much as my restraints allowed.

"Yes. Hang that plain-faced head low." Epistola had taken her place at the wooden podium. The *Necronomicon* and *Eldritch Grimoire* sat open upon the polished surface before her. Next to them was a very ornate, very sharp looking knife. It glistened as if forged from some metal not found on Earth.

The tall, shrouded, coffin-like structure I'd seen on Crystal's screen was gone. In its place stood a low, long shape. The incongruous tarp covering it made it seem as though it were added to the scenery in a hurry. I did not like the look of it.

Epistola pointed a long red-nailed finger at me. "Bring *that* over here."

There was motion behind me, and then I was tipped back suddenly. The jerky movement made me feel nauseous, but the tilt halted at fifteen degrees or so, and then I was rolled forward. One of the cultists wheeled my hand-truck to the podium, and dropped me roughly back upright. I gagged aloud as the chains across my midsection squeezed the wind out of me. Once again, I was but inches from the vile woman. The proximity made my skin gallop.

"That was an ugly sound, darling," she sneered. "But only the first of many that will be escaping that shapeless little body of yours tonight. If we hit our marks right."

So my suspicions were true. "You're going to torture me?" I tried not to whimper.

"Without a doubt. But there is so much more to it than that! There is to be utilitarian *and* recreational torture. Do you see this?"

She tapped the low covered shape with the toe of her ridiculous boot, producing a hollow *tink*. She looked at me for a moment, then rapped sharply on my forehead with her knuckles.

"*Hello?* Teacher has asked a question, darling. *Do you see this?*"

"Ow! Yes! I see it!"

"Good, very very good. Well, it's been brought to my attention that young Miss Slate suffers a certain irrational phobia."

Oh god. My face must have reflected my sudden surge of terror, because her loathsome grin widened.

"I see what I've been told is true," she preened. "Well, let me tell *you*, my dear, I was overjoyed to learn about it. For you see, our performance tonight happens to feature, as its centerpiece—"

She whipped the tarp away.

"—an anti-baptism. Death by drowning, dear."

She'd revealed an ancient bathtub that looked like it had been scavenged from some dilapidated dressing room in the theatre's bowels. It was filled with brackish water and covered in the same arcane runes that danced over the floor and walls.

I now had my answer: I would not have been able to walk into the ocean. My desire to live had never been so strong, if only to survive long enough to not die like *that*. Submerged. Suffocated by that hideous element, its icy tendrils working their way into all my inner hiding places. I began to shake. I began to cry again. Hope followed in the wake of love and likewise utterly abandoned me.

"Yes, please do cry, little girl. It is delicious. It nourishes me. But allow me to sprinkle a bit of seasoning, just for extra flavor," Epistola crowed. "I'll bet that little swimwear model of yours and his obnoxious old uncle thought that I'd been beaten, no? That I'd been deprived of my reprisal on existence for these years of unbearable scorn, when Dead Cthulhu refused my call?"

She grabbed the *Necronomicon* from the podium and thrust it violently in my face.

"Well," she sneered, "apparently they haven't read this moldy old thing as deeply as I. For you see, you sad scrawny child, I have discovered a loophole. Discovered it, of course, with assistance from my lovely put-upon Vivek." She glanced past me to where Vik stood, still drone-like with the other cultists. A slinky smirk sashayed across her face. "Such an obedient pupil. Of course, unless you're even more brainless than I thought, you must have figured out by now that it was Vivek who unlocked the key to my avengement. You see, after you so callously stomped upon his tender spicy heart, he found comfort in me. Such comfort. And oh, *my dear*, he's told me everything. It's thanks to him that I've now unmasked the deeply disappointing secret identity of the Priest All-High. You would not believe my shock, my appall, to deduce from errant flecks of pillow talk, that Dead

Cthulhu was once a student on my own class roster!" Yet another of her repugnant conspiratorial winks. "Loose lips, string-bean."

Stupid, stupid girl! I screamed inside. Of course, so much now made sense. I'd told Vik about New York and the cultists, about Neil's shop, about hiding the *Eldritch Grimoire*. The precious secrets had poured from my mouth like water from a tap. I'd acted as a spy against myself, and against Riley. I was so stupid! It was no wonder one such as Riley would maroon the likes of me on the island of my empty life, never to gently rock in his boat again. I truly deserved whatever bodily torture awaited me.

"Thanks to *you*, you twit of a slip of a girl, I now know that I don't need Dead Cthulhu at all. And I need not wait for the hour of Alignment! I have discovered that Dead Cthulhu is not the true conduit to Azathoth. Dead Cthulhu is merely the vessel. Dead Cthulhu's *heart*, roughly speaking— you must understand that biology becomes complicated when discussing beings who straddle multiple dimensions—his *heart* is the conduit."

She placed the book back on the podium, and stroked my hair again, making my scalp crawl. "And you, my silly little lovesick simpleton... You possess the heart of Dead Cthulhu."

I understood so little of what she was saying, I had been so far out of my depth for so many days now. But that last thing made so much sense that I was afraid I'd misheard. Did she mean that *I* possessed the heart of the thing that was also Riley sometimes? Did that mean I possessed *Riley's* heart? Did...

Did Riley somehow love me, after all?

With an almost physical jolt, a spark of hope returned to me. As it radiated from my reborn heart to the rest of my body, I worked to contain it before it could reach my face and tip my hand to Epistola.

But as I looked away to hide my expression, my gaze fell once more upon the tub. Immediately, my bubble of hope collapsed back into the nothingness of despair. I was deluding myself.

Stupid, stupid girl. Riley was gone. If ever I'd possessed his heart, that time was also gone. If Riley's heart really was the key to Epistola getting what she wanted, she would be denied her desire as surely as I had been denied mine. It was the coldest of comforts.

"You're wrong," I sniffled. "I don't have his heart. He doesn't want me." My voice splintered into a thousand shards. "I'm useless to him. Which I guess means I'm useless to you, too."

Epistola looked thoughtful for a moment.

"No... no. Useless generally, yes, but not to *me*. Dead Cthulhu did not resist my call, did not turn his back on ultimate fulfillment of his destiny, to simply cast you aside *immediately after*. Even constructed as you are for single-use, like a Kleenex." She shook her head in firm denial. "No, you *are* the holder of The Heart. You *will* act as the conduit. You *will* die, thrashing, screaming, submerged. And I, *Scarlett Louise Epistola*, will bring cosmic negation raining righteously down upon this world and all others!" Her cackling rose to the rafters. "It will be a night to remember."

I barely heard her as the tub gaped at me, seemed to stretch to unimaginable size, the murky water within it rippling threateningly.

"And to think," Epistola was *still* talking, "all these years I've spent worshipping the Priest All-High! Only to discover that he is nothing more than a hormonal child, so captivated by the first homely young strumpet he meets who's not a squirming mass of eyeballs, that he abandons his sacred duty. A pity. But! Let us not dwell."

She slowly lifted the knife from the table, caressing it gently, moving her long fingers dancingly from the tip to the base of the blade. The look upon her face was one of hunger, and there was a droplet of moisture at the corner of her crimson mouth. With great relish, she pricked the inside of one of her wrists, drawing a bead of blood to the surface. She pressed the wrist to my forehead. I gagged and tried to escape my skin, but to no avail.

"You are now anointed, you pallid little addlepate. The Heart of Cthulhu."

"*Orr'e Cthulhu!*" the dark cultists echoed around her.

Epistola turned to address the rows upon rows of empty seats. She lifted her arms in a Y-shape, a look of animal ecstasy upon her face. "Oh, at last! The humiliation I've endured. The trials I've overcome. The *scorn* which I have carried like a white-hot coal in the pit of my being for all these iniquitous years! All shall be revenged!"

Her minions accompanied her proclamation with a wild alien cry.

"Let the doom of all commence!"

Chapter Twenty-One
Cataclysm

"*C'THARANAK ORR'E CTHULHU… C'THARANAK ORR'E Cthulhu… C'tharanak Orr'e Cthulhu…*"

The dark dozen chanted rhythmically as they circled an iron pit in the center of the stage. I'd watched them light a great bonfire within it and its flames grew higher and higher, illuminating their swishing robes in the burning glow. The alien hieroglyphs that adorned the walls and floor pulsed with unearthly power.

"*C'tharanak Orr'e Cthulhu… C'tharanak Orr'e Cthulhu… C'tharanak Orr'e Cthulhu…*"

A few of the ominous chanters, Vik included, broke off from the circle to light more candles. I'd never seen so many candles in one place in my life! I glanced nervously to the dusty red curtains, to the old wooden boards of the stage floor, to the rickety catwalk, flashing in and out of sight above the tall lapping flames. One or two wayward sparks, and the whole place could go up in as many moments! I tried desperately to get Vik's attention, to get any of them to listen to me, but to no avail.

"*C'tharanak Orr'e Cthulhu… C'tharanak Orr'e Cthulhu… C'tharanak Orr'e Cthulhu…*"

Epistola came down from her podium and spread her bare arms to the fire.

"Oh greatest of the Great Ones!" Her breathing was labored and her words breathy, building into utterances that seemed both painful… and pleasurable. "We who are nothing, who are but your dreams, we call to you!"

The enormous fire belched higher as if in answer.

"Hear us, Nuclear Chaos!" she ululated. "We bring you the Heart of Cthulhu!"

"*C'tharanak Orr'e Cthulhu!*" the cultists cried.

But I wasn't the Heart of Cthulhu! I struggled futilely against my chains. Why couldn't I make them understand? I was *nothing* to Riley. Even if he had cared for me once, I no longer made his song take flight. It was over now. Our beautiful music of the night had ended forever.

"Listen to me," I cried. "This won't work! He doesn't love me."

"Your lies cannot save you, my dear girl," Epistola chuckled tauntingly as she returned to the podium and opened the *Necronomicon*. "You *are* the Heart of Cthulhu. And you will awaken the mighty Azathoth. Vivek!"

Vik turned to her in blind obedience.

"We begin." And she proceeded to read from the book, the alien words sliding past her moist lips like thick snakes.

Vik took up the largest of the candles and walked toward me with dull, shining eyes. The cultists began to chant more loudly.

"*C'fm'latgh ftaghu Cthulhu orr'ebthln… C'fm'latgh ftaghu Cthulhu orr'ebthln…*"

"Let the Heart of Cthulhu be purified with fire and water!" came Epistola's horrifying prayer. "*Orr'e d'faechlk!*"

Closer and closer, Vik came. We locked eyes. His were cold, lifeless, enslaved. I tried to fill my own gaze with sympathy. I tried to bring him back with just one look.

"Vik… please," I whimpered, tearing, "don't do this."

"You're wasting your breath," Epistola sneered down at me. "Vivek is *mine* now."

That thought terrified me more than the pain I knew was coming. It couldn't be true! Vik, *my Vik*, had to still be in there *somewhere*.

"Vik, please," I begged. "Try to *remember*… She has you brainwashed! Fight back! It's not just my life that's at stake. Don't you see? She's *insane*! She wants to destroy the whole world! All of existence as we know it! *Fight her!* Or you'll die too—"

He thrust the candle in my face, stopping only an inch from my skin. The heat of the flame clawed at me, and my words froze on my tongue.

"Yes." Vik leaned in close, the flickering light illuminating his features on the other side of it demonically. "I know," he spat. "I would rather die than exist any longer in this world which contains such pain as that which *you* and your selfishness have forced me to endure."

I knew he couldn't possibly mean them, but Vik's words lacerated me with the blades of a thousand cutlasses. Even if he could have fought Epistola's mind control, he did not *want* to. *Because of me.*

"*Orr'e d'faechlk,*" he hissed, and he lowered the flame of the candle to my embarrassingly bare stomach.

"Please," I sobbed. "Vik…"

"*Orr'e d'faechlk!*"

I screamed as he pressed the fire against my flesh. But the pain of the burn was nothing compared to the pain of knowing, fully and finally, that Vik was lost to me. My best friend was truly gone, taken over completely by that pathetic shell of a woman, a woman who was nothing but the casement of her skin and what little she did to cover it up.

I could only barely hear her next command over my own sobbing.

"Purify!"

A deluge of icy water fell upon me, filling every crevice of my body with wetness and dread. It was everywhere, permeating my very being. I could not escape it as the cultists poured and poured from some giant ceremonial shell.

When the last drops had trickled out, the chanting increased in volume. I was gasping for air erratically, sweating and shivering at the same time.

When I looked up, Epistola was on the stage before me again, her meteorite knife in one hand and the *Grimoire* in the other.

"Now," she recited, "let the flesh of the Heart be broken." She pressed the tip of the knife to the exposed flesh over my own heart. I winced as a droplet of blood oozed up around it. "Let it be marked with the Seal of Azathoth."

"*Y'hah! Azathoth! Nog! Y'hah! Y'hah!*"

As the cultists shouted their chorus of amens, Epistola scraped the knife along my skin. My eyes were glued to the horror of the lines she scratched into me, but my vision clouded with pain and I could barely discern the shape of the bloody Seal she carved.

When she was done, she threw back her head with a cry of ecstasy. I wanted to scream too, but my throat only made idiotic choking sounds. Shock came over me, shaking my body so hard the heavy chains around me clattered. Blood was running down my chest, past the burning welt on my stomach.

Epistola turned back to the fire and thrust the bloody knife into it. At the same moment, another downpour of frigid water assaulted me, drenching me further, flowing into the open wound over my heart. Now not even my innards were safe from that terrible liquid's reach. I could feel it clawing its way through my body, seeping into my bloodstream, consuming every fiber of my being. It seemed to go on eternally, and when it was done, stars filled my vision as I sputtered and wheezed, too shattered to cry anymore.

When my surroundings finally swam back into focus, the fire consumed my attention. There, in the heart of the inferno, where the knife burned, the flame had turned a very distinct shade of green...

Oh god, no!

How could it be? I didn't have Riley's heart. I didn't!

"AZATHOTH COMES!" the witch exclaimed ecstatically.

No... *It was working.* But it couldn't be working! Riley didn't love me. They were wrong about everything. I wasn't the Heart of Cthulhu! Unless—

Unless he *did* still have some sort of feelings for me and that was *why* he was letting all this happen. If I did possess his heart, he must hate me for it! He did not want to love me.

He'd made that indubitably clear. Maybe he had started to care for me a tiny bit after our time together, but once he'd made up his mind about how worthless I was, he needed to find a way to end it. End it definitely. Allowing Epistola to sacrifice me to awaken Azathoth was the surest means of eliminating the loathsome feelings he could not rid himself of. If the universe ceased to be, then so would I, and Riley would be free, as he longed to be. Free of the burden of caring at all for an ant like me.

"*Uln Azathoth! Spurg'scnduim! Uln Azathoth! Spurg'scnduim!*"

The green-hued flame shot upward, upward, upward, until it chomped at the chandelier. With a whistling scream, the whole thing came crashing down, slamming into the front of the stage. Crystal shards flew in all directions.

"*Uln Azathoth!*"

I was sure the stage curtains were about to ignite in wide, roaring flames, but then something strange happened to the fire. Its green hue paled and it narrowed into a tight, twisting pillar, as if being suctioned mightily from above. My eyes followed it up to the place where the chandelier no longer was.

It had become a place where *all* no longer was.

"*Spurg'scnduim!*"

A vast swirling pit of *absolute nothing* bloomed, portal-like, across the theatre's ceiling.

"Behold," Epistola cried, "the Daemon Sultan! He has slumbered through the long and dreary day of our pitiful existence, but now is the twilight of the universe! Now shall he awaken!"

Vik and two of the other cultists descended upon me.

Brutal hands grappled over my tortured body, pulling the chains from me, tearing me off of the hand-truck, lifting me high into the air above the tub. The briny water within it churned as if boiling with rage.

"*AZATHOTH! SPURG'SCNDUIM! Y'HAH!*"

And with that final cry of "Y'hah," I was thrown into the water. Vik, stronger than I ever thought, held me by the throat, preventing me from rising. I struggled and thrashed for the first few seconds, but quickly realized… there was no point. No reason left to survive. All my instincts abandoned me then, just as Riley had, just as everything that ever mattered to me had. I let the terror and the water consume me forevermore. It was over. My life… ended.

~*~*~*~

Don't lean over too far Andi, sweetie… Don't you know if you go too far, you might fall in? If you fall in, we'll never be able to get you back…

Never…

…Never be able to get you back…

~*~*~*~

As I felt the last faint glimmer of my livelihood evanesce into the dark emptiness of the waters, Vik's hand released my throat, and a very different hand reached down to encircle my shoulders. It lifted me up out of the darkness and into a new light.

I expelled what felt like very real water from my lungs, but as I looked up through my soaked hair, I beheld a vision of that which I knew had to be a dream.

Riley.

He gazed into my bleary eyes with those brilliant, green spheres of light—those spheres which reflected the eternal beauty of the cosmos, and everything beyond it.

Was this what the afterlife held for me? Oh, if I had known I would be so blessed, I never would have fought my end!

But then as my eyes focused, two details grew clear that told me at once—I was still alive and very much in reality.

The first was the look I began to recognize in Riley's eyes. The dark, simmering look of cruel contempt that had always filled them in the first days I'd known him.

No, if this were a restful plane for my poor soul after existence, that look would have been the last one I'd ever dream up for him to bestow upon me.

The second detail was the sight of Epistola over Riley's shoulder. She was standing beside the pillar of fire, bristling with rage in her red leather straps as the swirling ball of darkness above her began to crackle with livid lightning.

Chapter Twenty-Two
Cthulhu

"*RILEY!*"

My voice was little more than a hoarse gasp, worn raw from my screams, but his name felt like liquid paradise upon my tongue.

He leaned over me, his face inches from mine, and his eyes narrowed, his black brows knitting deeply. His lips parted as if he would speak, but instead his grip only clenched around me, and he drew me out of the water. I could feel the tension coming off of him in palpable waves.

As he set me down with confounding gentleness beside the tub, I caught sight of Vik's crumpled form against a column on the opposite side of the stage. There was a long streak of blood on the marble above his head. He wasn't moving. My attention was quickly pulled away by the sound of slow clap coming from the direction of the bonfire.

"Congratulations, *Great Cthulhu*, on your new bride."

SERRA ELINSEN

Riley released me and whipped around to glare at Epistola. He stood in front of me, his feet spread slightly—if it hadn't been for his anger, I almost would have called the stance protective. But I knew better.

I felt too weak get up, and I slumped against the tub, its porcelain cold on my back. I pushed my wet hair out of my face and leaned to look past Riley's thigh. The pillar of fire behind Epistola silhouetted her hourglass shape in the candlelight. Her eleven remaining demonic disciples flanked her like ridiculous dancers in a music video. She folded her arms across her cleavage and her gaze roved Riley up and down. *Ugh.* Could she have been any more obvious about undressing him with her eyes? I wanted to shout at her, to call her what she was, but I was still too shaken. Just trying to catch my breath took all the effort I could muster.

"You've spoiled my sacrifice," Epistola crooned at Riley, her words echoing eerily under the black wind that circled above. "But it is no matter. You are too late." She threw up an arm, thrusting a lacquered fingernail toward the maelstrom. "The mighty Azathoth has heard my prayer!"

Riley's fists clenched violently at his sides, and I could see how he trembled. "Impudent mortal!" he hissed. "You dare choose when to release the call, to decide the hour of the world's end? You are less than unworthy!"

So that was why Riley had come here... That was why he'd pulled me out of the tub. It wasn't me he cared about saving, of course. Epistola had robbed him of his most sacred duty. He'd come to rescue his pride.

"Azathoth has *deemed* me worthy!" the scarlet witch cried. "And I am mortal no longer!" For a moment it looked like she had begun to grow in size, but then I realized her feet had left the ground and she was rising above the stage. It seemed as if the swirling energy in the very air around her was offering an invisible stepping stool. The hooded figures fell back with murmurs of awe, and they began kowtowing before their goddess's power.

"I have looked upon the face of Azathoth and lived!" she crowed. "I am now the conduit, the incarnation of Yog-Sothoth! I control the gate!"

"INSOLENT HUMAN!" Riley bellowed, his voice louder and more resonant than ever before. "You know not of what you speak. You *dare* utter the name of the hollowed gatekeeper, who your pitiful mind cannot begin to comprehend?"

"I more than dare! I take control. The power of the gate is mine now!" She swept her arms up to the widening blackness above. "You are too late. I have succeeded where you fail. I have become greater than you. And now I will *destroy* you!"

"YOU DARE TO CHALLENGE THE MIGHTY CTHULHU?!" Riley's voice was so loud, I had to cover my ears, and I crumpled against the tub. I could feel the reverberations of his words pounding into the core of my being like thunderclaps.

"Mighty Cthulhu is not here," retorted Epistola, unfazed. "I see only a boy. A weak, small boy who surrendered his godhood for the first pathetic weakling nag he looked upon!"

Even though the blood on my chest had washed away, the raw knife wound throbbed and ached. 'Pathetic' was the understatement of the century. As wrong as Epistola was about everything else, it was undeniable how unworthy of Riley I ever was.

"*Mnahn'grah'n!*" she spat at him.

Though I could still feel the rage roiling off Riley, Epistola's last utterance had a strange effect on him. The alien word seemed to hit him like a slap in the face, but instead of lashing back at her, he became very still, and then after a frigid moment, he closed his eyes and lowered his head. As I gazed up at his profile, I was dismayed by the expression of conflicted anguish that twisted across his clenched features.

"Yes, you know it is true." Epistola took his silence as an opportunity to rebuke him further. "I used to *worship* you. But you are no Great One! I doubt now that you ever were. You were to bring about the end of the world, and I was to be your servant. And now, *look at you.*"

Riley's fists unclenched and his fingers straightened stiffly at his sides. I saw his eyes flash open, but he kept his gaze on the floor. "Look at me?" his words were low, almost too low to hear, but the venom they dripped was unmistakable. A moment later, a smirk spread slowly across his downturned face. "Is that what you wish? To look at me? Perhaps it can be arranged…"

"I grow tired of you," Epistola droned. "It is time we end this." She stretched out her hands to the chanting, swaying figures around her. "Minions, attack!"

They all became still, most only looking to her with dull-eyed confusion. Some seemed to understand her meaning though, and four broke off from the group to rush across the stage toward us.

Riley strode forward, and just as they jumped to tackle him, he sent them all flying into the wings with one sweep of his arm.

My mouth fell open in shock. It looked like he'd barely

touched them! But it seemed they would not be deterred as they all pushed back to their feet and immediately started for Riley again. It was then that I noticed his eyes had begun to glow.

They got within a couple feet of him, but just when it seemed they were about to leap for him again, they all froze in their tracks.

"Take him," Epistola shrieked from the fire. "The power of Azathoth will give you the strength!"

But none of them were listening to her, and I had difficulty paying her any attention either, as I watched their eyes widen impossibly and their faces contort in hideous agony. The four young men fell to their knees, gripping the sides of their heads, and then the screams began.

I looked back to Riley. The green fire of his eyes illuminated the smoky air around him, and his entire body seemed to surge with a power.

Episotla turned to the remaining cultists behind her. "Don't just stand there. Attack!"

There was an undeniable hesitation among the ranks, but then two of them charged at Riley. He knocked them down as if they were made of paper.

"Why do you send children to the slaughter before me?" His melodious voice rang clear, even over the screams. "Why do you not come at me yourself, *mortal no longer?*"

Was that fear I saw in Epistola's eyes as the two now on the floor began to thrash and writhe in torment with the others? Riley breathed deeply, as if inhaling some magnificent fragrance, and then stepped over one of them to start toward Epistola.

"You have no power over my mind," she decried even as

she backed away, shielding herself behind the remaining cultists. "I am the conduit!" She gave two of her minions violent shoves in Riley's direction before turning to circle the fire.

Riley stalked closer. "You should have known better than to hold the ceremony tonight." One of the cultists dropped before him with a scream as if both his legs had spontaneously broken. "If you had waited for the Alignment, perhaps I would not have had the power to resist your summoning." The second cultist fell even more painfully on top of the first. "Perhaps what you say could have been true. But you were impatient. And so your doom is sealed."

With each word Riley spoke, his voice was growing deeper, louder, more resonant, more intense. His frame seemed to radiate with strength that matched the cascading glow from his eyes, as if he had been finally set free from some long bondage.

I watched him reach the fire and, one by one, the remaining cultists toppled before him. With each mind he unhinged, each soul he consumed, I could see the power within him crest like ocean waves building impossibly.

On the other side of the fire, I caught sight of Epistola scrambling back to the books. She began flipping through them frantically. But my attention was pulled from her desperate chanting as Riley flung away one of the robed bodies that had piled up around him and fixed his radiating eyes on the last cultist, who seemed to have shaken free of his hypnosis. He'd escaped the stage and was running up the aisle between the house seats. I could hear his terrified cursing even over the din. Riley merely stared at his retreating back for a moment and then I saw a smile spread across his beautiful face. It was a smile of satisfaction.

The cultist stumbled and fell to his knees in the aisle. I saw him hug his ribs tightly and then he began to pound his forehead against the floor, his shrieks joining the chorus.

I looked back to Riley and it seemed that he grew larger before my eyes without actually changing size at all. It was as if the geometry of the space around us was slipping away, creating the illusion that he somehow filled the whole theatre. He lifted a hand as if he would touch it to his tranquil face, but then just looked at it. The light pouring from his eyes illuminated the flesh of his fingers green. His entire body began to quiver.

I could hear Epistola chanting madly from the podium, but Riley didn't seem to notice. I wanted to call out to him, to warn him that she was up to something, but before I could form the words, he abruptly gasped and bent double. He wrapped his arms tight around himself as if in pain, and I shrieked. The light that had before only been coming from his eyes now radiated from his entire body. It swirled out of him, concentrated in some places more than others, a great ball of it on his back.

He twisted around and locked upon my gaze. Even through the green blaze, it seemed as if his eyes had changed color, gone black. They looked unlike they ever had before, and yet somehow more familiar than I could fathom.

"Andromeda!" he called as the light shot out of his face in wild lashing tendrils. "Shield your mind." His voice was filled with incontestable command and yet, at the same time, more desperate than I'd ever heard it. "Look away!"

No! I didn't want to turn from him. How did the eleven screaming madmen that surrounded us have souls worthy to be consumed by him, but I did not? Why would he not let me too be driven mad? It was the one last thing I had left to desire! I was frantic for it, and I refused to be denied! If I would die here tonight, then at least I would die finally truly *knowing him.*

However, despite my resolve, a sudden painfully blinding flash made my treacherous hands cover my eyes on impulse.

I could still hear Epistola shouting alien incantations, but her voice was cut off by the boom of Riley's. "What was it you said? Look at me now?" he mocked. "LOOK AT ME?! AS YOU WISH."

No, it wasn't fair! I could not allow *her* to see him without seeing him myself. I forced my eyes open, although the brilliance was almost too much to bear. It shone all colors and no colors, and washed off Riley as if he were radioactive. Amid the sparkling storm, I first thought the dazzling green cast to his skin was a result of the glow, but as I focused, I realized that his flesh had actually *changed color.* My mind tried to grapple with the continued illusion that he was growing, the feeling that I was somehow shrinking, but then I understood that this time—this time, he was actually getting larger.

Energy bloomed behind him and first one, and then two, huge leathery wings unfurled from his back in an explosion of light and darkness.

The screams of the cultists were overwhelmed by a pulsing thrum, almost musical, that drowned out all other sounds. It seemed as if Riley were coming closer to me, but I realized that he was just continuing to literally inflate in size, his form spreading across the stage, stretching toward the catwalk. His limbs were thickening, larger than trees, his hands stretching into vast webbed things tipped with long razor claws, and his face…

His head transformed before my eyes, stretching into an inhuman shape, his hair disappearing, his nose flattening out, his eyes spreading to vast shimmering black rainbow orbs… and his mouth obliterated as countless tentacles spilled from his face, lashing with shimmering tendrils of pure iridescent energy.

I had seen this before, the prismatic creature that now rose to impossible heights before me… I had seen it *in my dreams*. Suddenly everything was clear to me. I hadn't dreamed of Riley rescuing me from a sea monster like the hero in the mythological Andromeda's tale. Riley and the creature were one and the same. They always had been.

My Great One.

The Almighty Cthulhu.

"BEHOLD!" he bellowed at Epistola, who had fallen from the podium. I realized in a delayed instant that the words I felt him speak weren't English; in fact, they weren't even sounds. He was somehow transmitting his speech in a way that was beyond my comprehension and yet sparkled clear as a bell to my understanding. I could only assume Episotla heard him the same way, as I watched her push up from the stage, her head ducked and eyes averted as she scrambled for the wings.

"BEHOLD THE TRUE FORM OF CTHULHU, NO LONGER TRAPPED IN R'LYEH, TO DREAM UNTIL THE ALIGNMENT."

It felt as if the whole building would tremble apart with his thunderous phrases, and I wondered how the roof hadn't blown off yet with his size. As cavernous as the theatre was, it seemed impossible that it could contain the greatness he had reached. The geometry of the space had ceased to make sense entirely.

I couldn't take my eyes from him, but Epistola craned away even as he lowered an enormous hand to block her path. She shrieked, "By the power of Azathoth—"

"IMPUDENCE!"

The clinquant hand closed around her body, and I saw her eyes bulge at the force of its grip. He lifted her high, holding her before his radiant face. The tentacles seemed to tear at her limbs, and she thrashed against his fingers, cutting her overexposed flesh on the gleaming claws.

"BEHOLD!" he thundered. "AND BE GONE!"

He turned her around and I could tell the instant she finally laid eyes upon his glory, because all her movements stilled at once. But only for an instant, and then her head fell back, her jaw seeming to unhinge to let loose the howls that accompanied her descent into madness.

The glow surrounding his massive body surged in brilliance, and with a great rush of air, the incandescent wings on his back stretched out to unimaginable swirling distances. He held onto her for a moment longer before spreading his great fingers and letting her slide from his grip. She plummeted, stiletto boots and all, into the orchestra pit, hitting with a sick *thwap*.

In a rush of wind, his hand came down over the pillar of fire, slapping it out. The iron pit that contained its origins shattered to shards under his blow.

I threw my arms up to shield myself from the flying debris, and it was then that I noticed the puckered wound over my heart was glowing. Glowing the same color as *him*.

The Seal of Azathoth.
The Heart of Cthulhu.

Stillness had returned to the theatre and all natural sounds seemed to fade completely under the musical hum that scampered through the charged air. It made me feel like I was floating in a space outside of time. The silence was so great that I would have feared I'd gone deaf, if I didn't recognize a second later that I could still hear my own ragged breathing.

Slowly, tenderly, I lifted my eyes to once more behold the Great One, glimmering in the candlelight like a viridian galaxy of stars before me. His wings seemed to pulse as he looked out beyond the empty seats.

"Riley?" I whispered. I cringed at how small my voice sounded, and if he heard me at all, he made no sign. I worked up my courage, and then tried again, "...Cthulhu?"

With a speed I never could have imagined possible for one so large, he whipped around to look down upon me. His nacreous eyes burned with imperial power, shining black with all colors and none. The depth of emotion that emanated from them made my breath hitch; it was as if they contained the concentrated essence of a million souls.

A giant fist came down before me, the stage boards cracking under its scintillating pressure, and his great weight shifted, making the building tremble. His other arm folded across his prismatic knee, and he leaned down over me, coming so close that the shimmering tentacles pooled in an effulgent mass of opalescence against the stage, inches from where I sprawled. I stared down at them, and I could feel the voltaic heat radiating from his vibrant body.

Was this going to be it? My heart leapt in my breast. Would he finally consume me now? I was ready. We would be joined, and the heart I possessed that was rightfully his would be returned where it belonged. He would be whole again, free, and I would be obliterated in his perfection. I wanted to get up, to offer myself to him properly, but my entire body felt limp and lifeless. Even in these last moments, I was failing him, unworthy even for consumption. I grimaced, hating myself for my weakness.

My expression seemed to have a strange effect on him— an emotion rippled across him that I could feel within me, our synchronicity stronger than ever. *Anguish.*

Slowly, I lifted my eyes. Even though his face was so alien to me, with the writhing mass of appendages and the great pupil-less eyes above, when my gaze finally locked with his, I understood the expression within as clearly as if he were human. He looked... afraid.

I held my breath, and watched as the fear dissipated after only a moment and shifted into something like confused concern. I frowned, my own confusion reflecting his.

What was he waiting for?

His gaze fell from mine, his bulk shifting as he looked away and sat back. The feeling that came from him then shocked me more than anything else I had experienced all night.

Shame.

My breath caught, and I forced myself to my knees. What could it mean? I floundered, at a loss for words. On impulse, I reached for the emerald hand on the floor.

With a quick, smooth motion, he pulled it beyond my grasp. I bit my lip as I craned my neck back to look up at him, and then using the edge of the tub, I pulled myself to my feet.

"Please…" I whispered.

He looked down at me again, and the sadness in his eyes was unmistakable. After a moment, and very slowly, his hand came back down as if he would touch me, but the tips of the glittering claws only brushed the air just above my head.

I took a deep breath and then reached up and snatched the edge of one of his fingers before he could pull away again. His verdant skin was soft and pulsing with warmth under my touch. He was frozen for a minute, and then he lowered his hand before me. I pulled myself into his palm before he could change his mind. For a moment I tensed, excepting his fingers to clench around me like they had with Epistola, but his hand remained open, and he lifted me as gently as if I were made of crystal.

High above the stage, I knelt before his face. The resplendent tentacles swirled about me, encircling my limbs, but staying an inch from my flesh, not one of them actually touching me.

The emotion coming from him then was one of utter amazement and wonder. I understood; I was gazing upon his true visage, and I had not been driven mad. Instead, I felt almost at peace. If it hadn't been for the pain in my body from the tortures I'd endured, I could have been perfectly content.

"You stopped her," I whispered. *You saved me…* "You came…"

"Of course I came, you foolish child." Again, his voice—his polychromatic song—surrounded me, filled me, with shimmering words that weren't words that I understood deep within the core of my being. "I had no choice."

I bit back a trembling breath and I looked down, tucking

some of my drying hair behind my ear. I nodded. "You had to save the world…"

One of the tentacles brushed me then, catching me under the chin and gently forcing me to look back up at him. Its texture was softer than satin.

The light in his eyes seemed to flicker. "You are the only thing in this world worth saving."

I blinked, and my lips parted speechlessly. I shook my head. "But, no… Why?"

Something that wasn't solid slithered against my back, like a feathery whisper of energy that yearned to press me closer to his face but did not dare.

"Isn't it obvious by now?" he asked.

I shook my head again, lost. Nothing was obvious. All was confusion.

His entire being seemed to sigh. "To allow you to be destroyed would be to destroy my own heart."

I tried to glance down at the throbbing Seal over my chest, but he would not let me, pushing my face back up with his silky smooth touch.

"Andromeda. Foolish, simple, itty bitty, little thing…" His eyes smoldered into mine. "I love you."

My mind had to be playing tricks on me. Did I misunderstand him? Even as they were the words I'd been desperate to hear in and out of all of my dreams, I couldn't bring myself to believe them. Or at least, he couldn't possibly mean them in the same way I meant them.

I took a shuddering breath. "But I thought you were done with me," I protested. "That I was unworthy of you, that… that you hated me for the fact that you cared about something so beneath you."

Tension gripped his great frame, his wings snapping out over his head. His fingers curled toward me, but did not clamp down. "No! Never," he said with severity. "I had to leave you, little one, to protect you, for I would only drive you mad. It was an inevitability I could not abide, *because I love you*. I tried to stop. If I could have stopped loving you, then you would be free... but try as I might, I could not. I cannot. I cannot *be* without you. I *cannot* be where you are not. Dream figment or no, you are the substance of *my* dreams. I would rather be forever in a dream with you than endure one moment more of reality without you."

A shudder seemed to course through him. "I feel as though we are linked," he intoned, "tied to each other by some unseverable strand. Your very being, insubstantial though it is, commands me, dominates my immensity. Overpowers me. I am *your thing*, tiny one. Though you are the mortal and I am the god, it is you who are worshipped *by me*."

I shook my head, not knowing what to believe anymore, overwhelmed.

My voice came out miniscule, "But you said..."

"I had to go," he repeated. "If I stayed with you, how could I hide myself from you forever? My true self. Your mind was too precious to me."

"But I'm looking at you now and my mind's just fine."

"Yes," he consented, the amazed confusion returning to his tone. He hesitated, but then when he spoke again, I was stunned by the profound dejection that filled his words. "Though perhaps it would have been more merciful if you had been driven mad after all... for now, you know me as I truly am... A monster."

I almost recoiled in shock. I pressed a hand against the raw cuts on my chest; the pain that was gnashing at the organ below them was far worse than that on the surface. My gaze drifted from his face. I looked intently at his elegant wings, his tentacled mandibles, his strong arms, his sharp talons and finally, back to his perfect eyes. The colors swirled like galaxies deep within them, so much more than the green I remembered, and yet still recognizable. Still perfectly and unendingly *Riley*. But they were so filled with despair.

"Madness or no," he whispered. "I wished more than anything to protect you—to spare you—from my true horror."

I reached out to him, grasping two of the appendages before me, and they responded immediately, swirling around my wrists. My heart felt like it was swelling beyond my chest. *His heart.* How could I tell him? How could I make him understand? His haunted visage held no horror for me now. How could it ever?

"No," I attempted, my voice almost breaking. "No, never." I shook my head. "My Great One." I lifted a hand to the flat of his face below his eye, feeling the muscles in his unearthly features respond to my every touch. "No horror. I see only... love."

I fixed my eyes on his, unwavering, and when I spoke again, my voice finally carried the tender strength I willed into it. "You are beautiful."

The whisper-smoke feeling at my back gathered against me then, entwining me. I was lifted off my feet by it, and had never felt more cradled and secure. It drew me to him and I leaned forward in anticipation, my heart beating almost through my chest. The delicate, beautiful tendrils of his face caressed my cheeks, combed through my hair, wrapped gently around my ears. Each of their touches was a silken kiss against my skin, enveloping me in a curtain of wriggling warmth and love.

I closed my eyes in bliss, and felt a breeze brush past me. The beating of leathery wings enveloped me like an embrace. A few moments later, arms came around me that at first dwarfed my body, but gradually seemed to condense until they fit me perfectly.

And then soft, ardent lips were upon mine, and I could feel the stars swirling in the cosmos above us in response.

I realized in a distant way that the hands that moved up into my hair were human hands again, but I was so lost in the kiss, it didn't matter. My beautiful Great One loved me. Loved *me*.

Nothing else would ever matter again.

The perfect moment was rudely shattered by a loud crash beside us, and a flood of water suddenly rushed across my feet. I looked over at the tub and saw it had been knocked over by thick chunks of broken ceiling beams. Another crash on our other side rendered the podium to splinters. I tilted my head back to look up. I screamed. The catwalk was swinging precariously above. Two of the cables supporting it snapped and it swung toward us.

Faster than I could comprehend, Riley pulled me away to the far side of the stage by the marble columns. A second later, the structure plummeted down to smithereens. We looked to the theatre's ceiling, to where the chandelier used to be. The swirling black abyss was even larger and more tumultuous than it had been before.

"What's going on?" I cried.

Riley's grip on my arms tightened painfully. "Azathoth yet comes!"

"But how?" I exclaimed, looking from Riley to the cultists who were scattered around us. They all seemed oblivious, twitching mindlessly where they sprawled about the stage.

"She was right," I heard Riley mutter. "I was too late."

"Do something!" I gasped.

"Stay here." He pressed me against the safety of the column, and my heart twisted as he pulled away from me. In a dazzling cascade of light, I watched him grow and change again, and his magnificent true form filled the theatre, his shape stretching up to disappear into the black abyss. The wind began to pick up the shattered debris, swirling the dangerous objects in a violent tornado. I ducked down, turning my face against the column, shielding my head.

Thunder filled the air above me accompanied by a sound like screaming, but the voice was unlike anything I'd ever heard before.

"Riley!" I gasped.

As if in instantaneous response, his arms came around me, and he pulled me into the protection of his embrace. He was his human self again, but as I looked up at him, I was shocked by the haggard appearance of his chiseled face. He looked exhausted... drained.

"It has become too strong," he whispered raggedly at my ear. The nightmare sounds continued to swarm around us with the wind and destruction, but nothing touched us, as if his strength provided a protective bubble over the place where we stood. "There is nothing I can do. I do not have the power to lock the gate. And even if I did, it is too far open now."

"So…?" I whimpered.

"The Nuclear Chaos will awaken."

"No!" I sobbed, and clutched desperately at his shirt, burying my face against his muscled chest. "No, it's not fair!" Finally, for the first time in my pathetic existence, I had a reason to live! And so soon it would all be torn away.

Riley's arms gathered me against him. He turned his face into my hair, and I felt the hot moisture from his eyes. "I have failed you," he wept. "I meant only to protect you always, and now you will disappear into the ether from whence you were dreamt."

I was crying too, my fingers twisting into his shirt, my heart breaking with the irony of our fate as I listened to the world falling apart around us. But even as I knew I was mere moments from my inevitable end, I was content to at least be with Riley. I only wished that he would keep holding me tightly—never let me go—until it was over. In his embrace, I would sink into sweet oblivion. In perfect love, I would die.

"I love you," I whispered. "*I love you, I love you, I love you, I love you…*"

I felt his trembling fingers in my hair, pressing my head against his shoulder, his fervent lips at my temple, our tears intermingling in our final, precious moments together…

"Oh, for the love of—" A sharp voice rang out behind us with an exasperated sigh. "Get a *room*."

Chapter Twenty-Three
Choices

RILEY PULLED BACK FROM OUR EMBRACE, THOUGH continued to clutch me protectively. I twisted around to follow his gaze, and beheld the man emerging from the wings. Neil. His dragon-headed cane tapped syncopatedly against the debris-covered floorboards as he approached us, stepping around a few of the twitching cultists and the toppled beams that buried them. Like with us, the hurricane of destruction didn't seem to touch him, as if he moved through a protective pocket of air.

He glanced to the chaos swarming above and then tsked at me and Riley. "Of all the times and places," he muttered, though the gleam in his eye belied his excitement as he tilted his face back as if in reverence to the abysmal vortex. "Sorry if we're interrupting a Kodak moment here kids, but I think we have more important fish to fry."

Riley's hands clenched my arms, pulling my back against

his solid chest, and I felt him take a sharp breath.

"You mean…"

"Well, I was thinking…" Neil tossed him a grin. "How about a little of the fight chaos with chaos, eh? Whattaya say?"

My heart leapt with new hope. "You have the power to stop him?" I asked excitedly.

"What?" Neil snorted and shook his head. "No." He glanced to Riley with a roll of his eyes and then fixed his gaze on me, enunciating very slowly. "None of us do."

"But…" I whimpered, confused and afraid and a little bit offended. If the world was really about to end, I didn't want to spend my last minutes being patronized by Riley's uncle, when we could have been alone together instead.

"That is," Neil added before I could say anything more, a sharky smile spreading across his face. "Not alone."

A teenage girl popped out of the wings behind him and waved at Riley. "Hey loser!"

I felt him stiffen against me. "Chloe."

Riley's sister! She looked a couple years younger than me and was dressed in a ruffly skirt and pink tank top. Like Riley, she was unnaturally pale, but her raven's-wing hair was cut short and spiky, styled in a sort of half-mohawk that complimented her heart-shaped face in a girlish way. Her dark eyes twinkled mischievously, and as she got closer I noticed four piercings in one of her ears, five in the other, and one each in her nose and lower lip.

"So this is the meat?" she queried, looking me up and down before giving me a friendly wink. "Niiiiice ceremonial garb." Despite her smirk, the impression I got wasn't at all one of sarcasm or derision. She actually meant it. And her smile grew more cheerful, as if to prove that point.

I could only shake my head, bemused. I'd completely forgotten about what I was wearing, and I flushed with shame. I wasn't about to thank her for the compliment, but if she had really come to help save us, I didn't want to offend her either... My hopes were steadily rising.

Riley seemed unsure what to make of her attitude, and he looked back to Neil. "But even with our powers combined," he said tensely, "we three do not possess the ability to lock the gate."

My hopes sank like a shipwreck.

Neil rolled his eyes again. "You think she's the only backup I brought?"

Chloe put her hands on her hips, scoffing. "Hey!"

Neil shook his head with a chuckle. "You're feisty, kid, but we need the big guns. So I rallied the whole crew. Well, the awake ones, anyway. And let me tell you what a romping good time *that* was. About five minutes ago, out under the Sahara—"

Chloe cut him off with an enthusiastic nod. "Getting our grumpy old cousins to agree to work together when they've been avoiding each other for centuries? Hoo boy..."

Riley still seemed uncertain, but I could feel how his tension was dissolving into guarded optimism. "Even the Deep Ones?" he asked.

"Better," said Neil. "I wrangled everyone's favorite curmudgeon."

"You don't mean..."

"Yup." Neil grinned. "Yog-Sothoth."

"The Gatekeeper," Riley murmured, low and reverent.

"You owe me bigtime for this one, kid."

Riley's family! He hadn't so much as spoken to them in ages, but they were all coming here now to try to save the universe. To try to save *us*. Could they possibly have the combined strength to close the portal? How I wished I could feel more assurance from Riley.

Instead I suddenly felt a strange ripping in the air, as if the dimensions had begun to shift. Preternatural thunder crashed all around us.

Chloe bounced excitedly on the balls of her floral-print Doc Martens. "Here they coooome!"

Before I could process the dizzying effect the rumbling was having on my senses, Riley pushed me back over to the shelter of the marble columns.

"You will be safe here," he said as he released me.

"No, don't go!" I begged, clutching his arm desperately. The thought of him joining the others in battle when I didn't know the first thing about what could happen to him up there terrified me beyond endurance. I wanted to stay in his arms until the last moment. If they failed, I couldn't die alone!

Riley looked as pained to leave me as I felt. "I must try," he winced. "I may provide the last bit of strength required." He reluctantly pried my fingers from his arm and slipped back, his eyes glistening with unshed tears. "Do not move from this place," he commanded.

I slid down the pillar with a whimper, wrapping my arms around my bare knees, but I kept my eyes glued to his every move.

Neil glanced back at us from where he'd positioned himself at the apron of the stage. "You might want to look away for this," he said to me. "I mean, only if you want to keep your marbles. It's time we all slipped into something a scoch more comfortable."

Riley crouched before me, taking my face in his hands, and his lips brushed away each of my hot tears. "Whatever you do, Andromeda," he said between kisses, "do not allow your eyes to fall upon the chaos. My heart may not protect your puny mind from the insanity of the other Old Ones." His hands clenched the sides of my face urgently, his glowing eyes boring into mine. "Swear to me!"

"I swear!" I gasped.

He held me that way for a trembling moment, his look almost violent with the passion of his concern for me, but then he released me with a great shudder and slipped away to join Neil and Chloe. All three of them had begun to glow. I watched Riley intently for a second before realizing I was doing exactly what he'd just told me not to.

But I couldn't look away!

Immense amorphous shadows were trickling into the cavernous expanse of the theatre independent of the widening darkness above, as if they would attempt to blot out the light that poured off the three of them. And then it seemed as if the very air began to fissure, and time ceased to have meaning.

As if outside of my own mind, I caught the barest glimpse of the horrors that lurked beyond the spreading cracks as they began to ooze out into our world. The whole room felt turned upside down and inside out at once. Nausea clawed over me, and with all the will I had left, I forced myself to tear my eyes away, squeezing them shut as tightly as I could manage.

I pushed to my feet, keeping my back against the pillar and began to slide around it. With any luck, I could place its sheltering structure between myself and the temptation to look into the chaos.

The slamming and crashing and crunching of the theatre falling apart around me were soon drowned out by those now-familiar eldritch sounds of cataclysm—almost musical, but this time multilayered in a psyche-bending symphony— that accompanied the charged air crackling against my skin. It purred at me, enticing me to gaze upon it, but I resolutely kept my eyes closed as I inched my way to the opposite side of the fat column.

But then I stumbled over something, and my eyes snapped open.

Terror shot through me for an instant until I realized I was out of sight of the vortex and still in possession of my mind. I let out a whoosh of relief and looked down to see what I'd tripped over.

A black-cloaked body.

I yelped and jumped back, but then a second later, I realized whose body it was.

Vik.

The floor shook under my feet, and even with the column's support, I couldn't stay standing. I fell to my knees beside Vik, and without even thinking, rolled him onto his back. He was dead weight in my hands, and his eyes were closed, his face lifeless. But he was warm. Almost too warm.

I hesitated, but then pressed my ear against his chest. I could hear nothing over the thunderous humming that sparkled the air. I clenched my teeth and concentrated, but then even though I couldn't pinpoint his heartbeat, I realized after a minute that his chest was rising and falling under my cheek. He was breathing! I exhaled in relief and found myself burying my face against his chest, clutching at the fabric in gratitude before I realized what I was doing. I pushed back abruptly, uncertainty flooding me as I stared down at him.

He doesn't even look like Vik anymore, I thought. Not really. Not my Vik. He was some uncanny *new* Vik that had grown up overnight, leaving me behind.

Blood was trickling from his hair in a line down his temple. I felt the urge to wipe it away for him, but I refrained. I bit my lip, my hands shaking. He looked so innocent lying there, his long black eyelashes resting against his tawny cheeks. Hardly the vicious torturer he'd been only minutes ago. My flesh whimpered at the memory. How much of what he'd done, his hateful words, had been the cult's brainwashing, and how much had contained some seeds of truth under the surface? I shuddered, but then jumped as something unnaturally loud crashed against the wall behind us.

Oh god, how could I even be thinking about these things when I didn't even know if we'd ever make it out of this alive?

I threw my arms over my head as a spray of something that felt like liquid ice flew past me. The chill of it penetrated the marrow of my bones, but before I could even begin to shiver, a sluice of heat rolled past me in perfect opposition. On its heels came a glittering wave of pinkish light that seemed to bubble the heat forward as it cascaded over me. I closed my eyes, but it was so bright that I could still see it in all its rosy ferocity through my eyelids.

I buried my face in my hands and tried to take slow

breaths, straining my ears to grasp at the last wisps of the music in the air. The violence of the wind was rapidly overpowering it, and soon it was so loud that it seemed sound stopped completely. But not in silence—in infinite noise.

It opened up around me, engulfing my being like the great, steamy maw of a creature made of sound. Even though I knew my eyes were still closed, I could see everything. The light had become infinite darkness.

Infinite nothing.

Utter chaos spun around me and I watched it in horror. Everything was gone. The column was gone, Vik was gone, the whole theatre was gone.

There was no sign of Riley or his family. No wind, no sound, no color—only absolute negation.

Beautiful insanity.

And me.

I was floating in the center of it, supported by nothing, containing nothing, and I understood completely. Azathoth's dream had ended, and I had returned to the ether. I was in space that wasn't space. The essence of what I was had slipped between dimensions, and I hovered at the brink of dissolution into less than atoms, less than thought. Figment no longer.

Although I retained an odd sense of my former body, as if it were still somehow whole, I could not see it. And yet, I *could* see. Even though there was nothing to see. For there was *nothing* to see. I saw the nothing.

Did I still somehow possess my eyes? I tried to wiggle my fingers. The part of me that should have been my hand seemed to respond. I felt it brush against something like smoke made solid. I would have gasped if there had been air to draw in or lungs to draw it. I stretched my not-fingers out further, reaching for the elusive tendril of energy. It slithered by me again, too far away to catch.

No! Come back!

And as if it could hear every last one of my desperate thoughts, it obeyed.

It enveloped my fingers, twined around my wrist. And then I felt my not-self embraced by countless shimmering phantom arms. They wrapped all around me, gathering me, buoying me, drawing me down, down, down, down…

~*~*~*~

Down, down, down…

…back onto the stage with a thump.

And I was no longer alone. Riley's arms were around me, cradling me in a fervent embrace. He brushed my hair back from my face as he peered into my eyes, his expression desperate as he sought to assure himself that my mind was intact. I managed to give him a little smile.

He relaxed visibly and returned my smile wearily, his warm fingers brushing over my cheeks. If I thought he'd looked drained before, he looked ready to drop now.

"The gate has been secured," he whispered as he drew me to my feet. "Azathoth slumbers."

I leaned against him, suddenly feeling almost as tired as he looked. "But I felt him wake up," I said, taking a confused breath. "I was so lost, Riley. Everything was gone… You were gone."

"No, little one. The Old Ones ensured he was not

awoken. They ensured our love would endure…"

Our love.

For me and Riley, his strange family would fight to keep our little world spinning. Defy the prophecies. Risk the wrath of the gods. It was worth it to them… for love.

I realized how silent the space around us had become. "Where are they?" I asked.

I heard a raspy cough and Neil emerged around the column. He wiped his mouth with his sleeve before screwing the dragon head back onto his cane. "You think they'd stick around this dump?" He glanced over the ravaged space, the settling debris and the gibbering splayed forms of the mad cultists. He shot Riley a look. "After all, you already cleaned out the buffet."

Riley's gaze slipped from me to follow Neil's to the black-robed shells of former zealotry. I felt him release a distantly contented sigh.

A feminine yawn caught my attention and I saw Chloe hop up from the orchestra pit. "I'm out of here too," she said, joining us by the wings.

Riley nodded to her appreciatively. "I thank you, sister."

She shot him a sleepy smile. "Happy to help." She turned to glance at me studyingly. "I'll have to come back and visit soon. I definitely need to know more about this… *uncanny* human of yours."

I couldn't help blushing, and Chloe giggled.

"Hey," she said, "it's not every day you get to meet someone whose love is strong enough to change everything we thought we knew about the multiverse! You and I *must* hang out sometime. But… after a nap…"

As strange as she was, I found myself feeling that if she

actually thought she could be friends with me, I might like that. I felt Riley's hand tighten possessively around my arm as Chloe's eyes wandered over me, but there was nothing judgmental about her childlike look, just benign curiosity. Her gaze paused at the wound on my chest and she nodded approvingly. "Niiiice. That's going to leave one awesome scar. If you're lucky."

"Goodbye, Chloe," Riley said, and I could feel how he forced his voice to stay even.

She looked up at him with a very genuine smile before punching him playfully in the shoulder. "See ya, losers!" And then with a crack that was like thunder and not at the same time, she was gone.

My gaze fell to examine the raw cuts over my heart. *The Seal of Azathoth.* I'd almost forgotten it was there. I winced as I brushed my fingertips over the torn skin. Riley caught my hand before I could cause myself anymore pain. He sighed and shook his head at me, but then kissed my fingertips, making tingles run all the way down my arm.

Neil's voice by the column shattered the sensation. "Speaking of the buffet, looks like you missed one."

I pulled my eyes from Riley to see Neil prodding Vik's body with the tip of his cane. A faint moan escaped Vik's unconscious lips, but he did not move.

Riley's entire frame tensed and he slowly turned to follow my gaze. "So I did," he said, his voice low, lethal.

My breath caught as I recognized the look that began to grow in his eyes. The pain over my chest twisted. He pulled away from me and stepped forward, his smoldering gaze locked on where Vik lay. I could feel the power begin to build in him and before I knew what I was doing, I jumped in front of him and grabbed him by the arms. "No!"

Riley froze. His body became granite under my touch.

I heard Neil groan behind me. "Oy, not this again…"

I reached up to Riley's face, trying to tilt it to make him focus on me instead. "Please?" I beseeched.

"You wish me to spare him." His voice was cold and dark. It was not a question.

"Please…"

He shook his head, though I could see the conflict in his eyes. "He is no different than these insignificant fools," he gestured to the other cultists.

"He is to me," I insisted, though my voice was tiny. "He's… he's like my brother!"

Or at least he was… But I tried not to dwell on those thoughts as I pleaded with Riley. "To me, he's family…" Surely Riley could not deny the importance of family after tonight.

He studied me uncertainly, and a very long moment passed, but then the glow in his eyes began to fade and I felt the tension seep from his frame. He gave a dismissive nod and glanced away. "The human authorities will deal with him when they arrive for the rest."

I exhaled the last of my anxiety and threw my arms around him in gratitude. His arms encircled me automatically, our bodies molding against each other.

"Soooo…" Neil's voice abolished our moment *again*. "You really did give a mortal your heart. Yeah, smart move there."

"She *is* my heart," Riley corrected him vehemently.

Neil gave a consenting shrug and an indulgent smile. "Weeeelllll, one of three, at least, eh Octoboy?"

What did he mean by *that*?

I stiffened, but as Riley's arms tightened around me, I was too distracted by the strength of his embrace to ask.

"Stop it, Neil," Riley said, though his voice sounded too weary to hold any real frustration.

"Alright, alright," Neil chuckled, then he winked at me. "Just kidding, peaches. You're his one and only."

A thrill coursed through me at the thought of it.

"But the question is," Neil asked Riley, "what will you do now? You've still got a sacred duty, you know. Your house at R'lyeh is waiting. Or... will you devote yourself to this mortal instead?"

A stone hand gripped my heart and I looked up at Riley's face in alarm. What did Neil mean? Was it possible that Riley had to give up his godhood to stay with me? I knew our love would change what he *did*, that was the prophecy after all. But I didn't realize it would change who he *was*. Could he really let that go after eons of existence? There was no way I was worth *that*.

I saw a dark cloud descend over Riley's perfect features, and his arms slipped from me as he took a step back. I began to shake.

"To choose?" He hesitated, his flawless eyelids drooping as his gaze slid from me to look past Neil. He slowly scanned the ruined place where we stood. I recalled what he'd said to me in the driveway earlier about having to slumber. He looked more tired now than ever before. Regardless of whether or not he wanted to, could he even go on, being so drained of his powers?

Neil cocked his head expectantly. I had stopped breathing altogether.

Riley lifted his hands to his face, as if he could rub wakefulness back into it. He took a long, slow breath. And then he spoke:

"I choose..." He fixed me with a defiant look. "Love."

The word fell like heaven from his lips.

"But—" I protested weakly, though before I could say anything more, his eyes seemed to snap to alertness and he looked down at me with a firm shake of his head.

"I'll sleep when I'm dead," he said determinedly.

"Attaboy!" Neil laughed. "Though you'll have to be prepared for the consequences, of course. Like that one crazy time I..." And he started going off then about eldritch monstrosities or some other stuff, but I was too lost in the look of pure affection pouring from Riley's verdant eyes to listen to a single other word he was saying.

"Besides," Riley murmured as he tucked a strand of my hair lovingly behind my ear, "how could I slumber now?" His perfect eyebrows rose and his perfect lips smiled down upon me. "I do believe there is a certain Ball that requires our attendance."

My heart—*his heart*—soared.

Epilogue

Complete

THE ANNUAL PORTSMOUTH PUMPKIN FESTIVAL WAS exactly what you'd expect something called a Pumpkin Festival to be. Most of the activities were clearly meant for little kids: a straw maze, a hayride, face painting, and of course, pumpkin carving. But after nightfall the adults had the Pumpkin Ball to look forward to. Also, there was food everywhere; I spotted Bree working her way down a long table covered in various baked goods. She waved at me before getting distracted by a blackberry pie.

It was easily the largest gathering of people I'd ever seen in Portsmouth. Practically the entire town had shown up. I stood off to the side, watching my neighbors laugh and play, and shuddered when I thought of how differently this day might have gone.

"None of them have any idea how close they came to dying," I said softly.

Riley put his arm around me. "That is for the best, don't you think?"

I nodded. I wouldn't wish some of my memories from the last few days on anyone.

"Do you still feel, you know... like you want to end the world?" I asked hesitantly as I glanced up at the darkening sky. Soon the stars would emerge.

"Sometimes," Riley admitted. "The pull of the Alignment is undeniably strong. But in those moments, I simply look at you."

Before I could really digest that information, he pulled me out of the shadows.

"Come," he said. "This is an evening for celebrating, not fretting over what might have been."

"Where are we going?" I questioned.

"The Ball, of course."

The next street over had been completely blocked off. An old-fashioned folk band was set up on a platform at one end. The rest of the space was already filled with dancing couples.

"Honestly, I wouldn't have guessed you'd be so into this," I said.

Riley raised his eyebrows. "Whyever not? You humans didn't invent dance, you know."

I had danced with a boy once before, at my cousin's wedding, and it was the most uncomfortable experience of my life. I never knew where to direct my gaze, and when I rested my hand on the boy's shoulder, his shirt was damp with sweat. I couldn't wait for it to be over.

But with Riley, dancing, like everything else, was completely different. There was nothing awkward about it. I just put my hand in his, and away we sailed across the dance floor.

I wanted to stay like that for as long as the band kept playing, but after a particularly lively number left me red-faced and out of breath, Riley insisted that we stop.

"You require rest and hydration," he proclaimed. "Wait here while I fetch you water."

"Thanks," I said, giving his hand a slight squeeze before letting it go.

As Riley disappeared into the crowd, I found a spot to relax along the wall. Watching other people dance was nothing compared to dancing with Riley, but it was still entertaining. That was when I noticed Vik standing on the other side of the street.

I froze like a deer in headlights. It was the first time I'd seen him since the theatre; he hadn't shown up at school for the rest of the week. Bree had gotten word that he'd had a Vespa accident and was recovering from concussion. I hadn't contradicted the story when she passed it on to me.

He was watching me, but not with the cold, hard stare I'd last seen him wear. His expression was one of worry and remorse. Could it be that the boy I knew and loved was back?

I walked slowly across the dance floor to his side of the street, but I stopped with a good five feet still between us.

"Hey," I said.

"Hey," he replied.

An uncomfortable silence fell upon us. There'd never been an uncomfortable silence between me and Vik before. For the first time, it really hit me what I'd lost, and it filled me with sadness to think I might never regain it again.

"I would say I'm sorry," Vik said at last, "but I know that would be way too little, too late."

Those two words did seem like very little after all that had happened. But he looked so miserable that my heart went out to him.

"You were hypnotized. You didn't know what you were doing," I said. "I forgive you, Vik."

"Really?"

"Really."

He chuckled bitterly. "Well, that's great. But I don't think I'll ever forgive myself."

I didn't know how to respond to that. It seemed so unfair that this sweet, kind-hearted boy was saddled with so much guilt, probably for the rest of his life, because he simply trusted the wrong person.

"It's all *her* fault," I said, anger bubbling up inside me. "*Scarlett Epistola.* I'm just thankful she's locked up where she'll never be able to hurt anyone again."

Vik gave me an odd look.

"What?" I asked.

"You haven't heard?"

"Heard what?"

"She escaped," he said. "On the way to the asylum. They can't find her. She's on the loose somewhere."

My stomach lurched. For the last four days, I'd been walking around like I had a bubble of protection over me, and now that bubble had burst.

"I have to find Riley," I said. I began looking around frantically, but he was nowhere in sight. Before I could take off running to seek him, Vik's strong hands grabbed me by the shoulders.

"Don't be afraid, Andi," he said. "Even if she comes back here, I won't let her touch you. I won't fail you again."

Instantly, I felt a little bit calmer.

"I know you won't," I said sincerely. "You and Riley both. You'll protect me."

At the mention of Riley's name, Vik flinched.

"You really like him, don't you?" he said, releasing me.

"No, Vik," I said gently. "I *love* him."

"But he's..." He hesitated as if trying to choose from a thousand different things he wanted say against my boyfriend. He settled for a soft but determined, "He's dangerous, Andi."

"No, he isn't. Not to me."

Vik sighed, resigned.

"Okay," he said. "I'll back off. But if he ever hurts you, I'll be here."

For some reason, I found myself blushing.

"That won't be necessary," I said. "But thanks."

Just then, Riley reappeared across the street, holding a water bottle. His eyes narrowed when he saw who I was talking to.

"See you later!" I said to Vik as I hurried away. The last thing I wanted was for him to end up like Travis.

"What did he want?" Riley demanded. "What did he say to you? Did he hurt you?"

"Of course not!" I said. "*I* approached *him*. And all he did was apologize."

Riley snorted. "Apologize! Does he imagine a simple apology can erase what he did?"

"No, he doesn't," I replied. "But I forgave him, anyway."

I tried to explain again what it meant that Vik and I had been best friends for as long as either of us could remember, that he was the closest thing I had to a brother, and that one mistake, even a mistake this big, didn't cancel all that out. I don't think Riley really got it, but in the end, I at least convinced him to leave Vik alone.

"We have bigger problems, anyway," I said. "Riley, Epistola escaped."

Riley sighed. "Yes, I know."

My jaw dropped. "You knew? How could you not tell me?"

"I wished to keep you from worry, little one," he said. "There's no need for alarm. The woman's mind is broken. She is a mere shadow of what she once was. She could not harm anyone now, even if—" He stopped short.

"Even if what?" I asked.

Riley tried to change the subject, but I wasn't going to let him off that easily. I could tell he was holding something back. Finally, he relented.

"There is to be another Alignment next year," he said.

My heart sank. "You mean we might have to go through this whole thing again?"

"No!" He shook his head vigorously. "I told you, the Epistola woman is no longer a threat."

"But what if someone else—?"

"Andromeda, trust me," he said. "There is nothing to fear."

I wanted more than anything to believe him. So I told myself that I did.

Riley took my hand. "Let's get away from this crowd, shall we?"

We walked down to the beach, leaving the noise and light of the Pumpkin Festival behind us. There was no one else in sight. Riley's hand was strong and sure around mine, and the sea was calm under the stars. For the first time in weeks, I felt truly peaceful.

"There is something I want to give you," Riley said suddenly. He reached into his jacket and pulled out a small box wrapped in silver paper topped with a gold bow.

"You got me a present?" I gasped. "What for?"

Riley looked deep into my eyes. "I thought that was obvious by now," he said sincerely.

I blushed. "I mean... I wasn't expecting... I don't have anything for you."

"Your existence is the only gift I require."

"And you think I don't feel the same way about you?"

"Why must you always make everything so difficult?" Riley huffed. "Just open it!"

Smiling, I took the box from him and plucked off the bow. Then I began to carefully pull up the tape, trying to preserve as much of the beautiful wrapping as possible.

"The paper is mere packaging," said Riley. "It is acceptable for you to tear it."

I laughed. My family and friends had teased me all my life about not understanding the concept of wrapping paper, but Riley sounded like he might be wondering if I actually knew.

Finally, I managed to pull the paper off without destroying it. Inside was a plain white box, but inside of that...

"Sea glass!" I exclaimed, holding the stone up to the moonlight.

Sea glass is what happens when you leave broken glass on the beach. The waves and sand wash over the shards again and again, day after day, for years on end. Gradually, nature wears down the sharp edges, leaving a perfectly smooth piece of frosted glass. This particular piece was about three inches long, one inch wide, and bright green.

"It matches your eyes," I told Riley.

"Yes, but that's not why I chose it," he said. "Well, not entirely. I must admit, the idea of you carrying a constant reminder of me is appealing."

"I'll bet it is," I said teasingly. "So what's the other reason?"

"This is no ordinary bit of sea glass," he explained. "It did not come from a broken beverage bottle left by a careless human. You hold in your hand the fragment of a statue that once stood in the central square of Atlantis."

My eyes widened, though by that point, nothing should have surprised me.

"The statue depicted the city's patron goddess," Riley continued. "All Atlantians worshipped her, as she provided for them and kept them safe. They loved her, all of them."

I ran my fingers over the glass, trying to wrap my head around its story.

"What was the goddess called?" I asked. "Atlanta?"

"No."

Riley wrapped his hands around mine, so that my fingers pressed against the cool glass on one side and his warm skin on the other.

"Her name was Andromeda," he said.

For the first time in my life, I felt grateful to my parents for my ridiculous name. Maybe they knew what they were doing, after all.

"But that is not why I chose it for you," Riley continued. "A millennium ago, this glass was all flat sides and sharp edges. Beautiful, yes, but you would not want to hold it in your hand. Since then, the ocean has washed over it and transformed it into something new. Just as you have transformed me."

What could I say to that? Absolutely nothing. So instead, I simply reached up and pressed my lips to his.

My life had finally begun.

That is not dead which can eternal lie,
yet with strange aeons even death
may love.

ACKNOWLEDGEMENTS

There are so many wonderful people who aided me on my writing journey, but I know exactly where to begin:

To my husband Linley and my five precious children, Marianne, Josh, Allison, MattA and MattB, you are all such trouble and always getting so dirty and leaving such a mess for me to clean up, but you are all worth it. Sometimes I don't know how you survived the novel-writing process in our home, having to endure so many nights of Chinese take-out and Dominoes!

To my mother, who helped me keep house and look after my family while I was writing my book. I know how impossible it is to expect little blessings to look after themselves and pigs will be flying before my husband takes charge on anything! Mom, without your help and support, I would have been lost.

To my writer's group—my *current* group, and only the current group—no past groups need apply! It took me a long time to come to this group after having gone through so many others who seemed to delight in savaging the words I had taken such time to lovingly craft. My current group, you have given me nothing but love, validation and support, for which I cannot thank you enough. I could not have done this without your constant encouragement.

Thank you to my dear Internet friend Gary, who guided me through the works of H. P. Lovecraft. You did everything you could to make this story flow with his words. Making sure everything in my book worked within the mythos wasn't easy, but it was our hope not to offend or be untrue to the spirit of Lovecraft. We worked very hard, so any readers who might take issue should bear this in mind--knee jerk reaction might tell you the fault is with me! But we did all we could, and realistically the best you could expect.

Some credit of course must go to Sir Andrew Lloyd Webber, who inspired so much of this dark Beauty and the Beast story (his work even got a little cameo!). Truly, a more inspiring work of art has not come along in this century.

But above all things, I must thank our Lord the Lamb, who has blessed me and my dear ones above most other people in so, so many ways. I take pity on those who have not received the same blessings that we have, and pray that all shall know his grace and light.

May the Bridge of the Lamb Fall Upon you all!

SERRA ELINSEN

lives in Trotwood Ohio with her husband and their five rambunctious children. She earned her degree in English literature from Dayton University. Having spent a good deal of her adult life in the maternity ward, she has not had the opportunity to use her studies until the Lord blessed her with the inspiration that led to the completion of her award-winning first novel, *Awoken*. When she's not packing lunches, playing chauffeur or writing, she is an avid matryoshka doll collector.

Her website is www.serraelinsen.com
"Like" her on Facebook: www.Facebook.com/SerraElinsen
"Follow" her on Twitter: @SerraElinsen

21937608R00189